FRACTURED HORIZONS

SAVAGE STARS BOOK 2

ANTHONY JAMES

Illustration © Tom Edwards
TomEdwardsDesign.com

THE VENGEANCE

The alien warship *Vengeance* was parked on the western fringe of the Adamantine base's enormous landing field. Surrounding the vessel's 1200-metre length were hastily erected walls of lightweight metal sheeting to prevent ground-level observation of the activity concentrated on the spaceship. The Human Planetary Alliance was already deep in the crap and neither the Representation, nor the military's high command were ready to deal with the consequences if the wider population got wind of the existence of an as-yet unencountered third species. The Daklan alone were more than the HPA could handle.

Viewed from above – where the walls didn't reach - the dark alloy vessel, with its angled plates of combat-scarred armour, gave the impression it was crouching low to the reinforced concrete, like a fierce predator waiting to pounce.

In and around the spaceship, thousands of personnel swarmed, from maintenance crews to technical teams, weapons designers and many other specialists. Each team had its own area of expertise, but the overriding goal was to unlock the secrets of the alien technology in order that humanity could copy it and put it to use against the Daklan.

In the two weeks since Captain Carl Recker brought the *Vengeance* back from the far planet Tanril, the work had continued ceaselessly. So far, the efforts had come up short. The spaceship was packing weapons – missiles, countermeasures and other types unknown – but Recker's security clearance he'd obtained when first activating the alien vessel didn't permit him to use them or even to learn their capabilities. It was frustrating for everyone.

Meanwhile, the Daklan continued whittling at the understrength human fleet and only a few hours ago news had come through that the aliens had knocked out the defensive fleet protecting a major ternium ore processing facility a short lightspeed jump from Fortune – a planet with a population of twelve billion. Every day that went by, the risk data became less palatable and it seemed inevitable the Daklan would soon locate a major HPA population centre. What would happen after that didn't bear thinking about.

High up and alone on one of the base's small passenger shuttles, Recker studied the warship's aggressive lines and angles, with a mixed sense of yearning and anger. He knew it wasn't *his* spaceship, but damnit, he was the only one who could fly it. Unbelievably, he'd been only reluctantly included in the investigation and in a fringe role. The HPA was at total war, and still the pettiness continued.

Spotting something emerge from the back of an armoured transporter vehicle, Recker adjusted the focus on the underside sensor and followed the progress of a two-metre cube-shaped obliterator processing core as it floated on its own gravity propulsion towards the *Vengeance*'s forward boarding ramp.

The core was a new design – built specifically to smash through encrypted data arrays – and had been brought from Earth on the battleship *Sledgehammer*, which had landed only an hour ago and then departed from Lustre, its destination known only to high command.

Recker had a feeling that the obliterator core would be no more successful at extracting the warship's secrets than anything else the military had tried so far. What would happen afterwards, he had no idea. Just perhaps, Fleet Admiral Solan would - in the interests of the HPA - put an end to his own son's manipulation of Recker's career. It hadn't happened yet and didn't seem likely now.

Realizing the situation was chewing him up, Recker turned off the autopilot and banked the shuttle towards one of the vacant landing pads in the built-up area of Adamantine. The base mainframe sent him a friendly reminder that the density of air traffic meant he should hand off control. Not wishing to pick an argument with a computer, Recker agreed and sat back while the mainframe guided him towards his destination.

Although it had the benefit of precision, the flight control system didn't take risks and the return journey took a couple of minutes longer than if Recker had been flying the shuttle on manual. During the flight, he reflected on this frustrating period. The military didn't have a warship for him, leaving him a man with no duties beyond the interminable day-to-day activity of inbox maintenance and whatever busywork came his way.

More than anything, Recker wanted to be out in space, fighting the enemy. When that opportunity would come again, he didn't know. It was beginning to feel like he'd been permanently side-lined, forgotten and left to moulder, despite his hard-fought victories at Etrol and Oldis.

With the slightest thump from its compressing landing legs, the transport set down and Recker exited onto the landing pad. The overhead sun blazed and the buildings which rose all around seemed to trap the heat and magnify it, making him feel an immediate prickling of sweat on his scalp.

Halfway across the landing pad, the communicator in Recker's pocket started vibrating, whilst playing its irritating alert tune which he never remembered to change. He dragged the device out of his pocket, flipped it open and stared briefly at the words on the screen.

Outer Admin 7. Sub-5. Room 12-C. Immediately. Telar.

Admiral Telar had something for him. Whatever it was, Recker was sure it would significantly increase the chance of his death, though in the circumstances any change was welcome. He quickened his stride.

CHAPTER ONE

THE SUBTERRANEAN LEVELS of Outer Admin 7 were more akin to a prison in appearance. The stark, undecorated corridors were lit too brightly and the sound of Recker's footsteps echoed crisply off the smooth floor, which was covered in a hard-wearing, light green composite material, patterned in a bad replica of natural stone. Signs dangled overhead, directing personnel to such enticing destinations as *Stats & Sys 3* and *Storage & Repository 4-9*.

Security-locked alloy doors broke up the walls at regular intervals, hiding secrets which Recker had no interest in unearthing. The breakout areas no longer contained seating – anything spare had been ripped out to furnish the newly occupied offices – and clusters of forlorn personnel queued at the replicators, hoping to find solace in reconstituted proteins and orange-coloured fluids that tasted almost like fruit.

If the temperature above the surface had been too hot,

here on Sub-5 it was the opposite. The natural chill exuded by the metal-clad rock from which the underground passages had been hewn was heightened by the constantly droning air conditioning, making the place uncomfortably cold. Recker hardly noticed and headed towards Room 12-C, which the map on his pocket communicator informed him was found along a turning from one of the main corridors.

Only two weeks ago, this underground warren was half-empty – a place mostly forgotten and ignored, home to a few teams of lesser-known branches of research or statistical analysis. The personnel in these teams were uncharitably referred to as eggheads – the sort who got excited by spreadsheets, yet who nevertheless had an important role in the military.

Following the transition to total war, space was suddenly at a premium and, as he made his way through the passages, Recker was forced to avoid numerous flustered-looking former civilians, who hurried this way and that as they became accustomed to their new home.

As he neared his destination, a woman carrying a huge box of files, with a framed photo of a smiling family perched on top, veered unexpectedly and nearly collided with him. She apologised, asked for directions and then resumed her travels to one of the offices in a faraway corner.

By the time he approached the corridor leading to Room 12-C, Recker's patience was wearing thin and he asked himself for the dozenth time why the hell Admiral Telar had chosen to host the meeting down here – underground and in one of the minor administration buildings on the edge of the base -instead of one of the countless more easily-accessible locations elsewhere on Adamantine.

He entered a passage which was wider than most others and flanked on both sides by doors. Armed guards in full combat suits stood watchfully as a small army of site maintenance operatives brought computers, cabinets, communicators and all manner of other kit, into the offices.

"Sir?" asked one man, an admirably alert corporal with pale blue eyes and a nose which had been broken at least once in the past. The soldier held his rifle with reassuring ease.

"Captain Recker. I'm expected. 12-C, Telar."

The man didn't even check a handheld for confirmation. "Yes, sir. This way," he said, turning and marching along the passage.

Recker followed and the soldier stopped outside Room 12-C.

"This was all done at short notice," said the man without turning. "And they're having problems updating the security, so I'll have to get you through the door."

With that, he brushed his gloved fingertips over the access panel and the door opened. The soldier disappeared inside and emerged ten seconds later.

"All yours, sir. The Admiral will see you."

"Thanks," said Recker, brushing past.

Beyond the door, a short passage led to a second door, this one already open. Recker didn't stand timidly on the threshold and he entered without introducing himself.

"Carl," said Telar mildly. "Take a seat."

Recker glanced around the room, wondering if this was meant to be a permanent home, or a place for whichever transient officer happened to get here first. The room was as uninspiring as was possible to imagine, with grey painted walls, a green-tiled floor, a desk and a few pieces of tech, some of which hadn't yet been connected to the base network.

The indicated seat appeared to be one of those taken from the breakout areas and Recker lowered himself carefully onto the meagre padding. His sitting position was so low that Admiral Telar was completely hidden by his desktop communicator.

"I'll stand, sir," said Recker, returning to his feet.

"As you will." Telar was dressed formally in blue and he looked out of place in the drab surroundings. "I'm sure you've asked yourself why I chose level Sub-5 as the location for one of my new offices."

"A trigger point got breached," said Recker, wondering why he hadn't guessed the answer sooner. "Somewhere, a computer or a research team came up with a risk figure that suggested the likelihood of a Daklan attack on one of our bases became too high to ignore. The mitigation is to stay away from the usual command and control areas and go underground."

Telar smiled thinly. "And if the risk figure climbs much further, I'll soon have to abandon this office and find one off-base."

"Topaz station?"

"Or Amethyst."

"I've been here too long, sir," said Recker, not one to hang back in a discussion. "You told me if I didn't cause any trouble, I'd have a new ship and a chance to discuss matters with Admiral Solan."

"Discuss? I recall your intention was to land a spaceship on his car and fire a full cluster of Ilstrom missiles through his window and into his display case of *undeserved medals*," Telar quoted mildly.

"You promised me a spaceship, sir," Recker repeated accusingly.

"To kill the Daklan, Captain. Not to commit an act of murder on a superior officer."

"Instead," Recker continued as if he hadn't heard, "I've been grounded for two weeks, while a thousand technicians poke around on the *Vengeance*, which is security-keyed to my biometrics. Two weeks wasted because of a personal vendetta from..." He paused, unable to recall exactly when his issues with Gabriel Solan had started. "Years ago," he finished.

"We'll discuss these matters later," said Telar with an edge to his voice.

Recker had no intention of alienating Telar and he took a deep breath. "The fleet has spare riots, sir. I watched the technical teams complete the handover of one last week."

"Who's to say there's a mission for that spaceship to go on?" asked Telar softly.

"The fleet is still on defensive duties only?" asked Recker. He'd done some digging but had no access to the flight plans from other military bases away from Lustre.

"I didn't say that." Telar raised a hand when he saw that Recker was about to object. "We'll return to your question shortly. Are you aware of the change in the command structure?"

The question caught Recker by surprise. "No, sir."

Telar nodded in apparent satisfaction. "The details were only finalised yesterday. I'd hate to think our security protocols weren't up to the task of keeping top-level planning away from the watching eyes of the entire military."

The man's cynicism was grounded in truth and it was an old joke that if you asked any soldier in the HPA what Fleet Admiral Solan had for breakfast during his morning meeting with the Representation, they'd have a ninety percent chance of providing the correct answer.

"In order to ensure continuity in the event of a Daklan attack, certain responsibilities and accountabilities have been updated." Telar smiled, though it lacked humour. "As of late yesterday, I was given sole command of the Adamantine facility, including the shipyard."

It was a significant increase in Telar's personal authority, but also came with other, more worrying implications.

"This sounds like we're planning for defeat, sir."

"You don't think that's wise, Captain?"

Recker shook his head. "Not if it distracts us from turning the war around. We've swapped one commander for a dozen."

"I understand why you might have that impression. However, we've always had dozens of competing decision makers, Carl. The Representation likes to have its say on how the tax money of our citizens is spent."

"And how have things changed now, sir?"

"Not everyone in high command is so easily blown by the wind." Telar let that hang in the air for a moment. "I assure you, the most important elements of the military are now pulling in the right direction."

Recker tried to grasp the underlying message – the words that Telar *wasn't* saying. He felt himself going cold at the possibilities. It sounded like Fleet Admiral Solan had been railroaded by his officers into accepting a new approach.

"Does that mean I can get more involved with work on the *Vengeance*, sir?"

"Not yet. That particular asset is still considered an outlier."

The words were delivered with the unmistakeable message of *don't push it*.

"What happens from here?" asked Recker.

Telar smiled again, though with a little more warmth. "Take a look at this."

He pointed at one of the screens on his desktop communicator and Recker went around to see what it was showing.

"A star chart," he said. "What does the highlight on that planet represent, sir?"

"The outcome of our analysis of the data you brought back from Oldis, Captain."

Recker's previous mission had seen him attacked by a Daklan annihilator, forcing him to take shelter in a mysterious cylinder – a tenixite converter – created by an unknown alien species. From the cylinder, he'd extracted data which might lead to another converter on the network.

"It's taken two weeks to pinpoint the location?" he asked.

"You're disappointed?"

"No, sir. I know the work involved. We had to narrow down the location across a vast distance and infinite planets, then have one of the monitoring stations check out the list of possibilities. I think we've done well to finish so soon."

"We have," said Telar, his tone suggesting that the effort was in fact much greater than Recker had guessed.

"Pinvos?" said Recker, leaning across the desk so that he could make out the tiny text label on the planet.

"It was originally called RT2-R332-W," said Telar. "I had them rename it to something that wouldn't slow down every briefing in which it was mentioned."

"You're sending me to scout the place?"

Telar had the good grace to look fleetingly pained. "This is too important, Carl. We're going out there in force."

"What happened to *risk aversion*?"

"Like I told you, the military is pulling in the right direction."

"When is it happening?"

"Soon. There are one or two obstacles yet to overcome. I anticipate we'll be ready to depart in less than twenty-four hours."

"Pinvos is a long way from home."

"Ten days at the speed of the slowest ship."

"My ship?"

Telar leaned back. "As it happens, you won't be commanding the slowest warship in the task force. Have you heard of the *Expectation*?"

"Yes, sir. A riot class currently in the trench outside."

"It's not a riot class. Not anymore. The name was originally assigned when the funds were allocated, and, as far as my superiors are concerned, the riot class *Expectation* will rise from its trench in twenty-seven days."

"I don't understand, sir."

"I reallocated the name to a shard class destroyer, Carl. The vessel was signed off five days ago on Fortune and it landed on Adamantine a few hours ago. Until this morning when I completed the paperwork, it was awaiting a captain and a crew. Now it has both."

"Thank you, sir." Recker didn't know what else to say.

"You deserve better than you've been treated. While I'm in control of Adamantine, things will be different."

"I appreciate that, sir."

"And now you're going to ask me *what's next*."

"Yes, sir. I was."

"Go and see your warship, Carl. I expect the final mission go-ahead to arrive soon and I want you ready to depart. I won't go through the mission briefing with you – the documentation will unlock at the right time."

"Yes, sir. What about the *Vengeance*? If I die, there's nobody else can make it fly."

"It's a single ship, Carl. One way or the other, we'll take what we need from it."

"You're underestimating..."

"No I'm not," Telar interrupted. He sighed. "I can't keep you grounded while I wait for the situation to be resolved. The HPA needs its best officers fighting the Daklan."

Recker had more to say but he didn't argue. The meeting was over and he glanced towards the door.

"One more thing," said Telar.

"Sir?"

"The *Expectation* is the first of a new design - we've got a lot of people interested in how it performs. On top of that, I've ordered the installation of some modifications. They're untested, but perhaps you'll find a use for them."

Telar stared unblinking and Recker could see he was going to have to find out the answers for himself.

"I'll do my best."

"I know."

Recker headed for the door, his head swimming with the apparent shift in his fortunes. Outside, the cold air hit him like a shock and he stood for a moment.

"Sir?" It was the same corporal from earlier.

"I'm fine," said Recker.

He got his bearings and headed for the exit.

CHAPTER TWO

THE *EXPECTATION* WAS PARKED on the western side of the landing strip, not far from the barriers which surrounded the *Vengeance*. At 800 metres and with a mass of a little over a billion tons it was much more imposing than a riot class. The *Expectation*'s design was significantly altered from other destroyers in a way which made it look a hundred years older than most other vessels in the fleet. As he stared at the low-profile hull bristling with weapons emplacements, Recker thought that the *Expectation* had real potential.

"Looks neat," said Lieutenant Adam Burner, standing a short distance from Recker. Burner was clean-shaven for once, though his curly hair looked more unruly than ever.

"Neat?" said Commander Daisy Aston, adjusting the band holding her dark ponytail in place. "It looks tough."

"A mean son of a bitch," Lieutenant Ken Eastwood confirmed. "See how they angled the plating by another few degrees to deflect Terrus slugs? That should help it resist armour-penetrating warheads as well."

In space, an attack could come from any direction, which meant that angled plates were of limited effectiveness. Still, Recker thought that a skilled pilot could take advantage by altering the warship's orientation so that inbound missiles were more likely to glance off the sloped edges.

"Back to the old design," he said.

"It's what's inside that counts, right?" said Burner, tapping his chest.

"Like those two Hellburner tubes?" said Aston.

"Made to crack open the hardest of nuts," said Eastwood. "It'll be good to have something with a bit more punch."

The shard class destroyers weren't anything like so well armed as a cruiser or battleship, but they weren't meant to be cannon fodder. In the right circumstances, those Hellburners could split open a Daklan heavy cruiser. The hardest part was surviving long enough to deliver the payload.

"We should head onboard," said Recker.

He climbed back into the front seat of the pool car which had brought them here. The *Expectation* was a few hundred metres away and he didn't have the patience to walk it.

"It's great to have you back!" said the vehicle's navigational computer, the falseness of it making Recker want to put his fist through the dash-mounted display.

"Shut up," he growled.

The computer didn't take the hint. "Oh I do love a good space battle," it said.

Recker reached for the mute button on the dashboard.

"And I see we're starting work on two new spaceships in those far trenches," the car continued. "Big ones."

"What new spaceships?" asked Recker, his finger halting an inch from the mute button. "And how come you've heard about them and I haven't?"

"Oh I just pick things up," the car babbled. "Always in the right place at the right time. You know how it is."

"What about the new ships?"

"Like I said, sir. Big ones."

"That must be the technical term," said Burner from the back seat.

"You should check it out, sir. Find out what they are," said Aston from the adjacent seat. She gave Recker an encouraging nudge with her elbow.

"Maybe I will," he said, stabbing the mute button with relish. From this minor encounter with the car he came to a sudden realization. "Ever since I joined the military, it's been an ongoing joke that if something's going on, everybody knows about it." He tapped the cheap plastic dashboard. "And here's the culprit. Whoever programmed these cars forgot to add some coding to make them keep their mouths shut."

"There's got to be more to it than that," said Eastwood. "Someone would have noticed by now."

"I'm not sure I want to think about it, Lieutenant."

Recker took manual control of the vehicle and gave it some power. The gravity car's engine whined smoothly as it accelerated over the landing strip. The journey wasn't long, but Recker had to steer around numerous obstacles, from piles of crates, to maintenance crews, cabins, trucks and everything else required to keep a warship armed and ready.

On the left, his view was blocked by the looming barrier around the *Vengeance*, while to the right, Recker found his gaze returning to the skies over the construction trenches, several kilometres away. He narrowed his eyes at the sight of a huge lifter shuttle, with an even larger propulsion block attached by an invisible gravity chain, and wondered what would rise from those trenches in a few months.

A hundred metres from the *Expectation*'s lowered front boarding ramp, Recker brought the car to a halt.

"Let's go check it out," he said, pushing open the door and stepping onto the landing strip. Hot sun beat down and the dense, shimmering air throbbed with the pressure of a hundred nearby propulsions.

Recker strode towards the squad guarding the warship and the stifling heat made him long for the frosty corridors of Sub-5. Even stepping beneath the shadow of the destroyer didn't provide much relief - if anything, it became more humid and, knowing that the spaceship's interior would be cool, Recker quickened his pace.

A man detached himself from the squad of fifteen watching over the spaceship.

"Sergeant Tracker," said Recker, remembering him from before.

"Captain Recker," said Tracker in acknowledgement. He half-turned and nodded towards the *Expectation*. "Nice looking ship, sir."

"Nothing that a high-speed flight through a sandstorm won't fix," said Recker with a brief smile. The destroyer's alloys were dull and unreflective, but they were also clearly new and unmarked. "Anyone onboard?"

"Sergeant Vance, sir. He and his men arrived fifteen minutes ago and I directed them to quarters."

"Thank you," said Recker.

Tracker didn't hear the response. His eyes widened and he whirled around so that he was looking north, towards the landing strip perimeter. In alarm, Recker looked too and all he could see was more of the base.

"What is it?" he asked urgently.

For a moment, Tracker didn't respond. "A couple of spaceholes, sir," he said eventually, tapping the side of his helmet to indicate he'd heard about it via the comms. "Sounds like they were attempting a flyover in a civilian shuttle."

"What happened to them?"

"The flight control mainframe brought them down into the waiting arms of Lieutenant Cider and a whole bunch of pissed-off soldiers."

"I hope they get five years," said Eastwood. "We're at war, damnit."

The arrival of the spaceship spotters was a minor, yet unwelcome distraction and Recker put it behind him.

"Come on," he said.

At the lower end of the *Expectation*'s boarding ramp, Recker paused.

"Well folks - another new ship for us," he said. "It's becoming a habit."

Up the ramp he went, his eyes fixed on the airlock. He

entered a space that wasn't much larger than the equivalent in a riot class. A foldable metal bench on one wall provided temporary seating, while a sealed locker contained combat suits, gauss rifles and a few other useful spares. The combined low-level hum of engines along with the faint vibration of technology made him feel instantly at home.

"Before we go any further, let's get suited up," said Recker, sliding open the locker door.

He grabbed a suit and set the helmet down near his feet. Then, he took off his cloth uniform and, after a couple of minutes struggle with the stiffly elastic polymers in the combat spacesuit, finished getting dressed. Aston was ready at the same time, then Eastwood. Meanwhile Burner cursed everyone under the sun and accused the suit of being too small, even though they only came in four different sizes and he'd chosen his usual.

"Too much high living on base," Eastwood commented.

"Maybe he's been working out," said Aston without any indication she really believed it. "All those muscles won't fit in medium suit."

Eastwood looked at her in mock-concern. "There's still time to get your eyes checked out before lift-off, Commander."

Still complaining, Burner rose from the bench, made a few last adjustments to his suit and declared himself ready.

Recker was impatient to be off and he readied himself to open the inner door. He'd been on every type of warship in the fleet and knew what he was going to find.

Even so, the excitement was there. With his fingertips, Recker activated the security panel and the door slid open. A gust of cold, sharp-scented air rustled through, drying the beads of sweat in his hair. He smiled.

Beyond the door, a short, narrow passage with a low ceiling led through solid metal to an intersection, where Recker turned left. As he walked along the blue-white lit passage, he tapped his knuckles against the walls to feel the reassuring solidity that only came from enormous blocks of dense alloy and ternium.

"No pipes, no cables," he said.

Rather than finding a different way to route these intrusions, it seemed as if the designers had instead lowered the ceilings and hidden the conduits in the space they'd gained by doing so. Recker guessed he had about six inches less headroom than normal and when he stretched out his arms, he thought that a similar amount had gone missing from the width.

"If they keep making the crew areas smaller, in a hundred years' time, they'll have to design a one-way system for warships because there'll be no room for two people to pass," said Aston.

By the time they arrived at the steps leading up to the bridge, Recker was convinced the *Expectation* had even less overall space for the crew than a riot class. He shrugged – the fewer rooms and corridors the builders had to fit inside, the larger the Hellburner magazines they could accommodate, and Recker would gladly swap high ceilings for more ammunition.

The square door protecting the bridge was shut. Twin, stubby-barrelled miniguns spun lazily in their alcoves to either side, promising a nasty surprise to either Daklan invaders or overachieving spaceholes.

Without hesitation, Recker touched the access panel and the blast door opened.

"Someone pinch me," said Eastwood. "I just got back on the *Finality*."

It was an accurate observation. The bridge area was almost identical to that of a riot class, though Recker noted that the *Expectation* was fitted with newer-design consoles and, in a nod to luxury, the seat coverings were probably only four degrees of separation from real leather, instead of six degrees on a riot class.

"Why mess with a good design, Lieutenant?" asked Recker.

"No reason, I guess. I just thought they might have rearranged the furniture in the six or seven years since I last served on a destroyer."

"The more familiar it is, the easier it'll be for you," said Recker, marching onto the bridge. "Find your stations, folks. I want to know everything about this spaceship. More importantly, I want to know you're ready to fly it the moment we receive the order to go."

Recker took his seat and brought the command console out of sleep. Barely had his screens fired up than Lieutenant Eastwood called for his attention.

"Sir, come and have a look at this."

"What is it?" asked Recker, standing again.

"This."

A box constructed from thin metal was sitting on the floor at the base of Eastwood's console. Wires emerged from one side and they were patched into a small, open hatch, low down. A keypad and green-lit screen on top of the device gave away no immediate clue as to its purpose.

"Admiral Telar said they'd fitted some last-minute modifications," said Recker.

"*This* is what passes for a modification these days?" said Eastwood, nudging the box with his foot. "It looks like a college student's first attempt at building an ATM hacker."

"Leave it for the moment, Lieutenant. Get ready to fly."

Recker had hardly got himself seated when Burner relayed a message from the Adamantine flight controller.

"We've been given a thirty-minute departure slot, sir. Starting now."

"I didn't know Admiral Telar was in so much of a hurry," said Aston.

"Neither did I," said Recker. "I only left the meeting three hours ago."

"Adamantine is expecting a classified arrival, sir," said Burner. "They must need our space on the landing field."

"Fine. Acknowledge the order and instruct the ground crews to get clear. If it's safe for us to go, we'll go."

Recker returned to his pre-flight checks. The *Expectation*'s magazines were fully loaded and every status light was green. Whoever had brought it over from the shipyard on Fortune had taken the vessel through its riskiest first lightspeed jump. In theory, the warship was as ready to go as it ever would be.

Twenty minutes into the departure window, Recker was confident enough to order the lift-off.

"Once we're up, we can finish any remaining checks," he said.

The crew were ready and so was Recker. He held the controls, ran his eyes across the width of his console and then drew the alloy bars towards him. The underlying grumble from the engine rose in volume and the *Expectation* rose from the ground, its ternium propulsion carrying the warship upwards like it weighed the merest fraction of its billion tons.

"All sensors locking and focusing within expected parameters," said Burner.

"Propulsion output at 99%," said Eastwood. "I don't know where that final one percent got to."

"A calibration problem on the monitoring hardware?" said Aston.

"Could be. I'll check it out once we're in orbit."

The *Expectation* climbed steadily and the underside feeds betrayed the level of activity on the Adamantine base far better than was possible from ground level. It seemed to Recker as if he were watching a huge crowd dancing to an unheard tune, the ordered steps teetering on the brink of chaos.

"The car was right," said Burner. "They're making preparations for two new hulls in those far trenches."

"We're about to find out what the HPA can achieve when given the motivation," said Recker.

"Motivation and funding," said Eastwood. "The military's been lacking both."

"Not anymore," said Recker. He'd seen the determination in Admiral Telar's face. A change was coming and it was going to sweep everyone on the Adamantine base along like an unstoppable tide – a tide that Recker welcomed with open arms.

Gradually, the base dwindled and Recker turned his attention upwards. The *Expectation* left the planet's atmosphere, where it joined the twenty-five-strong defensive fleet of destroyers, cruisers and the *Granite* battleship.

"Any sign of those mission files unlocking?" asked Aston.

"Not yet, Commander."

"Check out the forward feed, sir," said Burner with sudden excitement.

One of the screens on the bulkhead was locked onto a huge spaceship with square edges and flat sides. The angle was such that Recker could spot the multiple laser housings and the twin rows of enormous inverted chutes which ran along the vessel's underside.

"Planetary dredger," he said.

"That one's the *Atlas*. Seven klicks from nose to tail and a fifty-billion-ton load capacity. The Daklan aren't the ones who can build them big," said Eastwood.

"What's it doing here?" asked Burner. "We've got no major ore processing plants on this side of Lustre."

"I think I can guess," said Recker. "They're going to use those rock-cutting lasers to make a new trench for the shipyard. Hell, they've got room for two new ones if Admiral Telar thinks he can fill them with warships."

"Damn," said Eastwood. "If you're right, that's taking a big gamble. Those dredgers aren't made to draw fine lines."

"I could be wrong, Lieutenant. If I'm not, all that dredger needs to do is cut a rough hole and suck up the debris. It'll save the teams on the ground a couple of months at least."

"That would be interesting to watch," said Eastwood.

The opportunity never came.

"We've received coordinates and orders to reach them at the earliest opportunity, sir," said Burner.

"So much for twenty-four hours," said Recker under his breath. "Acknowledge the order." He checked the *Expectation*'s distance from Lustre. The spaceship was far enough away to activate the ternium drive. "Lieutenant Eastwood, program in those coordinates and then tell me where we're going."

"All done, sir. This is to be a three-hour journey and the arrival point is nowhere in particular. On the plus side, we're fitted with a high-spec processing core and the warmup calculations will be done in twelve minutes."

"Any improvement's welcome," said Recker, and he meant it.

"Sounds like we're going to a rendezvous," said Aston.

Recker checked the mission files again and gritted his teeth when he found they were still locked. He resisted the temptation to request a comms channel to Admiral Telar and decided to wait it out. The files would unlock soon enough.

Twelve minutes later, the *Expectation* entered lightspeed.

CHAPTER THREE

THE NAUSEA of the transition seemed muted, as if the size of the warship – or a more capable life support unit - offered a buffer against the physical stresses placed on the human body by the abrupt shift into the semi-theoretical realms of high-speed cosmic travel.

Shrugging off the clenching in his stomach, Recker checked the status panel and discovered that it was uniformly green.

"Whoever is responsible for ensuring new active duty spaceships are genuinely safe to fly, they're doing a good job," he said.

"Amen to that," said Eastwood. "Everything's holding together. We got another good one, just like the *Punisher.*"

"Three hours until rendezvous," said Recker. He didn't bother checking the mission files again – they were locked in the moments leading to the transition and the comms system was unable to receive unlock codes during lightspeed travel. "Anything you need to test or investigate, now is the time to do it."

"There's nothing new with the comms hardware, sir," said Burner. "While the sensor arrays are bigger, better and more than what we've had before."

"Commander?" said Recker. "Give me a run down."

"Nothing you don't already know, sir. We're packing eight clusters of ten Ilstroms, six Type 1 Railers, disruptor drones and twin ass kickers," she finished, giving the colloquial term for the Hellburner missiles.

"350 thousand klick lock range, eight thousand klicks per second non-boost and twelve thousand on-boost velocity," intoned Eastwood. "Just waiting to smash open the side door of a desolator and ruin the enemy's day."

Despite the bold words and the huge payload of the Hellburners, they weren't nearly so effective against the Daklan's newest warships. Even so, Recker felt much better now that he was piloting a warship that had some real firepower. Watching a dozen Ilstroms detonate fruitlessly against the armour of a heavy cruiser was one of the most frustrating experiences he'd ever dealt with.

"Have you found out what that device on the floor is there for, Lieutenant Eastwood?" he asked.

"No, sir. I got distracted talking about Hellburners."

"Check it out as a priority."

"On it, sir."

"Any idea who we're meeting up with?" said Aston.

"None," Recker confessed. "Admiral Telar sprung news of some big changes on me. Last I heard, the fleet was on guard duty only and now we're on a mission to a planet that's ten days out from Lustre."

"Think we'll be joining a big fleet?"

"I don't know," said Recker. "I think these are the baby steps, so I'm not anticipating too much."

"Better than sitting on our hands," said Burner.

"Got bored over these last two weeks, did you?" said Aston.

"I've got no family there, Commander, just like the rest of us. And all FTL comms bandwidth was reserved for military use, so I couldn't even phone home."

"Yeah, that was bad," said Eastwood with real bitterness. He fished in his pocket and pulled out the frayed photo of his family and stared at it. "One day – if it ever happens – I'm going to turn up on my doorstep and Elsa's going to look at me like I'm a stranger." He shook his head and tucked the photo away again. "Even if we turn this war around, I'll be asking myself if it was all worthwhile."

"No you won't, Lieutenant," said Aston quietly. "You know it's worth it."

"Yeah. Maybe," he said. "It's just you expect victory to be a good thing and all I'm seeing is separate roads leading to the same place."

"You can't let yourself think that, Lieutenant. None of this is decided yet."

"I know. Doesn't make it any easier."

"And this is what you signed up for, right? To keep your family safe from species like the Daklan?"

"That I did, Captain. Sometimes I like to let off a bit of steam, that's all."

"Just find out what that device does, Lieutenant. Sometimes it's best to think about the now, rather than the future."

The conversation ended and Recker tried to shake off his own dark thoughts which had been given strength by Eastwood's low mood. Recker had no wife and no children, but he had family on Earth and he missed them. He couldn't remember – had stopped trying – when he'd last seen any of them.

As a distraction, he opened a channel on the internal comms to Staff Sergeant James Vance.

"Glad to have you onboard, Sergeant," he said.

"Glad to be back, sir," said Vance, his tone offering Recker the perfect degree of uncertainty about whether he meant it.

Recker smiled. "Another mission. We're on our way to a rendezvous. After that, expect ten days of boredom, followed by the high possibility of death and then – if we make it through – another ten days of boredom on the way back."

"Nothing changes, sir. The squad got reinforced to fifteen. Maybe you could stop by and make the introductions at some point."

"I'll do that, Sergeant," Recker promised.

He cut the channel and turned just in time to see enlightenment cross Lieutenant Eastwood's craggy features.

"You figured it out," said Recker.

"I did, sir. This box is an overstress toggle."

Recker had more than a passing interest and he left his seat in order to stand at Eastwood's console.

"How does it work?"

"The buttons on this top keypad allow me to switch all six of our propulsion modules into an immediate but limited overstressed state for a short duration, and then it switches them back to unstressed."

"Sounds straightforward."

"Not so much. It's definitely experimental and from the time stamps on the code, they only finished writing the control system addon a couple of days ago. There are plenty of warnings and disclaimers about potential module failures, like the programmers didn't want anything coming back to bite them. I don't think this was ever intended to be hard-wired into an on-duty warship."

"Admiral Telar must want to fast track it," said Recker. Even though he was being used as a guinea pig, his admiration for the speed of implementation was genuine. "What limits are on the overstress?"

Eastwood gave one of his noncommittal grunts. "The answer isn't simple."

"Sure it is," said Burner. "You're just buying thinking time."

"That's not helping," said Eastwood.

"You have ideas," said Recker.

Eastwood nodded. "The programmers added explanatory text to each section of code. The intended outcome of the overstress activation is for the processing unit in this box..." he gave it another nudge with his foot, "...to judge the atomic health of the ternium modules, at which point it will decide what level of overstress they can handle and for how long."

"Atomic health?" asked Burner.

"It was the most appropriate phrase I could come up with," said Eastwood testily. "So when this overstress unit decides the engines have had enough, it shunts them back into their normal state. Or that's what it's meant to do."

"That's a lot of uncertainty, Lieutenant," said Recker. "From what you've said, this new feature is nothing we can rely on."

"I think that's an excellent summation of the tech, sir. It's an option that may or may not help in a pinch situation. There's something else."

"Which is?"

"This new unit is now the only way to set the engines into overstress. They've deleted the option from these main consoles." Eastwood absently patted the top of his station.

"I'm not surprised," said Recker. "If word gets out what you did on the *Finality*, sooner or later every captain in the fleet will be testing the method."

"It's not ready for prime time," Eastwood agreed. "And the military doesn't intend its warships to be single-use."

Recker remembered something else. "The propulsion output is 99%. Does this overstress module have something to do with that?"

"Yes, sir. Part of how it works involves reserving a fraction of each propulsion module for ongoing monitoring of the *atomic health*. That monitoring helps determine how much overstress the engines will handle."

"One percent," said Recker. "It sounds insignificant, but I'd rather have it available."

"Maybe the designers thought it was a price worth paying," said Eastwood. "Though it's more likely they didn't have time to figure out a more elegant solution."

"Do some more poking around, Lieutenant," said

Recker. "If we're field testing the experimental kit, I'd like to learn everything about it."

"Will do, sir, but I don't think there's much left to find. The coding is only a few thousand lines – like a really cut-down version of a full control system - and the processing unit is the same as we install in some of our sensor arrays."

Recker didn't immediately return to his seat. Instead, he stopped at the food replicator, which was a slightly more advanced model than the one found on his last ship, the *Punisher*. Without much enthusiasm, he ordered it to vend. An acrid-smelling coffee and a sorry-looking sandwich appeared, which he carried back to his station and promptly forgot about.

The three hours passed without incident and Lieutenant Eastwood declared himself certain that the overstress box held no further secrets. Recker accepted the man's judgement and hoped he wouldn't be required to activate a device with so many associated maybes.

"Prepare for re-entry to local space," said Lieutenant Eastwood as the scheduled arrival time approached. "Ten seconds."

"Everyone ready," Recker warned.

The ternium engine cut out exactly on time and the *Expectation* entered local space. Without prompting, the crew got to work scanning the area and Recker took the precaution of pushing the warship to maximum acceleration, in case the Daklan had a presence in this part of space.

"You can let up on the controls, sir," said Burner. "We're joining a local battle network."

In front of Recker's eyes, the tactical populated with the HPA warships which had arrived first.

"Battleship *Trojan* leads," he said. "Plus two cruisers and three destroyers, including the *Expectation.*"

"And the heavy lifter *Titan*," said Burner. "Vice Admiral Fraser commands the *Trojan*, sir. I've got him on the comms."

Recker held in a sigh. He'd dealt with Fraser twice before and on both occasions the dislike had been one-sided, palpable and demonstrated, though Recker hadn't done anything to anger the other man. "Bring him through."

Fraser's voice was cool. "Captain Recker. Going up in the world, I see."

"Yes, sir." Recker wasn't in the mood to provoke a confrontation so he determined to keep this as brief as possible.

"Your mission files have unlocked. Make sure you read and understand them."

"Yes, sir."

Fraser's voice suddenly became angry, like he'd been waiting for an opportunity to get something off his chest.

"And I won't have any of your pissing about, do you hear me, Recker? This will be a professionally-run mission and I will not tolerate dissent from my officers!"

Recker's own anger came in a surge and with it, a cold calmness that he usually only felt during combat. "That's *Captain* Recker, sir."

"What?" spluttered Fraser, caught off guard.

"You will do me the courtesy of referring to me by name and rank. Sir."

"Very well, *Captain* Recker. This mission will run smoothly and you will dance to my tune, do you understand? We've lost enough *good* officers already without losing others because some personnel don't know how to play by the rules."

"Sir, I will do what it takes to ensure this mission is a success."

"Make sure that you do, Captain."

The comms went dead and Recker shrugged. "You heard the admiral."

"That we did, sir," said Aston.

Recker shook his head at the absurdity of the situation. The HPA was on the brink of losing a war and he was still having to deal with crap like this. Vice Admiral Fraser was rumoured to be one of Admiral Solan's drinking buddies, but he should learn how to do his damn duty, whatever he believed about Recker.

"We're expecting one more spaceship, sir," said Burner. "The *Shock and Awe* is inbound from Hope. ETA: ten minutes."

"Just time to read the mission briefing," said Recker, sitting down and accessing the files.

Some mission documentation was so detailed it ran into dozens of pages when two would have been enough. The files for this mission were distinctly light on specifics and Recker had no idea why high command felt the need for them to remain locked down for so long.

"Fly to Pinvos, recover any alien artifacts we find. Engage the Daklan only as a last resort," he told his crew in summary.

"Last resort?" said Aston incredulously. "What's that supposed to mean?"

Recker didn't like it either, since it gave Admiral Fraser the opportunity to find the easy way out of any situation. If he caught wind of something - even a Daklan destroyer - he could order the task force to turn tail and run on the basis that he suspected larger numbers of enemy warships were on their way. Maybe Fraser was made of sterner stuff. Recker hoped so.

With several minutes to kill before the *Shock and Awe*'s arrival, Recker accessed the sensor controls and focused the arrays on each warship in turn. The two destroyers – *Barbarian* and *Claymore* - were parked side-by-side, approximately eight thousand kilometres from the *Expectation*. They were older models with fewer angles and a higher profile, though they carried equivalent armaments.

The 1800-metre Teron class cruiser *Harken* looked mean and with enough minor damage to its armour to suggest it had come through a multitude of engagements. As the war progressed, the veterans – meaning both space-ships and crews - were becoming increasingly hard to find and it seemed that hardly any of the older members of the fleet remained.

The battleship *Trojan* – four thousand metres in length and with a thirty-five-billion-ton mass – first rose from its construction trench five years ago, according to Recker's memory. Fraser had been its first and only commanding officer, which probably explained why the warship looked clean enough to eat a twenty-course admiral's banquet off the plating. And it seemed to Recker that a thousand or more ground crew must be kept permanently occupied polishing the hull.

That aside, the *Trojan* looked like a real bruiser. HPA battleships had plating so thick it was occasionally speculated that you could fly one clean through a small moon without realising it. Alongside that, they carried enough missiles to wipe out a hundred cities, as well as two charge cannons that could put an enormous crater in the surface of a planet and cause real problems for any opponents too slow to get out of the line of fire.

The *Trojan* was the type of warship that could go head-to-head with a Daklan annihilator and stand a chance of coming out on top. In Recker's mind, the military needed to push a few of those engagements in order to learn how best to combat the enemy. More than anything, they needed victories. Personnel wanted to see human warships slug it out with the best of the Daklan fleet, rather than hide away in fear of defeat.

"I bet even the ceilings have carpet," said Aston mischievously. "Probably leopard skin."

"Yeah, and there'll be more chefs onboard than soldiers and crew combined," Burner added.

"Enough," said Recker. He could tolerate the minor insubordination but thinking about the situation made him feel tired and angry in equal measures.

"I bet Admiral Fraser is shitting himself that he's been pushed to the frontline," said Eastwood.

Recker had no sympathy. "He should embrace the opportunity, Lieutenant."

Maybe he'll come out of it a better man.

"Here comes the *Shock and Awe*," said Burner.

"Monitor the particle wave," Recker instructed. "Just in case."

"Definitely one of ours, sir."

The *Shock and Awe* entered local space a hundred thousand kilometres away and began executing evasive manoeuvres at once. The cruiser joined the battle network and the commanding officer banked to join the fleet.

"We've been issued a synchronisation code, sir," said Burner. "The destination checks out as the Agarvand system."

"Home to Pinvos," said Recker. "Accept the code."

The synch codes ensured that every ternium drive on the battle network would fire at the same time and with the same output. It was an excellent method to ensure a fleet arrived in the same place and at the same time. Variations happened, but generally not enough to cause problems at the destination.

With the *Expectation*'s lightspeed drive whining at increasing volume, Recker checked out the final ship in the fleet. The heavy lifter *Titan* wasn't as large as the Daklan equivalent which had arrived at Etrol and Oldis, but at 10,000 metres, it was no minnow. In terms of design, it bore a striking resemblance to the planetary dredgers, and Recker believed they shared many components. Where the dredgers had lasers and gravity suction chutes, the lifters had massive underside doors.

"It's going to be tight squeezing a tenixite converter in there," said Eastwood.

"I'm sure someone did the maths, Lieutenant."

Despite his outward confidence, Recker wasn't so sure one of the alien cylinders *would* fit. Lengthwise there should be room, but the converters had a 2000-metre diameter and that would present a challenge to the lifter crew.

"Can't worry about everything," he muttered.

A few minutes later, the *Expectation*'s ternium drive achieved a state of readiness. The synch code held the launch for long seconds, presumably because the other destroyers were fitted with slower cores than the newer *Expectation*.

"Come on, come on," said Recker, tapping the arm of his chair impatiently. The howl of the engines filled the bridge and he could sense their eagerness to be unleashed.

At thirteen minutes, the drive fired and the fleet entered lightspeed.

CHAPTER FOUR

AFTER TWO WEEKS on the Adamantine base, Recker was already coiled up and realized that a ten-day journey would be a test of his willpower. Rather than permit circumstances to rule his state of mind, he determined to keep himself occupied. Unfortunately, the options were limited. The *Expectation*'s small gym was in high demand and the ceilings of the interior passages were so low that it wasn't easy to run circuits. Aside from that, the options were reading or watching shows from the on-demand TV databanks. With such a short list of distractions, Recker made the best of what was available.

One morning, halfway into the journey, Recker was on the treadmill, with Aston running alongside. The gym was tiny and the only other equipment was a surprisingly unutilised rowing machine.

"This place could do with some music," said Aston. She had a good pace going – enough for a sheen of sweat to form on her exposed skin.

"It doesn't help," said Recker.

"Not a lover of music, huh?"

For some reason, the question had Recker stumped. "I don't know."

"You don't know?" Aston grinned. She had an open manner and could ask prying questions in a way that didn't offend. The way she fitted in everywhere made it easy to forget she was only twenty-eight.

"My parents never listened to it at home," Recker admitted. "Maybe it passed me by."

"That's the trouble with being an only child - you get a sheltered upbringing. And music *never* passes you by. One day it'll sneak up and before you know it, you'll think it's the best thing ever."

"I'll watch out for the moment, Commander. I need something other than bare walls."

"Bare walls and enemies, sir."

"Here it comes," said Recker dryly.

Aston said her piece, like she'd been waiting for the right moment. "Even when he's a trillion klicks away, he's got you, sir. I'll bet Admiral Solan enjoys every moment of life." Her face twisted. "And it's not fair."

"I promised myself it would change, Commander, and it will."

"You should be on the fast track to promotion, sir. Instead, years of your career have been wasted because of this..." she hesitated and then came out with it. "...asshole and his bunch of sycophants. Cowards every one of them and they're going to cost us this war."

"They're not all cowards."

"Cowards for what they're doing, sir." Aston gave a

short, bitter laugh, then stepped off the treadmill and came over to Recker. "Most of them are cowards when it comes to the fighting as well. If we had less like them and more like you, we'd be in a different situation. Instead, the brave ones die and the others live and perpetuate the same old shit, not once committing themselves to facing the enemy."

"Except Vice Admiral Fraser."

"Like Ken said it, Admiral Fraser doesn't want to be here." She sighed. "You say things are changing, sir, and it can't come soon enough. Maybe Admiral Telar is doing the right thing, whatever it takes."

"He's a man I can respect," said Recker. "For a time, I wasn't sure which way he fell."

"It's only a shame it took him so long to reveal his hand."

Recker pushed a button on the panel in front of him and the treadmill stopped. He picked up the towel he'd hung over the machine's side rail and wiped his face. "And I might yet be wrong about him."

"I don't think so."

"Nor do I. We'll find out soon enough."

They left the gym and went separate ways. Recker stopped at the mess for some breakfast, where he found Corporal Suzy Hendrix and Private Ken Raimi swapping tales they'd probably told a hundred times before. The soldiers were dressed in combat suits, their helmets within easy reach. They both remembered what happened when the heatwave swept through the *Punisher* and weren't going to make the same mistake as their squadmates who died.

"No sign of the new boys and girls," said Recker, sitting down with his fruit juice and bacon-ish sandwich.

"You'll see them soon enough, sir," said Raimi. His cheeks had a touch of colour which the overhead lights exaggerated. "The sergeant doesn't let anyone sleep past 6:30am."

"Yeah, he puts us through our paces in the deployment bay. Seven at a time," said Hendrix, telling Recker something he already knew.

"The bay's a shit place for exercise," said Raimi. "We just got back."

"Corporal Hendrix's face isn't red like yours, Private."

"Yeah well, I always work hardest. Everyone knows it."

Hendrix gave a derisive snort but didn't respond to the obvious exaggeration. Her hair had grown since last time and she had it tied in a short tail. She looked at Recker.

"Five days until what, sir? Some of the guys say we're hunting for relics, but I'd rather hear it straight from the head honcho."

Recker's mouth twitched upwards at the informality. "It's the same old, same old, Corporal. What we found on Oldis has got high command interested and now we're out looking for more like it."

"Super weapons to take out the Daklan," offered Raimi.

"I'd take those bastards out if I could. Easy as that," said Hendrix. She paused and something in her face changed, like a cloud drifting away from the sun. "Or maybe I wouldn't. Not unless I was forced to choose between them and us."

"Getting soft, Corporal?" asked Raimi.

"Nah. Just seems to me that a weapon which can take out an annihilator on its lowest setting isn't something we want to turn to maximum and aim at a populated world, no matter who's living there."

"Let's hope it doesn't come to that," said Recker. "Sometimes the threat is all you need to force peace."

"Peace ain't coming, sir," said Raimi. "I only dream of war."

"Bullshit, Private," said Hendrix, laughing out loud. "You've got a week's pay down with Drawl that we'll be drinking in a Daklan bar within the year."

"Hey, don't remind me," said Raimi, looking pained.

"I'll remind you not to lay bets when you've been drinking."

"A week's pay to find that out is a cheap lesson," said Recker.

He finished eating and took his leave, putting his tray into the replicator's disposal slot on the way out. He needed a shower, but since he wasn't due on shift for another hour, decided to take a walk around the ship. So far, the journey hadn't been so bad and he was pleased to find that the soldiers no longer greeted him with sullen stares and surly acknowledgements. There was nothing like a hard-fought victory to help people recognize the ones who were doing their best.

As well as the improved attitudes, the overall morale was better than expected given that the war was going badly and the common perception was that neither high command nor the Representation cared. Recker knew full well that most of them *did* care, they just lacked the leadership qualities required to turn things around.

With the HPA at total war, the shift in attitudes was slowly being recognized. Money was pouring in and suddenly the newfound determination to claw back the ground lost to the Daklan was visible wherever people looked. Recker couldn't allow himself to believe that it was already too late, but deep down, he was worried that the enemy hadn't so far been trying too hard and that once they realized the HPA was giving it everything, the Daklan would respond by turning the screw.

He thought back to his recent conversation in the mess room. Hendrix had grasped the ramifications of either side holding a weapon like the tenixite converters and Recker understood them just as well. The only thing stopping one species massacring the other in the war was the fact that each side had managed to keep their main population centres so well hidden. If that ever changed, Recker didn't know what would happen. With the amount of firepower in a modern cruiser or battleship, the destructive potential of the tenixite converters was distinctly overkill.

Taking the long route to his quarters, Recker stopped to watch Sergeant Vance putting half of his squad through their paces. The *Expectation*'s single bay was a fraction longer than the equivalent on a riot class. It was low ceilinged like everywhere else and the channel running along the middle of the floor made the space seem more akin to a confluence room in an underground sewer.

That channel gave access to the single deployment vessel. On top of that, a destroyer carried two Puncher medium tanks, these accessed through shafts in the port and starboard forward corners of the bay.

It was cold down here and the soldiers wore both suits and helmets. Sergeant Vance was animated, making angry chopping motions with his hand as he ordered the troops to sprint from one end of the bay to the other in a full loadout.

Recker didn't stay long and returned to his room where he showered and then returned to the bridge. Everything was running smoothly. Hardware failures at lightspeed weren't unheard of, but generally it was the into-lightspeed transition where they occurred and to a lesser extent when a spaceship re-entered local space.

"Five more days of this," said Burner, stretching like he didn't mind one way or the other. The edge of his console was piled with empty cups and a stack of trays was building where he rested his feet.

"Tidy that up, Lieutenant," said Recker. "You should know better."

He took his seat and went through the motions of a status check. The monitoring tools reported no concerns and that was enough. Naturally, the comms receivers had nothing new - when travelling at lightspeed, the comms didn't work in or out and the sensors wouldn't gather any data, leaving a warship effectively isolated from everything. It was a limitation which Recker hoped the HPA would overcome at some point before his death or retirement.

Recker often considered how strange it was that technology allowed a forty-billion-ton lump of metal and engines to travel at incredible speeds and arrive unscathed at its intended destination, yet nobody exactly understood what was happening during the process. Sure, the scientists talked about *mathematical vector tunnels* and *non-accelerative theoretical motion*. Other terms, such as *light-speed transition* were used freely in the military, like everyone knew exactly what was happening behind the words.

The remainder of the journey passed by – as they all did – and, as the re-entry time approached, the crew readied themselves. Recker noted the change in atmosphere. The bored humour fell away and the crew focused on what lay ahead.

"Ten minutes!" said Eastwood. "We're aiming for five million klicks from Pinvos. Given the length of the journey, we might see some divergence from the intended coordinates."

"We'll deal with whatever comes, Lieutenant." Recker turned towards Aston. "Run through the details again for me."

"Pinvos is planet three of six in the Agarvand system," she replied. "The star is larger than average and Pinvos itself is one-point-five billion klicks out, meaning it's going to be cold and barren. Other than that, we don't have much – Agarvand is outside the sphere of our usual star charts and we only have this much data because the team on Deep Space Quad3 was hunting for the destination of the Oldis cylinder's outward transmission."

Recker wasn't upset by the lack of detail – the HPA's area of influence was no more than a speck in the universe. It wasn't unusual for a mission to bring him to places like this – unvisited solar systems filled with uncharted celestial bodies.

"Once we arrive, the *Trojan*'s comms team will create the battle network," he said. "From there, we'll scan the planet and wait for Admiral Fraser's decision on the next step."

"Five minutes!" said Eastwood.

Recker settled into his seat. He didn't know what to expect from this mission and he hoped that for once, the HPA would get a lucky break by locating something both undefended and useful which they could load into the *Titan*'s bay and take home for study. He smiled inwardly – every gain was hard-fought and he didn't expect it to be otherwise at Pinvos.

"Ten seconds!"

The timer hit zero and the warship didn't exit lightspeed. Two tense minutes passed and Recker looked to Lieutenant Eastwood for answers.

"What's happening, Lieutenant?"

"I'm not sure, sir. The moment I know, you'll know."

No sooner had Eastwood spoken the words than Recker detected the ternium drive switching over. The *Expectation* entered local space and he gave the engines full power. The surging acceleration pushed him into his seat and he watched the sensor feeds, waiting for them to calibrate.

"Get on with those scans," Recker ordered.

"Still waiting, sir. The comms system is online and searching for a battle network. Looks like we got here first."

"We're two minutes late. We can't be first."

The sensors came up and Burner started a local area scan, while Eastwood watched for incoming particle waves.

"Local area scan clear," said Burner. He sounded puzzled. "We landed off the mark, sir. We're closer to twenty-five million klicks from Pinvos."

"Two minutes late and twenty million klicks off-target," said Recker. "I'd like some answers."

Aston and Eastwood got on it, while Burner extended his scan sphere. Once Recker was convinced there were no hostiles nearby, he slowed the destroyer and set it on a course that followed the distant Pinvos along its orbital track.

"I think I understand what happened, sir," said Eastwood after only a few seconds. "The synchronisation algorithm we received from the *Trojan* didn't detect that we were only at 99% of our maximum propulsion output. That screwed up the vector and we ended up here."

"If we're late, why's there nothing on the battle network?" asked Recker. "Please double-check we're in the right place."

"There's no doubt, sir," said Burner. "This is the Agarvand system and this planet here is Pinvos."

An image of the planet came up on the screen. The *Expectation* had more capable sensor hardware than a riot class, but twenty-five million klicks was too far for them to obtain a sharp feed.

"Another rock," said Recker. "So where the hell is the rest of the fleet?"

"I don't know, sir," said Burner. "We're in range to join

any HPA battle network, even if we consider a worst-case divergence over the ten-day journey."

"And we were only two minutes later than expected," said Aston. "That's not enough time for the fleet to have travelled blind side."

"Send an FTL comm to base," snapped Recker in sudden anger. "Tell them we've arrived, but there's no sign of anyone else."

The FTL comm had a long way to travel and he was under no illusions that he'd receive a response any time soon. Recker wasn't planning to wait it out. On the other hand, the situation was completely unfathomable. The fleet was either late or it was elsewhere and Recker refused to countenance the idea that the other warships had somehow been destroyed in the two minutes since their arrival.

Despite his refusal to accept the possibility, the idea wormed its way into his head and he couldn't shake it out.

CHAPTER FIVE

"COMMANDER ASTON, I want you to assist Lieutenant Burner. Focus on the area where the fleet was meant to arrive and keep scanning until you find something.

"Are we staying at 25 million klicks?" asked Burner.

"For the moment. This isn't a time to fly in and hope for the best."

"This is going to be like looking for a needle in a haystack, sir."

"I know – do what you can." Recker twisted in his seat. "Lieutenant Eastwood, I need to be sure that the synch algorithm didn't screw with something else that we don't know about. We weren't the slowest warship in the fleet, so maybe we did somehow arrive early instead of late."

"I don't think there's any doubt, sir, but I'll go over the propulsion output logs."

Recker left his crew to get on with it. He itched to

help, but he was needed at the controls. Even though the local area scans had turned up nothing, Recker didn't want his ship taken out in a surprise attack. Normally, he wouldn't have considered it likely, but with the mission task force apparently missing, he didn't want to discount any possibility, no matter how remote.

"The timings are worse than we thought," said Eastwood eventually. "If we assume a straight one percent reduction in our propulsion output and work that across the expected flight duration, we could be as much as 138 minutes later than the rest of the fleet."

"And that one percent loss in output translates directly to a one percent increase in travel time?"

"Well, it's a little more than one percent," said Eastwood. "On top of that, we're not down an exact one percent on our maximum propulsion – it's more like a 0.98 percent reduction. When you throw it all together, it ends up at 138 minutes." He looked pained.

"What else, Lieutenant?"

"When it comes to the interaction between the synch algorithms and our own processing core, things start to get fuzzy. We thought we were two minutes late, but the timer itself has been wrong from the outset. We could be more than 138 minutes late or less than 138 minutes late and I can't give you a definite answer one way or the other."

"This was always a ten-day journey," said Burner.

"But when you say *ten days,* what you could mean is nine days and fifteen hours. Or ten days and six hours. Humans talk in round numbers and rely on the computers to keep track of the specifics."

Burner opened his mouth and then closed it again. He

scratched his head. "Things went wrong and we don't know how badly."

"It's likely we got here a little more than two hours after the rest of the fleet," said Eastwood. "All that other stuff I said was just the possibilities."

"Let's work on two hours," said Recker. "As you said, humans get on better with round numbers. I don't plan to come much closer than this to Pinvos for a while, so if it turns out that we're actually early, then we'll see the rest of the fleet when it gets here."

"I hope we're early, sir. I really do," said Eastwood.

"Me too, Lieutenant. Keep working on the figures and see what comes out."

"Yes, sir."

"Commander Aston, Lieutenant Burner, it's down to you. Find something and tell me we're not alone out here."

"Since we're here to investigate Pinvos, that's where I'm concentrating my efforts, sir," said Burner. "The planet isn't large, but the surface is rough and there's still a lot of ground to cover."

"And it's not easy from 25 million klicks. I know how it is," said Recker. "The transmission from Oldis led us here, so there's a good chance you're going to find another tenixite converter."

"Yes, sir. I've been searching for a pattern of cylindrical holes. Those should be easier to spot than the cylinder itself."

"Don't forget we didn't see any holes on Etrol."

"I reckon that was a dead node," said Aston. "Either that or it was never called upon to activate its depletion burst."

Recker didn't have an opinion one way or another. Certainly if the Etrol node had failed, it meant the Daklan were in possession of non-functioning hardware and that could only be a good thing.

"You don't suppose our fleet was destroyed by a depletion burst, do you?" said Eastwood. "I didn't want to be the one to ask."

"I already considered that same question, Lieutenant. Remember that the Oldis converter didn't fire until we instructed it from the command station."

"It performed an automatic core override on the Daklan shuttle, sir. The cylinder wasn't all manually controlled."

Recker hadn't forgotten. The core override had knocked the enemy craft out of the air without causing any outwardly apparent damage, leaving him to guess as to what effect the weapon had on its target.

Two hours went by. The missing fleet didn't turn up and neither Burner nor Aston located anything significant using the sensors.

"There's a chance I missed something," said Burner. "But given the circumstances, maybe we'd be safer trying for a long-distance scan of the current blind side."

"That would mean a lightspeed jump or a long time on the sub-light engines," said Recker.

"Or we could stay where we are, sir," said Aston. "If the fleet arrives, we'll see the clustered ternium clouds from here."

"I don't think they're coming, Commander. I think they got here ahead of us and something happened."

"If there's wreckage, we might not find it," said

Burner. "All depending on size of debris and post-destruction trajectory."

"Or they were turned into dust by a depletion burst and the tenixite converter got taken blind side by the planet's rotation," said Eastwood.

Recker grimaced. He had plenty of variables to consider and he wasn't yet sure how he was going to play this one. Having witnessed the effects of the depletion burst on Oldis, he was ready to accept that the weapon could turn an entire fleet into particles so small that the *Expectation* would never locate them – particularly from this range.

Aside from a depletion burst, the Daklan were a second possibility. If the aliens were here with sufficient strength, they could have taken out the HPA fleet. In which case, there'd be wreckage, which may or may not be spread across a few million kilometres. Depending on the lateness of the *Expectation*'s arrival, some of that debris might have impacted with Pinvos and with sufficient velocity to leave visible cratering.

He growled in anger and wished things were clearer.

"A lightspeed jump will leave a ternium cloud that increases our visibility to enemy ships a thousand-fold," he said at last. "It's a risk I'm unwilling to take – not yet. We're heading in on the sub-lights – directly for the planet."

"That's a five-and-a-half-hour journey," said Eastwood.

"We're not going all the way, Lieutenant. I'll aim for twenty million – maybe a bit closer. If the fleet doesn't arrive in that time, we can say with near certainty that they're either not coming or they got here first."

"At twenty million we'll achieve better scan results," said Burner. "It won't be perfect."

"I've got faith in you, Lieutenant."

With his decision made, Recker fed in the power and the *Expectation* accelerated to its maximum velocity of 1300 kilometres per second. Thoughts of the overstress device jumped into his head, but he wasn't even tempted to give the new hardware a trial run.

After ten minutes, Burner spotted something on the sensors.

"What the hell?" he said.

"I need details, not questions, Lieutenant."

"I caught a hint of a moving object between us and the planet, sir. With the sensors at maximum zoom, they don't track too well and I'm doing what I can to establish a lock."

"How far away is it?"

"I'd guess it's two million klicks over Pinvos, sir."

"That's got to be one of our ships," said Eastwood. "Or a Daklan one."

"I don't think so," said Burner. "I'm not sure what it was."

Recker didn't like the unexplained and he felt a rising sense of alarm. "I'll bring us to a halt," he said. "Until I know more about that object, we're not going in any closer than this."

"I've got a lock on it, sir. Whatever it is, it's huge and travelling fast along a high orbital track around Pinvos. Altitude confirmed at two million klicks and I'm putting it up on the screen."

An *object* appeared on the bulkhead screen. Recker couldn't think of a more precise way to describe the peculiarly shaped mass of dark grey that sped around the planet. Burner's assertion that the discovery was huge seemed like an understatement – if this was a spaceship, it was several times the mass of anything in the HPA or Daklan fleets.

"Can you enhance?" he asked.

"That is enhanced, sir. The clarity will increase if we get closer."

"How fast is it going?" said Recker.

"Approximately 870 klicks per second, sir."

"It could be a spaceship," said Aston. "Or a satellite."

"If it's a satellite it could reach that velocity with the help of a gravity slingshot," said Eastwood. "Otherwise whoever built it fitted enormous propulsion modules."

"Estimating the mass based on the density of ternium and the dimensions of the object, it could weigh upwards of two hundred billion tons," said Burner. "And that's being conservative."

At first, Recker's brain didn't want to believe. This mission had come with the intention of finding alien artifacts – weapons to be precise – so he knew he shouldn't be surprised to discover something out of the ordinary.

"How long before it's out of sight again?" he asked.

"Approximately fifteen minutes. It's got a two-hour orbital period and I didn't detect it straightaway."

For once, Recker was stumped about what to do and he drummed his fingers, aware that a window to act might be slipping away. "A two-hour orbit means that whatever that thing is, it might have been on this side of the planet when our fleet came out of lightspeed."

"If the timings were right, our fleet could have arrived in the path of the object we're tracking, though at a much greater altitude," said Eastwood.

"I'd have called those timings *wrong*, Lieutenant," said Recker, becoming increasingly convinced that the missing fleet had been destroyed and that this object was responsible.

"We should let it go, sir," said Aston. "That'll give us two hours to scan the planet's surface for anything we might have missed. Then we should consider a lightspeed jump to the blind side and resume scanning."

"What about the object?" said Burner in surprise.

"We'll deal with it when we're ready. I'm proposing we avoid a potential confrontation until we're ready."

"It's the strangest damn satellite I ever saw," said Burner. "Whatever we find out about it, I don't think we're going to like the answers."

"When was it ever different?" asked Recker. "Here's what's going to happen – we'll let the satellite go on its way. A two-hour orbit gives us enough time to finish our intended approach to twenty million klicks."

"That means we'll be a minimum distance of eighteen million from the satellite," said Burner. "It's got such a high orbital track that it'll be further away for much of the visibility window."

"Yes. We should be in place in plenty of time for you to determine exactly what it is."

"Eighteen million klicks might not be close enough, sir."

Recker offered a concession. "What about fifteen million?"

"If you're offering fifteen, that'll have to be good enough. Whatever we've found, it probably destroyed our ships and we owe it to the HPA to find out what we can."

"Well said, Lieutenant."

Recker took the controls and resumed the approach to Pinvos. The *Expectation*'s sensors tracked the satellite for as long as possible, until it vanished around the planet's blind side. Once the object was gone, the tension which had crept up on Recker lessened significantly and he exhaled loudly.

Halfway into the journey, Lieutenant Burner came up with a discovery that shocked everyone.

"Sir, I've been studying the recorded feed of the satellite," he said. "You're not going to believe this."

"I can't leave my seat, Lieutenant. You'll have to spell it out for me."

"I told you it was the strangest satellite I ever saw and that got me thinking. I manipulated the feed recording and tested a few hypotheses, and I believe it's a collection of different objects, rather than just one."

"I don't understand the significance," said Recker.

"Let me explain, sir. Once I came up with that conclusion, I tried to break the whole into its component parts and I believe it comprises nine separate objects. Spaceships."

Recker suddenly realized where Burner was heading with this. "The missing part of the task force comprises only six members, Lieutenant."

"I know that, sir, but I've been able to produce a rough

estimate of the mass and dimensions. One of the components is the *Titan*. I'm sure of it. Two of the others conform to the dimensions of a Teron class cruiser."

"And the others?"

"The *Trojan* and our destroyers. I could be totally wrong about this, but I thought I should let you know."

"Assuming you're correct, that leaves three you haven't mentioned," said Recker.

"Desolators, sir. Three components are the same approximate size as Daklan heavy cruisers."

Recker had no idea if Burner had added two and two, and come up with fifty-six, but the whole idea of these warships being somehow bound together on an orbit of Pinvos only added to the mystery of the situation.

"We'll find out soon, Lieutenant."

"I guess we will, sir."

The *Expectation* flew on.

CHAPTER SIX

AT SEVENTEEN MILLION kilometres from Pinvos, Recker brought the destroyer to a halt. The satellite should have been visible for the last twenty minutes, but Burner was having a hard time locating it.

"I don't know where it is, sir," he admitted. "It's easy enough to predict where it'll emerge from the planet's cusp and it was travelling at a constant velocity, but it's not where it should be."

"Could it have shifted orbit?" said Aston suddenly.

"That would explain why we haven't located the target," Burner nodded.

"I'll move my search radius to the north-west, Lieutenant. Let's see if I'm right."

"And I'll go south-west."

A few seconds later, Aston located the satellite. "Got it. I don't know what the hell happened, but it's on a different orbital track. Same altitude and velocity as before. Our current distance to the target is eighteen million klicks."

"Get me a feed," said Recker. "I don't like this at all."

"Here we go."

At eighteen million kilometres, the feed was noticeably cleaner than it had been from twenty-three million and when he studied it, Recker was left in no doubt that Lieutenant Burner's theory was far from madness.

"You were right, Lieutenant. I can see the individual shapes of the warships and for some reason they're all aligned the same way."

"Yes, sir and I believe they're arranged in a rough sphere. There're approximately twenty klicks between each of the spaceships and I'm certain those last three are Daklan heavies. Either that or they're a different sort of warship with near-identical mass and dimensions."

"It's possible they're something else," said Eastwood. "The existence of the *Vengeance* means these new aliens had – or have - a fleet of their own."

"If any of our ships are receiving comms, they're not responding," said Burner. "Which means they're either completely out of power or..." He tailed off.

"Or their crews are dead, Lieutenant. Let's not sugar-coat what it is we're up against." Recker didn't take his eyes off the feed. "If those hulls form a sphere, what's in the centre?"

"The sensors aren't detecting anything, sir."

"That's not the same as there being nothing to locate."

"No."

"Lieutenant Burner, concentrate your efforts on the imagined centre. If there's something inside that sphere with advanced sensor deflection, I'd like to know what it is," said Recker. "Commander Aston, check out the surface. Find what there is to be found."

"Anything capable of holding nine warships in place and hurling them around a planet at 870 klicks per second isn't going to fit inside a teacup, sir," said Eastwood. "It's going to be bigger than big."

"In which case it should be easy to find." Recker had another thought. "Lieutenant Eastwood, is there any way to obtain hull readings from those warships?"

"Not from here, sir. You're thinking this is a core override."

"Maybe. The *Vengeance* was brought down by an override. It was like the off switch had been pushed at the same time as all the onboard systems were returned to how they were before the software was configured."

"What we're seeing could fit in with that," said Eastwood.

"Which means we could suffer the same outcome if we get too close," said Burner. "Did the technical teams find out anything from their examination of the *Vengeance* that we could use?"

"No," said Recker. "There was no trace of the override – like it happened and that was it. No audit logs, no nothing."

"If those ships were shut down, how come they ended up so neatly arrayed?"

Recker shook his head. "That's something I can't answer, Commander, and I would dearly like it to be otherwise."

"If we're up against an alien weapon, it would be good

to have an idea of the activation range as well," said Burner. He cursed in frustration. "Too many unknowns."

The satellite sped around its orbital track, coming steadily closer to the fifteen-million-kilometre minimum. While the *Expectation*'s crew had lost a few minutes' visibility because of the orbital shift, the object wouldn't be out of sight for a while yet.

As Recker watched, one of the smaller shapes – a destroyer if the theory was correct - detached from the cluster. It accelerated at an incredible rate until it reached a peak velocity of three thousand kilometres per second, heading directly away from Pinvos. A moment later, the second destroyer followed.

"What the hell?" said Recker. He racked his brain trying to figure out the reason for this unexplained development. "Lieutenant Burner, attempt contact with those destroyers."

Lieutenant Burner didn't require prompting. After a few tense seconds, he looked up. "Still no response, sir."

In front of Recker's eyes, the first of the destroyers to be ejected from the cluster was hit by a weapon from an unknown source. The warship's hull went rapidly from red to orange and then white. A moment later, the stresses of heat expansion tore it into indistinct pieces of debris, which dispersed in an arc as it sped away from the other spaceships.

Recker guessed what was coming next and so did the others of his crew.

"Oh crap, no," said Aston.

The second destroyer went the way of the first, becoming an incandescent storm of wreckage, doomed to forever travel through space with its carbonized passengers reduced to no more than a memory of what they'd once been.

With a snarl of fury, Recker crashed his fist against the top of his console. "No!" he roared. He closed his eyes and imposed control on his emotions. Anger had its place, but not here. "Find me the source of that weapon," he said. "Do it quickly."

"On it, sir," said Burner, his bared teeth indicating he was struggling with rage of his own.

"I'll assist Lieutenant Burner," said Aston.

"I want something I can act on before we lose sight of the target again. By the time it comes back it might have *disposed* of our other ships."

"The satellite is almost at its fifteen million klick minimum range, sir," said Burner. "I'm picking up ghost traces of an object in the centre."

"Something's deflecting our sensors," Aston confirmed. "If we didn't have an idea of where to look, I doubt we'd have detected it even from a million klicks."

"What are we facing?" asked Recker. "Tell me."

"We won't find specifics from here, sir."

Recker couldn't sit and he paced three steps one way and three the other, while his brain roiled with unformed ideas.

"If we could predict the target's next orbital shift, we could send a couple of Hellburners to meet it when it completes another circuit," he said.

"We lack data to predict the shift, sir," said Aston. "And since our missiles won't lock from this range, we're relying on them heading to pre-programmed coordinates.

The level of precision required may be beyond our hardware."

"I know, Commander, I'm thinking aloud," said Recker. He gritted his teeth – the Hellburners' travel time from here to the target location was more than thirty minutes. Expecting them to hit an object with an 870 kilometre per second velocity using pre-programmed coordinates required a great deal of optimism, especially given the presence of the other warships around the satellite. Besides, using the Hellburners would mean allowing the enemy object to complete another two-hour orbit, during which time it might well destroy more of the captured task force.

"We could lightspeed to the far side of the planet in order to intercept the target and strike at it from a much closer range," said Aston.

"Which means creating a huge particle wave," said Eastwood. "If we're undetected now, we won't be after that." A split second later, he gave a shout of alarm.

Recker didn't understand what was wrong, but he spun towards his console in time to see thousands of lines of text rolling upwards on every one of his screens. He sprang into his seat and his eyes scanned the activity, trying to make sense of it.

"We're shutting down," he said in disbelief. His fingers jumped from place to place and he called up status menus on his screens. Within seconds, he knew what was happening. "Core override."

"I can't stop it happening," said Eastwood.

"Nor me, sir," said Aston. "I'm locked out of the weapons."

Recker did what he could. First, he attempted to isolate the critical systems from the rest of the warship's network. Somehow, the core override had already affected every piece of hardware, like it had appeared everywhere, rather than spreading from an initial source. In truth, Recker wasn't sure if the weapon was hardware or software based and his ignorance hampered the efforts to counter the attack.

"I'm applying admin level protection on every file to prevent manipulation or deletion," he said.

"That's going to take too long, sir."

"I know. It's something."

A few moments after applying new permissions to one of the data arrays, Recker's link to the hardware was cut. He tried again on a separate array with the same outcome. "Damnit!"

The core override was unstoppable and it swept through the *Expectation*'s hardware. In less than sixty seconds, Recker was unable to access anything using his console. Whatever he attempted, he got no response to his commands.

"We're powered up, but we can't control anything." Recker fought the temptation to punch his console. "I want answers," he said. "Failing that, ideas."

Eastwood already had an idea. "The core override was selective, sir. At first, I thought the attack was intended to purge our control systems, but if you look at your console you can see that all the monitoring tools are operational. If the status readouts are correct, the *Expectation* is in full working order. We just can't do anything."

"Which makes me think the core override isn't just a

dumb shut-down weapon," said Aston. "I think it's a tool designed to subvert at the command and control level."

Suddenly, the propulsion note climbed in volume and Recker felt a surge of acceleration. "We're moving."

The monitoring tools were active like Eastwood said, and Recker accessed them. The propulsion output was stuck on 99% and stayed that way until the *Expectation* hit maximum velocity.

"Lieutenant Burner, can you access the FTL comms?" asked Recker, knowing the answer already.

"No, sir – same with all external comms in or out." He paused for a moment. "I'm into the sensors again!" Burner's excitement was short-lived. "I can't control them and they're fixed on the same settings as before the override. I'll attempt to estimate our course based on the position of the stars."

"We're heading to the same place as all those other ships," said Recker. "No place else we could be going."

"It'll take more than three hours to reach the closest point of the previous orbit," said Aston. "Sounds like we're in for a long trip."

"That gives us time to work on a solution, Commander." Recker turned. "Lieutenant Burner, can you access the internal comms?"

"Yes, sir. Those aren't much more complicated than two tin cans connected by a wire. They're working fine."

"I want you to speak to Sergeant Vance. Tell him to check out the deployment vehicle and the two tanks in the underside bay. I want to know if they're affected as well."

"I'll pass on the order, sir."

Recker proceeded with his investigation into the

extent of the core override's effect on his warship. It didn't require expert evaluation to realize that the weapon was sophisticated and he experienced a fleeting hopelessness over the situation. This was the same attack which had incapacitated not only the HPA fleet, but the Daklan heavy cruisers as well. And a weapon which had brought down the *Vengeance* eighty years ago.

"The *Vengeance* crashed onto Tanril because of the core override," he said, hoping that talking would spur on an idea.

"And when we found it, it was like someone had done a fresh install of the control systems," said Eastwood.

Recker drummed his fingers. "When we were flying it home, we suspected that the warship had done a complete and automatic reinstall from backups, and the shipyard concluded likewise."

"We have the control software install package on one of our data arrays," said Aston. "Checking…damn, it's been deleted."

"That would have been too easy," said Eastwood angrily.

"Someone on one of our spaceships would have already figured it out," said Recker. "If not us, then the Daklan."

"Whoever built the *Vengeance* must have had a lot more experience combating the core override than we have," said Aston. "Somehow they figured out a way to get their backups online."

"Too late to prevent the crash into Tanril."

Recker grimaced. "And the shipyard found microscopic traces of biological matter across the bulkhead.

The crew of the *Vengeance* were likely killed in the impact."

"Which means the core override can be selective in what it does," said Aston. "When it came to the *Vengeance*, the override switched off the life support prior to impact, ensuring everyone onboard got killed."

"And the same could happen to us." Recker swore again. "For the moment, it seems like we're being taken towards that ghost satellite. Why?"

"Information," said Burner. "We're being brought in for interrogation. Once that's done, we'll suffer the same fate as the *Barbarian* and the *Claymore*."

"Why were the other ships spared?" wondered Recker.

"It seems Lieutenant Burner is right about an interrogation, sir," said Eastwood, his voice thick with worry. "Check out the utilisation on our main core."

Recker didn't need to check. "It's up and down. I thought that was a result of the core override attack."

"I had a closer look and our own core is actually working to break the encryption locks on some of our critical data arrays."

"I thought the core override had control over those already?"

"That's what I thought as well, sir. In fact, it seems like the attack was specifically designed to take over our command and control systems – effectively locking us out in order that a further attack can take place on our encrypted data."

"The command and control system doesn't have

access to the encryption keys, sir," said Aston. "They're tied in with our biometrics and also encrypted."

"So our attackers are using our own core to brute force into our data," said Recker, clenching his fists. He swore again. "Those arrays contain our star charts."

"The analysis of which might lead a hostile species to our home worlds," said Burner. "Shit."

A chill gripped Recker, constricting his entire body. If this conclusion was accurate, the core override might eventually crack open the encryption locks protecting all kinds of data that humanity didn't want falling into the wrong hands. Once that happened, all bets about the future were off.

Unable to prevent himself, Recker gave his crew an extended demonstration of the language he'd picked up as a ground trooper many years ago.

CHAPTER SEVEN

FOR TWO HOURS, the crew worked ceaselessly, not only to regain control of the *Expectation* but also to prevent the warship's own core from extracting the sensitive data from its arrays. So far, they'd had no luck and though Recker wasn't about to give up hope, he was fully aware that the crews on all those other captured warships had been doing the same thing for longer and without apparent success.

Meanwhile, Sergeant Vance had investigated the lower bay and reported that all three vehicles were fully operational. Either the core override hadn't noticed them or it wasn't interested. It was possible the holding clamps wouldn't accept the command to release, but they could be easily blown in an emergency. Recker had passed on the order for the soldiers to board the deployment craft and await further commands.

As he thought about the mountain of problems, he pulled at the controls in frustration. He'd tested the response numerous times already and nothing new happened on this occasion - the engine note changed fractionally and the propulsion output dropped a little before jumping once more to 99%. Recker tried again and this time the output gauge didn't move.

"The core override is learning and reacting," he said.

"That's exactly what it's doing, sir," said Eastwood. "If I had control-level access again I could probably disable it given enough time." He laughed bitterly. "Except there are no backups to restore from, so the repair work might take hours, days or weeks."

"I wonder if the satellite destroyed the *Barbarian* and *Claymore* because they had no more secrets to give, or for another reason," said Aston.

"Those destroyers were fitted with earlier-generation cores," said Eastwood. "It might be that they'd take decades to brute-force an encryption lock." He tapped his console. "The *Expectation* has a new core, fitted with a dedicated number cruncher unit."

"How long until our core breaks open those arrays, Lieutenant Eastwood?" asked Recker.

"I don't know, sir – this is a totally unprecedented situation. What I can tell you is that the *Trojan* has many times our processing power and last we saw, it wasn't destroyed."

For the hundredth time, Recker cursed the design of the spaceship. He knew where the data arrays were stored, but they weren't intended to be physically accessed from the interior. Once installed, a core and its associated arrays were assumed to be in for the life of a warship and replacing them required shipyard facilities.

"Can we disable the sensors?" asked Recker in desperation. "Assuming that any stolen data has to be broadcast and since the comms route through those arrays, maybe it's something we can do."

"We have physical access to some, but not all, of the comms antennae, sir. The enemy will only require one functioning antenna in order to transmit what we assume they're trying to steal."

"There's got to be a way," said Recker.

Another hour went by and still the crew were unable to regain control of the *Expectation*. Had the destroyer been alone, Recker would have focused his efforts on ways to detonate the weapons magazines in order to take out the data arrays. With so many other HPA warships involved, the successful destruction of his vessel – if achievable - would have been little more than a pointless gesture.

"Assuming the enemy satellite didn't deviate from its orbital track or change velocity, we should have another ten minutes before we're brought into the cluster," said Burner.

"Time's running out, folks," said Recker.

The crew had worked hard to overcome the effects of the core override and knowledge of their failure rested heavy upon each pair of shoulders. Recker wasn't disappointed in their efforts and he made sure they were aware of the fact.

"But we're still screwed," said Burner.

"Not yet we aren't, Lieutenant. I'm convinced we can fix this." The words were easily said but Recker was finding it increasingly difficult to maintain the belief. "Has anything come into the sensor viewing arc?" he asked. "I'd like to see my enemy."

"Without control over the tracking, we're relying on luck, sir. I'm sure when we're brought in with the other warships, we'll see what fired the core override."

"I feel it'll be all over by that point, Lieutenant."

"It's not like we're in charge right now," said Eastwood.

Recker didn't want to argue and didn't attempt to impose his view. He stood in order to stretch his muscles, and a shape, protruding into the aisle, caught his eye.

"The overstress device," he said, pointing at it.

Eastwood glanced down as if he'd forgotten it was there. "I've been using it as a footrest, sir."

"You mentioned it had a cut-down version of our engine control system built in."

"Yes, sir, it does," said Eastwood, blinking as his mind began working.

"Do you still have access to the device?"

Eastwood entered a command into his console. "Yes, sir. The rest of the command and control system doesn't even know this box exists."

A faint hope crept into Recker. "What would happen if you activated the overstress?"

"The processor would squirt in the control program in order to set the engines into their new state."

"What would happen then?"

"That control program would sit alongside the main controller, maintaining the overstress state until it decides the propulsion has had enough, then it'll shut down again."

"At which point the main controller resumes control."

"Exactly." Light dawned and Eastwood's expression changed to one of excitement. "If I activate the overstress, you'll have a period during which the *Expectation* will respond to the controls."

"Which might be a long time, or not much time at all," said Recker. He was trying to keep his own excitement contained, though he didn't yet have an idea how to take advantage of the new possibilities.

"And we won't have control over the weapons or anything else, sir," said Aston. "If you were planning to put a couple of big holes in the enemy satellite, I can't offer you that."

"I'm aware, Commander."

A plan was forming in Recker's mind. It was risky and borne out of desperation.

The best plans always are.

He announced his intention.

"We're going to let that satellite bring us into the cluster, then we're going to activate this overstress device and I'm going to use the *Expectation* as a battering ram to smash the enemy to pieces. If anyone's got a better suggestion, I'm happy to listen."

"I wish I had, sir," said Burner. "Believe, me, I wish I had."

Eastwood had other concerns. "Aside from the many flaws I won't mention, what happens if this overstress unit decides that it's not safe to increase the load on the engines?"

"That's an excellent question, Lieutenant." Recker glanced at the timer he had running on his console.

"You've got a few minutes. Is that enough to delete the section of coding that estimates the safe levels of engine operation?"

"Yes, sir. The coding is so basic I can do that in less than a minute."

"Go ahead - quickly." Recker smiled grimly. "I intend pulling through this, Lieutenant Eastwood, and if that means I need to destroy this ship or its engines, then so be it."

The code modifications were finished in the promised minute and Eastwood leaned back in his chair, with the air of a man who didn't quite believe what was happening.

"And I changed the 200% hard cap on the overstress to 500%," he announced. "There's no chance the engines will go that high, but I figured we might just need everything we can get."

Recker nodded. "Leave it at 500%," he said. "Our experience on the *Finality* suggests we're unlikely to see much beyond a 400% boost."

The crew spent a few minutes discussing their approach. In reality, they were only killing time before the moment came, and they weren't left waiting long. The *Expectation* had been coasting at maximum speed for the last three hours and the propulsion suddenly intruded.

"We've had an adjustment to our vector," said Burner.

"The engine output indicates we're banking," said Recker, glancing at his display.

"Let's hope the core override doesn't decide a crew is surplus to requirements and switches off the life support," said Burner nervously.

"If it was going to happen, we'd be dead already, Lieutenant."

"That's what I keep telling myself."

A minute later, the *Expectation*'s velocity was down to 1100 kilometres per second. The engines grumbled and Recker felt the on-off stresses as the life support stabilised the interior against a series of erratic course corrections.

"Whoever programmed the core override's flight behaviour shouldn't be allowed within a million klicks of a spaceship," he said. "This is like being on a fairground ride."

"We're slowing," said Aston. "Not long to go."

Recker turned and caught her gaze. She knew the moment was coming and was ready for whatever happened.

"Got something on the sensors, sir!"

A grey mass appeared on one of the starboard arrays. With Burner unable to make adjustments, the spaceship cluster remained outside of the sensor's focus for long moments and then it abruptly snapped into clarity.

Recker stared. The cluster was within a hundred kilometres of the *Expectation* and the first thing which caught his eye was the *Trojan* battleship, with the clear outline of a Daklan heavy cruiser seemingly within touching distance. Further away and at the edge of the feed, Recker spotted what he believed was the cruiser *Shock and Awe*.

"I'm unable to confirm if any other warships have been expelled from the cluster," said Burner.

"Keep watching," said Recker.

While he was extremely keen to find out what had befallen both the HPA and the Daklan spaceships, the most important target right now was the satellite which had captured them. Recker wanted to know what it looked like and what visible armaments it was carrying. The hulking beam of the *Trojan* limited the viewing angle, denying him a sight of his foe for long moments.

At last, the core override altered the *Expectation*'s orientation and Recker got a first glimpse of his opponent. At this range, even the best sensor deflection technology wasn't enough to conceal the target.

"What the hell is that?" asked Burner.

Recker didn't know. The satellite was a cube, made of an alloy so dark it was only distinguishable against the backdrop because the *Expectation*'s sensors automatically enhanced the colours and traced an outline around the alien vessel. At a little more than two thousand metres along its edges, Recker figured it had a mass of anywhere between 160 and 240 billion tons, depending on its composition, and every visible face was covered in sharp-pointed pillars, each 500 metres long and with square bases.

"Looks like a spiked mace from early Earth history," said Eastwood. "Except without a handle to swing it."

"I think those pillars might be antennae," said Burner. "Or maybe a type of sensor array I haven't seen before."

"Which would explain how they managed to detect us from fifteen million klicks," said Aston sourly.

Some bad news was apparent to everyone and since it was his plan, Recker felt obliged to mention it first. "I'd hoped that crashing the *Expectation* into our target would be enough to disable it," he said. "There's no way in hell we'd get through the armour on that thing, let alone break it into pieces."

"Maybe if we had enough speed," said Burner. "It might be hollow."

"It might be," said Recker.

"I don't believe it either, sir."

The final manoeuvring continued for another few minutes and at the end of it, the *Expectation* was on the furthest side of the satellite from Pinvos, with one desolator above and another below. On the positive side, Burner had confirmed sightings of every HPA warship aside from the two destroyers which had been ejected from the cluster earlier.

"Ever feel small?" asked Burner.

"Yeah," said Eastwood. "On mass alone, that satellite is probably beyond the HPA's construction capabilities. When you add in the core override, it's like having our noses rubbed in our technological inferiority."

"I would really like to know what this thing is doing at Pinvos," said Recker. "The ping from the cylinder led straight here."

"I have an idea about that," said Aston. "We believe the tenixite converters form a ringed network, with each in communication with only two others - for reasons of security. What if the creators of the network didn't want their opponents following the trail from one converter to another?"

"So they added this satellite into the network to catch the unwary," said Recker. "And we fell right into the trap."

It was a deeply speculative answer and he knew it. Regardless, it provided a small degree of satisfaction in a universe which suddenly seemed bereft of logic and where even the guesses were in short supply.

At that moment, a new plan appeared in Recker's mind, fully formed and breath-taking in its potential for destruction and carnage. He didn't know if it was viable and in order to find out, he spent a few moments examining the warship's propulsion charts.

He sat back, not daring to believe. This was going to be the longest of long shots, but in the absence of an alternative, he was desperate to put his plan in motion.

"Well, folks," he asked. "Do you want the bad news or the bad news?"

CHAPTER EIGHT

FOR A MOMENT AFTER HIS EXPLANATION, nobody spoke. Eastwood was the most technical of the crew and, like Recker expected, was the first to overcome his mental inertia.

"Have you checked the output charts and put the data into the simulator, sir?" he asked.

"The core override has locked us out of the simulator, Lieutenant."

"You added this up in your head?"

Recker nodded. "The engine charts indicate we're coasting," he said. "Except our velocity is way too high for us to remain in the planet's orbit. To compensate, the core override program is making constant, small adjustments to our course to ensure we maintain a constant distance of two million klicks from Pinvos."

"And you're assuming the satellite is doing the same thing," said Eastwood. "You're also assuming it's automated and that the automation isn't sophisticated enough to deal with what you're planning."

"There's no crew," said Recker with conviction. "I'm sure this entire tenixite converter network is either abandoned or the personnel died long ago."

"If that satellite is semi-coasting like we are, it might work," Eastwood conceded. "But you're forgetting that it made a substantial alteration to its orbital track on the last circuit. If it makes another, the control routine might attempt to stabilize the satellite."

"We won't know if we don't try and time is running out for all of us."

"It'll work," said Aston. "It's got to."

"We've got nothing better on the table, sir," said Eastwood. He gave a short laugh of disbelief.

Recker smiled thinly. "Activate the overstress device," he said.

Eastwood leaned forward and, with his index finger extended, poked the top keypad on the box. "Done."

The effect was instant and the engines took on the harsh edge Recker well remembered from his time on Etrol. Electronic needles jumped around on the status panel, settled, and then began a strong climb from left to right.

"200% on the engines," said Recker, shouting to be heard over the rising intensity.

He pulled the control bars, twisting them at the same time. Immediately, the *Expectation* banked away from the satellite and its cluster of warships. With no control over the sensors, Recker knew he was going to have a hard time keeping in sight of the enemy satellite.

"There!" yelled Burner.

Luckily, one of the forward arrays was aimed directly ahead and the satellite appeared in the centre of the screen, already dwindling. Controlling the destroyer's speed was tough when the engines were nailed on maximum and Recker fought the controls.

"The output gauge went past 300% on all six propulsion modules!" shouted Eastwood.

"I can feel it," said Recker.

"Signs of a reduced rate of change on three modules."

"What we've got is going to be enough," Recker said, like the words could turn hope into reality.

The *Expectation* had so much potential acceleration that it easily caught up with the cluster and Recker brought the warship into another tight turn which would put the spiked cube directly between the destroyer and Pinvos.

"Come on!" he said, focusing his mind.

One of the Daklan heavy cruisers lay across his intended path, with its immense forward and aft Terrus cannons looking terrifyingly near. Recker didn't want to screw up, but neither did he want this to take a moment longer than necessary. He piloted the *Expectation* directly over the desolator's topside, narrowly avoiding a glancing collision with a half-billion-ton slab of upper plating.

Then the destroyer was through the outer ring of warships and Recker saw the enemy satellite was directly ahead. He didn't want to impact with too much force and hauled on the controls at the last moment, hearing the propulsion howl its dismay at being restrained.

With the heaviest of thuds, the *Expectation* struck the

satellite between two of its pointed antennae. Ignoring the vibration which swept through the bridge, Recker steadied the destroyer and increased forward output. Still showing on the bulkhead screen, the fixed sensor feeds offered a view of darkness and jutting shapes, like the spaceship had crashed amongst a forest of geometric trees.

"Mass versus good old HPA propulsion," Recker growled. "Lieutenant Burner, I'm relying on you to keep us on course."

Burner's voice was filled with determination. "I won't let us down, sir."

Recker let the propulsion rise to maximum and the noise of it was deafening. For a time, nothing happened and he feared that the incredible mass of the satellite was too much for the *Expectation* to push off course. Either that or the target's onboard control systems were compensating for the unexpected change in trajectory. Recker didn't give up and he willed on the destroyer.

"Output stable at 320% on three of the modules," said Eastwood. "Looks like the other three will top out at 350%."

Recker's heart thumped in his chest when he noticed that the *Expectation* was slowly accelerating. The hull groaned and shook and he was required to make constant adjustments to keep the warship aimed in what he hoped was the direction of Pinvos.

"Shit, I think we're doing it," said Eastwood.

"You didn't believe?" asked Recker, feeling suddenly light-headed.

"Uh, sir, I don't know if you thought about this, but the other warships are coming with us," said Burner. "They're

ANTHONY JAMES

maintaining the exact same distance as before we started pushing the satellite."

Recker didn't know what to make of the news and he didn't have time to consider the ramifications. Deep down inside, he knew he was winging it and whatever the outcome, he had no option other than to accept the result.

"Those warships have life support, Lieutenant."

Over the next few minutes, Recker did his best to reduce the satellite's forward velocity and increase its lateral velocity. Every second, the huge cube's propulsion made adjustments of its own as it followed a pre-programmed routine for maintaining a stable orbit with a two million klick altitude. To Recker's enormous relief, the satellite made no effort to shift back onto its original vector and he kept pushing it towards Pinvos, with the much smaller destroyer fighting constantly to overcome the inertia.

"Forward velocity down to a hundred klicks per second," said Eastwood. "Lateral velocity has increased to three hundred klicks per second."

"How long till impact?" asked Recker. He glanced at the timer and realized he'd lost track of the seconds.

"Based on the current rate of velocity increase, maybe fifteen minutes," said Burner. "How fast are you intending to make this collision?"

"As fast as possible, Lieutenant."

A surge in resistance from the satellite brought Recker's attention back to the controls. "It's attempting an orbital shift," he said. "Damn, we're accelerating the wrong way."

Recker did what he could to counter the shift. If the

satellite attempted to make a full correction back to its original velocity and altitude, it was likely this attempt to drive the cube into the planet would fail.

"I won't fail," Recker said under his breath.

Twenty seconds later, the resistance lessened and although the satellite had regained some of its lost forward velocity, it was still only a fraction of what it had been originally. The greatest relief for Recker was that the target hadn't rotated, since that would have required him to reposition the *Expectation* against one of the other faces. Having managed it once, he wasn't in a hurry to test his skills for a second time.

"Five hundred klicks per second," said Eastwood. "You realize we're about to make an impact crater the size of a moon?"

"In for a penny, Lieutenant."

The *Expectation*'s velocity kept on rising and Recker felt like he was riding the wave. Each time the satellite attempted to correct its trajectory, he compensated automatically and by the time the destroyer approached seven hundred klicks per second, he'd eliminated the target's own forward velocity. Impact, when it came, was going to be head-on and it was going to involve more than just the alien cube.

"Any second!" shouted Burner.

Recker didn't want to let up, in case by doing so he allowed the satellite an opportunity to avoid the collision. He told himself that wasn't going to happen – if the target had the capability, it would have revealed it already.

At what he hoped was the very final moment, Recker dragged the controls directly towards him. The life support system reduced the strains on his body from the deceleration but not so much that he didn't know it was happening. The view on the forward feed made it seem like the satellite was racing away and then the *Expectation* was rocked by a momentous impact, sending the destroyer into a spin which tested Recker's reactions to the limit. He caught a glimpse of the desolator which had struck them go by, travelling so fast it was hardly more than flicker of grey on the sensor feed.

Recker swore and tried not to look at the swirling view on the bulkhead screens. The planet was visible now – so close that it stretched from horizon to horizon, a sheet of mottled browns and muddy reds that came and went with the rotation of the destroyer.

The controls weren't responding too well and Recker was certain the collision with the Daklan heavy had damaged something. Even so, he got the *Expectation* under control, just in time to witness the effects of five hundred billion tons of assorted warships and alien satellite strike the planet's surface at approximately seven hundred kilometres per second.

For Pinvos, the results were not positive. The battleship *Trojan* hit first, striking the centre of a flat plain of dark red, closely followed by one of the desolators which landed nearby. Visible shockwaves rippled out.

Before the shockwaves had travelled any significant distance, the cube landed with such force that the planet's surface sank inwards, as if the rocks beneath had suddenly become yielding like elastic. A new shockwave rolled from the impact point with incredible speed, and, in the blink of an eye, a crater three hundred kilometres across appeared.

Then, the rest of the warships impacted, forming new, overlapping craters and shockwaves.

"Shit," said Recker quietly, hardly able to believe the destruction he'd caused.

It wasn't over. The shockwaves continued, sweeping over the planet and lifting the surface into enormous waves of rock. Fissures jagged in every direction, like a hundred thousand lightning bolts had riven the planet's hard stone. After a few seconds, the view became blurry and indistinct, as trillions of tons of fragmented stone dust was hurled into the sky. Soon, the dust would obscure the impact zone and Recker could only imagine the ferocity of the winds carrying it upwards and outwards.

In the face of such devastation, part of Recker wanted to do nothing more than stare, to see the outcome when the dust cleared - if it ever did. Pinvos had been changed forever and no matter how much he reminded himself that it was only one planet amongst countless others, he still felt the significance.

"Sir?" said Aston.

Recker tore his gaze away. He glanced at the status panel on his console, which told him all he needed to know.

"The core override didn't go away." He closed his eyes and gritted his teeth.

"It was always going to be a long shot, sir," said Aston.

"I know it, Commander. I just thought that the destruction of the cube might be enough."

"The most important thing was to stop the satellite receiving and then transmitting the data from our encrypted data stores," said Burner.

"And the next priority was to prevent the destruction of more of our warships," added Eastwood. "I guess we didn't do so badly."

"I didn't want a half-victory, Lieutenant."

"It's what we got, sir."

Recker couldn't bring himself to feel happiness. This mission had started with high hopes of recovering some usable tech for the HPA and now that tech was cratered on a fringe planet, along with hundreds of personnel who were still trapped in their spaceships.

And when it came down to it, Recker had no way of confirming if the alien cube retained its destructive capabilities, or its ability to transmit.

"Too many unknowns," he said bitterly. He stared at the console in front of him and imagined the core override to be a disease coursing through the warship. The thought made him furious.

In the end, Recker had only a single option available. With no way to get home, he had to try and salvage something from the mission. He laid his hands onto the control bars again.

"Anyone want to go sightseeing?" he asked.

The crew didn't answer, already resigned to what was coming to them. Less sure than ever what his future held, Recker aimed the ship towards the dust storm and took them lower.

CHAPTER NINE

THE HIGHEST REACHES of the dust cloud extended several hundred kilometres over the surface and Recker dropped the warship steadily through the swirling particles. Luckily, the sensors were set to auto-adjust and they pierced a few thousand metres into the gloom with reasonable clarity, and a few additional kilometres at much-reduced precision. In addition, the altimeter was functioning along with the rest of the *Expectation*'s positional hardware. The core override had removed direct control, but the output of many important functions was still visible.

"Is there a plan, sir?" yelled Eastwood over the engines.

Recker didn't answer at once. He'd had enough of shouting and motioned for Aston to grab some suit helmets from the wall locker. Moments later, in the comparative silence of the helmet, he was left wondering why he hadn't done this sooner. Using the suit comms, the conversation proceeded without effort.

"There's no plan, Lieutenant," said Recker when every member of his crew was in the channel. "We're going to take a look and then decide."

Recker's tension hadn't lessened and it was an effort to take a measured approach. The destroyer sank ever lower into the dust and, although the warship was battered by the external conditions, the winds weren't nearly strong enough to be felt on the bridge of a billion-ton construction of alloy and ternium.

Whatever damage had been caused by the collision with the desolator it hadn't gone away and Recker fought against the warship's desire to enter a spin. The cause could be one of a dozen things, but the core override prevented the damage report from appearing and all he could do was compensate.

At an altitude of ten kilometres, Recker brought the spaceship to a halt. The lack of control over the sensors was frustrating, meaning he was required to adjust the *Expectation*'s orientation in order to direct the arrays in the direction he wanted. Murky shapes dotted the underside feeds and he spent a moment studying them.

"I believe this is the satellite's crater, and this might be the satellite," he said, indicating one of the larger shadows. "These adjoining craters were formed by our warships."

"Let's just get down there, sir," said Eastwood.

"This is as good a place as any to check out the lay of the land."

Even so, Recker took the controls again and continued the descent. The dust was thicker here and the winds stronger, with the result that the sensors struggled more than they had at a greater altitude. One moment, the shapes below were almost identifiable, the next they were lost in the cloaking dust.

"We're in the main crater," said Recker at last.

A long, broad shape became momentarily clear, lying in a huge crater adjoining the even larger one made by the cube. Much of the surrounding area glowed red with heat generated by the impacts.

"That's the *Trojan*," said Recker. "If we deploy the incision vehicle, is there any way the comms signal from a suit would penetrate the hull?"

"Definitely not, sir," said Burner. "Usually the external sensors would accept the transmission and route it to the intended recipient, but the core override has locked down traffic in both directions."

Recker piloted close enough to see that the battleship had ended up on its side. Its plating was extensively crushed - ruptured in places - and many of its landing legs were bent or snapped off. The starboard flank had taken the brunt of the impact and Recker had no doubt there'd be extensive heat damage. All around, the stone had a peculiar sheen, like it had fused with the airborne dust to form a rough glass.

"If the life support was active, the crew were in their suits, and Admiral Fraser knew what orders to give and when, most of the personnel should be alive," said Recker, acutely aware that any deaths were a direct result of his actions.

"The *Trojan* is carrying four heavy shuttles with missile launchers and chain guns," said Aston. "I'm not saying they should have attempted an attack on the cube while up in orbit, but I'd expect them to be deployed after impact – assuming they weren't too badly damaged."

"I notice you carefully avoided saying anything that might sound like criticism of Admiral Fraser, Commander," said Burner cheerfully.

"We're on the same side, Lieutenant. Even if, by all accounts, the man is an ass."

"This isn't the time," Recker said in warning.

"Those shuttles could have launched before we got here," said Eastwood. "We'd only spot them if we got lucky."

The launch of the shuttles would leave no visible indication on the battleship's exterior, so Recker didn't spend any time hunting for signs they'd been deployed. A few kilometres to the east, he made out what appeared to be the place where the *Trojan*'s impact crater merged with the one made by the *Titan*. The heavy lifter wasn't solid like a warship and doubtless the spaceship would be a crumpled mess.

Recker had always found particular tragedy in the ruins of huge constructions like these and he was assailed by the enormity of what he'd done. When he'd witnessed the helpless destruction of the *Barbarian* and *Claymore*, he'd felt driven into immediate action. Now that he was witness to the result of that action, Recker found it hard to cope. Questions jumped into his mind, asking if he'd done the right thing, or if another way had existed – a way which might have freed the trapped spaceships and ensured the survival of all personnel, not just the lucky ones.

Aston was perceptive enough to detect Recker's agitation from the set of his shoulders. "You can't let it drag you down, sir. Not now."

"This is too much to let go."

"That's for you to handle, sir. We were all involved and none of us thought of a better way. You're in command, but that doesn't absolve the rest of us."

The muscles in Recker's jaw tightened. "You're right, Commander. We can't allow events to rule us –if we have a debt, only the living can accept payment."

Recker felt the doubts and the guilt fade – they didn't disappear completely, rather they slid away into a recess of his mind. It was a burden for any man to carry and he promised that one day he'd deal with the accumulated darkness – a confrontation which would either break him or see him emerge stronger.

"The *Trojan* wasn't the only warship carrying shuttles," he said. "The cruisers and the *Titan* had their own."

"Let's not forget those desolators, sir," said Eastwood. "I can't imagine the Daklan waiting timidly for an invitation to come out and play."

"And again, there's no logical reason the Daklan would have attempted a shuttle attack on the cube while up in space," said Aston. "None of our transports have enough firepower to even scratch that thing."

"Which means we could have Daklan shuttles in the vicinity," said Recker. "They're too small to hurt the *Expectation*."

"And they're too slow to prevent us ramming them out of the sky," said Aston. "The difficulty will be spotting the bastards first."

"We've got to reach the cube," said Recker suddenly. "If the Daklan manage to launch their shuttles, they'll attempt an incursion."

"With what aim, sir?" asked Eastwood.

Recker guessed the answer. "If the satellite fired the core override, maybe it contains the way to recall it from our onboard systems."

The more he thought about it, the more convinced Recker became that he'd stumbled upon a possible way to escape this mountain of crap. Without further discussion, he banked the *Expectation* towards the place where the cube had impacted.

Rough estimates suggested the cube's mass was likely five to eight times greater than that of the *Trojan*. Consequently, it sat in the bottom of a far larger impact crater, with sloping sides peculiarly free of debris, as if the collision had thrown anything loose far away.

Recker piloted the destroyer lower, aware from his observation of the initial impact that the cube was about twelve kilometres below the original surface level. A dark shape loomed ahead, shrouded in thicker dust than they'd encountered so far and the heat glow from the cube's impact had faded until it was little more than the faintest tinge of red on the metal and nearby rock. The glassy sheen suggested that the temperature had originally been much greater.

"There it is," said Burner. "I hope it's smashed to pieces."

The bottom of the crater was almost flat in comparison to the steeper sides higher up, and here they found the alien satellite. It had landed on one face, with no sign that it had rolled afterwards. As a result, many of the spiked antennae had survived, though they weren't entirely intact. Most were bent or snapped partway up. Others lay scattered upon the ground.

The main structure of the cube was extensively damaged, and every visible face was bowed outwards as a result of the collision. Closer to the ground, the lower section of the satellite was crushed, and pieces – some of which must have weighed in excess of a billion tons - had splintered off and fallen nearby, all lumps and irregular edges.

"That's what happens if you mess with the HPA," said Eastwood.

"No more than it deserved," said Burner.

"Except we don't know why it was built in the first place, Lieutenant," said Aston. "Maybe it was constructed by the good guys in the fight against a bunch of murdering bastards – their equivalent of the Daklan."

"That would mean the species who built the *Vengeance* were the bad guys, Commander," Burner replied. "Personally, I don't care too much, as long as we find something that helps us beat our own enemies."

"Lieutenant Burner, speak to Sergeant Vance and make doubly sure he's ready for a possible deployment."

"Yes, sir."

Recker piloted the destroyer nearer to the cube, while keeping an eye on the sensors. The red-tinged dust storm didn't let up and here in the crater it whirled in a circle around the alien cube, as though the injured planet was directing its wrath against the object which had caused so much devastation.

"No sign of a breach on the visible side," said Aston.

"And no doors," said Recker dryly.

"Whoever built this, they got in and out. We've just got to find a way."

Hoping for a quick win, Recker flew the warship sideways around the cube at 1500 metres, keeping the forward sensor directed at the target. The second face had suffered more damage than the first and the vertical edges were bowed out so much that silvery stress fractures were visible, while most of the antennae were snapped or gone.

"Still nothing," said Recker, peering closely.

Movement on one of the starboard arrays caught his eye – it was a small shape moving rapidly at low altitude. Without hesitation, Recker turned the spaceship so that the forward array was pointing towards it.

"Daklan," said Aston.

Under Recker's control, the *Expectation* surged towards the enemy craft. The Daklan pilot was aware of the danger and had already put the shuttle into a steep dive, banking at the same time. For once, Recker felt like the cat instead of the mouse and the destroyer thundered into the flank of the forty-metre transport, knocking it towards the ground and out of sensor view.

A moment after the impact, Recker brought the *Expectation* to a halt and then flew it quickly backwards, hunting for the enemy.

"There," said Aston. "They hit the ground."

Daklan shuttles were tough and this one had survived the comparatively low-speed impact, though its hull was out of shape. It rose unsteadily from the ground and flew towards the cube, skimming across the floor of the crater.

Recker got no satisfaction from the second collision and this time when the shuttle crashed into the surface, he set the *Expectation* on top of the wreckage, ensuring one of the landing legs came down onto the enemy craft, crushing it utterly.

"Damn this shitting war!" he yelled. "Bringing us to this!"

Recker lifted the destroyer off the ground and resumed his circuit of the cube. The third face was the most damaged of all, and only one sheared-off antennae remained out of dozens. A few billion tons of debris covered the ground, and two of the broken spikes had somehow landed almost upright, wedged in position by huge slabs which had detached from the lower part of the cube.

"There's an opening," said Recker.

"Right down at the ground," said Burner.

"I'll bring us in for a closer look."

The lowest two hundred metres of the third face had crumpled like paper and ruptured, forming a long, narrow opening, 1200 metres long and ten high, starting about a hundred metres from the ground. With steady hands, Recker brought the destroyer in and aimed the forward sensor array towards the gap. Unfortunately, the array was angled slightly downwards and no matter how he adjusted the position of the warship, the feed didn't show much of what lay inside.

"The array is locked in that position, sir," said Burner.

"I know," Recker growled. "All I can see is alloy."

"We should check the fourth face, sir," Aston suggested. "Maybe there'll be another opening."

"And we didn't check out the top face too closely," said Burner.

Recker didn't delay and he guided the warship around the cube. The fourth face was bowed like the others and with plenty of stress fractures, though with no sign of a breach large enough for entry.

"Up we go," said Recker.

It was a similar tale on the upper face of the cube, where the antennae were more intact than elsewhere. A brief inspection was enough for Recker to be sure that they'd not be getting inside the satellite from above – it was tightly sealed.

He returned the spaceship to the third face and studied the opening again. "Is there a way of finding out if that leads anywhere significant?" he asked.

"You know the answer to that, sir."

Recker nodded. "I don't want to risk the squad until we've done everything we can from here."

"One of the rear portside arrays might see far enough inside," said Burner. "I think you'll have to land in order to bring the array low enough."

"Let's give it a try."

A few minutes later, Recker abandoned the effort. The rear portside array was about five metres too high and, though it offered a marginally better view than the forward array, it wasn't enough to reveal anything new.

"No sign of any more Daklan," he mused.

"Their shuttle-to-shuttle comms is probably function-ing, sir," said Burner. "That one we crushed would have got out a warning to the others."

"They're hanging back," said Recker. "But for how long?"

The Daklan didn't usually tolerate a standoff, however that was assuming an attack stood a chance of producing a successful outcome. Against the *Expectation*, even without its armaments, a hundred Daklan shuttles wouldn't be enough.

"It's time to move," said Recker. He climbed from his seat and strode towards the weapons locker.

"Sir?" said Aston, her expression one of confusion.

"Sergeant Vance and his squad are highly trained and skilled soldiers, Commander. What they are not, is trained in the use of alien technology. If they find something inside that cube, they lack the ability to extract the data."

Recker pulled a gauss rifle from the rack, checked the ammunition readout and grabbed some spare magazines.

"I should go," said Aston.

"Negative, Commander. I'd trust you to handle the *Expectation* against any opponent. A few Daklan shuttles won't cause you any problems."

Aston's lips tightened. Recker wasn't meant to leave the bridge except under specific circumstances and he could see she was trying to accept that the current situation permitted his departure.

"I'm going," he said firmly.

"I'll let Sergeant Vance know you're on your way, sir," she said.

For some reason, Recker found himself smiling. "Since that desolator hit us, there's a stern drift you'll need to watch out for."

Aston smiled back. "I'll handle it."

"You'll be comms blind once you leave the *Expectation*, sir," Burner reminded him.

"I trust you all to do what's right."

With the handover complete, Recker exited the bridge. He knew this was a risk, but the potential rewards were vast. Putting his misgivings to one side, he sprinted for the underside bay.

CHAPTER TEN

WITH RECKER AT THE CONTROLS, the incision craft dropped smoothly from the opening beneath the *Expectation*. The moment it emerged into the storm, he felt the winds pushing against the spaceship's flank and the sensors struggled to penetrate the gloom. Everything vibrated, though it wasn't from the conditions outside – the destroyer's overstressed engines produced a resonance that could be heard and felt even through the deployment vehicle's hull.

"Enhance the feed, Private Montero," said Recker.

"On it, sir."

The deployment craft's hardware wasn't nearly so capable as that on the *Expectation* and Recker didn't anticipate much improvement. Montero surprised him and the feed brightened, while shapes previously hidden by the thick, stinging dust became dimly realized on the screen. Overhead, the destroyer hovered unmoving.

"Comms are dead," Montero confirmed.

Sergeant Vance was the squad's usual pilot but, on this occasion, he was acting as backup. The man had his rifle propped against the wraparound console and his thick fingers tapped out commands into the control panel with surprising delicacy.

"No sign of Daklan," said Vance.

"That's for Commander Aston to worry about, Sergeant. All we have to concern ourselves with is getting inside a 250-billion-ton alien cube and finding a way to recall the core override from our spaceships."

"A walk in the park," said Vance, with a rare chuckle.

Recker turned the incision craft towards the third face, scowling at the broken antennae jutting from the surface. While the 800-metre *Expectation* was dwarfed by the enormity of this alien construction, the sixty-metre deployment craft was no more than a speck.

The opening to the cube wasn't hard to locate since Aston had positioned the destroyer directly above it, and Recker stared at the snaking line of darkness in front of his craft.

"Ten metres top to bottom. Not too tight," said Montero.

"Plenty of room for this vessel," Recker confirmed. "Not so much for a Daklan shuttle."

In truth, he believed the enemy transports would have a metre or two clearance. They'd likely scrape the paint-work if they were in a hurry, but otherwise, the Daklan wouldn't have problems.

Recker gave the engines some power and the incision craft accelerated gently for the breach. Montero continued adjusting the sensors, though the result was far from perfect. As far as Recker could see, the outer split appeared to increase in height the deeper it went and he got the impression it ended at a vertical wall. He gritted his teeth at the sight.

"We've got lights, sir," said Vance.

"Hold off on them, Sergeant. If the Daklan have any shuttles nearby, they'll see us easier if we're lit up."

"Roger that, sir."

When the incision craft's nose was only fifty metres from the opening, a huge slab of debris came tumbling down from above. Although the *Expectation* was overhead, it wasn't tight up against the cube.

"Shit," said Recker.

He tapped into the propulsion and the spaceship raced into the opening, entering smoothly and without impact. A flicker of movement on the rear feed indicated the debris would have missed anyway, but Recker's heart was beating hard regardless.

About a hundred metres inside, forward progress was blocked by a sheer wall of near-black alloy, but now that the incision craft was closer, Recker noticed that a long, vertical shaft had formed, running parallel to the outer face of the cube.

"I'll have to rotate the ship," he said. "And hope there's something up there worth looking at."

The manoeuvre was easy enough to complete and he got the small craft positioned at the base of the shaft. From here, the crew had a good view horizontally along the opening. The floor and ceiling were both warped, while the metal had a peculiar appearance, like it was covered in countless tiny scars.

"More stress fractures."

"I guess when you drop something this big at high speed onto something even bigger, something's got to give," said Montero. "Look at what's straight up."

What Recker had thought was a shaft rose for two hundred metres and then ended at a flat ceiling. From there, a new opening led horizontally into the cube.

"This satellite must have come down on the lower edge of this face," said Recker. "It's suffered some lateral force damage, like the interior armour and construction materials got pulled apart."

"Let's get up there and check it out, sir," said Vance.

Recker made a final alteration to the spaceship's orientation, to ensure it wouldn't hit anything when he flew it vertically. Movement to his left distracted him and he saw the *Expectation* drop directly opposite the opening. Then, it accelerated backwards and stopped after a few hundred metres.

"What the hell?" asked Montero.

The answer came in a blur of fast-moving dark metal. A Daklan shuttle hurtled into the opening a few hundred metres along from the deployment vessel. The last-second effort from its pilot to decelerate wasn't enough to prevent it from striking the inner wall at high velocity and the shuttle jumped with the impact, its angular nose flattening. At the same moment, the *Expectation* surged along the opening, stopped and then flew once more in reverse.

Recker understood. "Crazy Daklan bastards," he said, in mixed anger and grudging admiration. "They're flying at the opening from different directions in order to get past the *Expectation*."

"Let's see what they think of this," said Vance.

The deployment vessel's nose was fitted with a multi-barrel high-calibre chain gun. Aiming could be done manually and Vance used the backup control sticks to target the flank of the Daklan shuttle. The enemy vessel was damaged, but Recker was sure the life support had kept the crew alive.

A drone and a whine of motors presaged the onslaught. The nose gun opened up with a menacing rumble and unleashed a flood of hardened alloy slugs into the shuttle. Streaks of white connected the two vessels and the side plating of the Daklan transport began heating up at once.

The enemy crew was alert to the threat and the shuttle turned in the confines of the space. Sergeant Vance didn't release the chain gun trigger and the slugs continued pounding the enemy armour.

"Come on, come on," said Montero.

"Thick armour," grunted Vance.

To the left, the *Expectation* was still accelerating forwards and back, its propulsion resonance dislodging more loose debris from the exterior of the cube.

"How many shuttles did they bring?" asked Montero.

"A desolator usually carries four, Private."

Movement on the rear sensors caught Recker's attention and a second Daklan shuttle came hurtling into the opening. It glanced off the ceiling and then crunched into the facing wall at high speed, crumpling armour and knocking the vessel sideways.

Meanwhile to the front, the fusillade from the incision craft's powerful nose cannon punched a hole in the first shuttle. Recker saw it happen – heat softened plating sagged and then was torn apart by the bullets. To his horror, the sensor feed was sharp enough for him to distinguish the movement of enemy soldiers within the passenger bay. Vance wasn't about to give quarter and he aimed the deadly torrent at the Daklan troops, before concentrating his fire on the cockpit.

The shuttle's nose section – usually the strongest part – was damaged from the impact and the chain gun smashed the protective alloy, revealing blue illumination and shattered technology.

A glance at the rear feed was enough for Recker to understand the danger. The second shuttle was already rotating in the direction of the incision vehicle and he didn't like the idea of facing the enemy chain gun - the incision craft was built primarily for speed and wasn't designed to trade blows with a Daklan armoured shuttle.

"Going up" said Recker.

The deployment vehicle climbed vertically. Sergeant Vance was an old hand with a nose gun and the sudden movement didn't affect his aim whatsoever. The chain gun temperature gauge went into the orange and still Vance didn't relent in his attack on the first shuttle.

Recker focused on the controls. The incision craft reached the top of the shaft, and the opening continued sideways. A check of the upper sensor array presented Recker with a view that reminded him of massive steps, heading upwards. He guessed the outer walls of the cube had been formed from huge blocks which had been torn apart in the impact with Pinvos.

"The stairway to heaven," said Vance, finally letting off the triggers. He roared with laughter.

"The Sergeant gets this way sometimes," said Montero. "It's best to ignore him."

Recker wasn't paying too much attention. He piloted the incision craft sideways towards the next vertical and then pulled on the control to make the spaceship climb. Lines of white sliced through the air, coming from below and crashing against the alloy far overhead.

While the Daklan pilot didn't have a firing angle, Recker was shocked at the speed with which his enemy had brought the shuttle under control. He threw the spaceship forward as its altitude increased and tried to anticipate how the approach of the enemy craft would affect its firing angle.

The incision craft reached the next ceiling without being struck by chain gun bullets and Recker's eyes darted across the sensor feeds, hunting for a clue as to his enemy's location. The Daklan shuttle was out of sight and he tried to capitalise.

"Hold on."

Sharp movements on the control sticks swung the incision craft's stern wide. At the same moment, Recker sent the nose in the opposite direction in order to complete a 180-degree turn. He misjudged it a fraction and the rear corner thudded into the vertical face, glancing off as he got the spaceship under control.

The outline of the enemy shuttle appeared, rising over the edge of the step and much closer than Recker expected. It worked out in favour of Sergeant Vance, who hardly needed to do more than compress the chain gun triggers again. The rumbling started anew and hundreds of slugs crashed into the enemy vessel's flank.

Immediately, the Daklan pilot banked, hoping to bring the incision vehicle into the firing arc of his nose gun. Anticipating the move, Recker threw his own craft sideways, taking it away from the enemy weapon.

A patch of red heat on the Daklan shuttle expanded beneath the multitude of impacts, turning orange in the centre. Space was tight and Recker ran out of room. Once again, he pulled on the sticks and the deployment craft climbed strongly. The nose gun was intended for use against ground vehicles, so anything beneath was an easy target, and Vance made good use of his opportunity.

The Daklan shuttle wasn't finished yet and its pilot tilted the vessel so that its nose was aimed upwards towards the incision vehicle. Recker attempted to get out of the firing arc but could see that he was too late.

"Get ready."

A cascade of Daklan slugs filled the cockpit with an echoing clatter that made Recker's ears ring, even with the protection of his suit helmet. The sound continued for long moments until the deployment craft came level with the next step up and he was able to move it out of sight.

On the topside array, more of the cube's interior was revealed, though Recker didn't have time to stare. His Daklan opponent was challenging and would take advantage of any distraction.

"They're staying low," said Montero. "I'm attempting to track the engine note."

Recker knew how that was likely to turn out – with the howling of the *Expectation*'s propulsion all around, combined with the limited capabilities of the deployment vessel hardware, the Daklan shuttle wouldn't be easy to pinpoint.

Montero surprised him.

"That way, sir," she said, pointing over her shoulder. "They're flying backwards past us."

"You're sure?"

"Yes, sir."

Recker put his trust in her judgement and for a second time, he spun the incision craft 180-degrees. He was just in time – the Daklan shuttle rose into sight, white streaks lancing from its gun barrels. The clattering resumed, this time against the hull plates only a couple of metres in front of Recker. A moment later, the rumble of the incision craft's gun spat in response, with Vance aiming for one of the still-hot sections of alloy he'd targeted a short time earlier.

Unwilling to be a passive observer, Recker attempted to get out of the enemy's firing arc again. This time, the Daklan pilot was quick to react and he rotated to ensure his own gunfire wasn't interrupted.

"Getting hot," said Vance.

Although heat smoke poured from the barrels of the incision vehicle's chain gun, Vance wasn't referring to that. The cockpit air shimmered and the computer in Recker's helmet informed him the temperature was heading upwards and was already beyond safe levels for an unprotected human.

For what seemed like an age, the exchange of fire continued as the two craft manoeuvred in the confined space. Recker knew he'd been drawn into the slugging match he wanted to avoid and he swore loudly - the Daklan pilot possessed the kind of skill which should have likely seen him in charge of a fully-fledged warship.

Vance also swore and Private Montero demonstrated a rare talent for obscenity which she'd so far kept hidden. The entire front section of the Daklan shuttle burned bright orange, yet for some reason the plating refused to yield. A faint glow appeared on the bulkhead above Recker's head, telling him that the battle would finish soon, one way or another.

Just when Recker thought he'd taken a gamble too far, the nose section of the Daklan shuttle collapsed inwards. A huge hole appeared, like the superheated alloy was retreating from the focus point of the chain gun bullets.

"Down you go," snarled Vance.

The Daklan pilot couldn't hope to survive the flood of high-velocity slugs entering his cockpit and the alien shuttle spun around sharply, before crashing into the nearest wall. There it hung for long moments, uncontrolled yet with its engines pushing it into the hard surface. Vance kept spraying the hull, forcing a breach into the passenger bay and bringing death to the soldiers inside. A moment after, something failed on the enemy shuttle. Its propulsion cut out and the wreckage fell out of sight.

When Vance lifted his fingers from the triggers, it brought comparative silence into the bay. He leaned back, his expression showing no satisfaction at the victory.

"Them or us," he said, like it was a phrase he used to protect his mental walls.

"Them or us," Montero repeated.

Recker was alert for signs of a third shuttle, though the incision vehicle wasn't in a state to face another.

"Watch and listen!" he ordered.

"Still on it, sir." Montero assured him. "I'm not picking up anything other than the *Expectation*'s propulsion."

It should have been a relief, but it wasn't. The Daklan had shown their determination to enter the cube and Recker had no idea how many Aston had intercepted. It was possible the enemy had more than twelve shuttles and equally, they may have held some in reserve.

"We've got to be ready," he said. "There's a chance the Daklan will send others."

"And we'll give them the same treatment, sir," said Montero, though she was just going through the motions of bravado.

Vance wasn't prone to bluster and he kept his thoughts to himself. "Burned through half our ammo," was all he said.

With the known opponents dealt with, Recker turned his attention to what he'd seen on the feed earlier. Beyond the next *step,* the cube appeared to be at least partially hollow, though again, the viewing angle provided more hints than certainty.

"We're here to do a job," Recker said. "Let's do it."

Without further hesitation, he turned the incision vehicle and guided it towards the area above.

CHAPTER ELEVEN

THE INTERIOR of the cube wasn't solid and nor was it entirely hollow. Recker piloted the spaceship cautiously into a vast, cube-shaped area, perhaps 800 metres to each side. The space was unlit and the dark material of the walls made it harder to comprehend the shapes and lines which came up on the sensors.

Montero adjusted and enhanced the arrays and within seconds obtained a feed which told Recker some of what he needed to know.

A cube – exactly in the centre of the satellite - with a diameter of no more than two hundred metres, was held in place by dozens of spokes, each of which was no more than five metres in diameter. These spokes were connected to square housings fixed to the inner wall of the internal space. Recker believed these housings contained huge dampers, to allow the spokes, and therefore the central cube, a degree of movement. Generally, a life support system could cope with any kind of shock, so it struck Recker as odd to find such an arrangement within an advanced structure like this one.

"If there's anything to be found, it's usually in the middle," said Montero.

"Then let's take a look," said Recker.

Flying through the interior of the cube was one of the most alien experiences he could recall. True, there was nothing especially unusual about spokes and cubes, but when everything was combined – the impact with Pinvos, the crashed fleets and the staircase leading here – it made Recker's head swim.

"If we're to delete the core override from our space-ships, we'll need to locate an interface panel," he said.

"What if they didn't fit one?" asked Vance.

It was a possibility, but Recker didn't think it likely. "Even if this satellite was designed to operate without a crew, the technicians would have run onboard tests before sign-off. And those tests would have been initiated through control consoles."

"What if big alien robots built everything?" asked Montero.

"Let's not overthink things, Private. We're here and without other options. We'll push until we arrive at a dead end or we succeed."

"Get our heads down and run," said Montero, nodding like she suddenly understood. "I can go with that."

Uncomfortably aware that the Daklan didn't give up easily, Recker piloted the spaceship to midpoint between floor and ceiling and began a clockwise circuit around the inner cube. The spokes were numerous but the arrangement was regular and they were easy to avoid, as long as he took extra care.

After completing half a circuit, an unwelcome sight appeared on the sensors.

"Shit," said Vance. "Daklan shuttle."

Recker saw it too. The enemy vessel was less than 400 metres away, tight up against the inner cube and not moving. His heart thumped when he noticed that he was looking at the rear section of the shuttle.

"Take it down," he ordered. "Before they see us."

Vance didn't need a second invitation. He targeted and fired within two seconds and the nose gun's alloy slugs pounded into the Daklan shuttle's armour. Recker kept the deployment craft moving and readied himself for a response.

That response wasn't long in coming and the shuttle accelerated away from its berth, with a large section of its stern plate orange from the chain gun impacts. The moment it came to the edge of the cube face, the shuttle's pilot banked hard, hoping to buy some respite. A misjudgement sent the Daklan craft side-on into one of the pillars and then it spun into a second, the collision halting its momentum. Chain gun slugs crashed into the vessel and Sergeant Vance growled low in his chest.

In his pursuit of the enemy craft, Recker had brought the incision craft parallel to the cube face where the shuttle had been parked. He glimpsed an opening in the dark wall and his eyes detected a flicker of silvery movement.

Instinct told him what was coming and Recker hurled his spaceship lower, hoping to get beneath the cube. He was too late and a red streak of propellant etched a line through the darkness.

"Rocket!"

The Daklan missile struck the top section of the incision craft and Recker felt the craft lurch beneath the force of the blast. The cockpit alarm went off and warning lights appeared on the console. Through the open cockpit door, he heard the soldiers shouting questions and obscenities. That at least was a good sign – he'd never heard expletives coming from a dead man before.

"Finish that shuttle," snarled Recker, dropping the deployment ship beneath the cube. To his relief, the controls were responding and he hoped the shoulder launched rocket hadn't done any lasting damage.

Bullets spewed without cease into the enemy craft and its pilot made another attempt to fly into cover. Recker's room for manoeuvre was limited by the necessity to deny the rocket soldier another shot and he flew sideways to keep the fleeing shuttle in sight.

"They're turning," said Montero nervously. "Gonna hit us with their nose gun."

"No, they're not," said Vance.

The Daklan shuttle flew in a tight arc around one of the spokes and the pilot attempted to rotate the vessel at the same time. For a split-second, the support pillar interrupted the deluge of chain gun bullets drumming against the enemy armour and then it was out in the open again, this time with its nose pointed at the deployment vessel.

Recker braced himself and the clattering began at once, drowning out everything else. The deployment craft's nose hadn't cooled down from the previous exchange and Recker didn't think the spaceship was going to hold up for much longer.

The surprise of the initial attack, in combination with Recker's determination that he wouldn't lose this one, proved to be enough. Under the pressure of imminent death, the Daklan pilot made a second error and caught his vessel's stern against another pillar, knocking the bright tracers of incoming bullets a few metres wide of the incision vehicle.

When he saw it happen, Recker flew his ship in the opposite direction, while keeping the vessel's nose aimed at the shuttle. Vance's aim didn't waver and the chain gun shots punctured the Daklan armour, opening a wide, heat-rimmed tear across its cockpit and continuing into the flank plating.

A ternium drive could suffer incredible punishment and remain operational, and so it was here. The crew and passenger sections of the vessel were torn into pieces, but the shuttle stayed in the air. Without direction, it drifted gently sideways into a pillar, bounced off and began a slow rotation. All the while, Sergeant Vance raked it with bullets to make certain the job was done.

"Another one down," he said at last, releasing the triggers.

The series of confrontations, coming in such rapid succession, had left Recker feeling drained and his thoughts wandered to the booster injector he carried in one of his suit pockets. He ignored the brief urge and held the spaceship steady beneath the cube, while Private Montero spoke to the squad to find out about casualties.

"If curses were bullet holes, they'd all be dead a thousand times over, sir."

Recker hid a smile. "The monitoring tools report no hull breach, so we're ready to proceed. Sergeant Vance, are you ready to say hello to a Daklan rocket soldier?"

"I'll put my best foot forward, sir."

Despite the lightly spoken words, Recker was fully aware that what they planned was easier said than done. If the rocket soldier was alert, he might get off a second shot even if he was chewed up by bullets a moment later. Speed was the best way to reduce the risk of a counterattack, but in the confines of the inner cube, space was at a premium.

Taking a few deep breaths, Recker sized up his options and picked one. "Ready?"

"As ever, sir."

Recker took the incision craft lower into the cube and piloted it carefully towards the inner wall, using one of the support pillars as cover. When he judged the position was right, he positioned the craft underneath one of the diagonal supports that connected with the cube face where the Daklan soldiers were hiding. Slowly, he drew closer and stopped just before the place where he judged a soldier in the doorway would have a firing angle.

"Now," he said.

The chain gun had a tiny spool-up delay and Sergeant Vance anticipated by depressing the triggers immediately.

At the same time, Recker flew the incision craft rapidly sideways with its nose pointing towards the opening in the cube. Bullets flew into the opening and then Recker flew back into the cover of the pillar. A moment later, an immense explosion struck the far side of the spoke, illuminating the surrounding area in plasma-accelerated orange.

"Again," said Recker.

Before the explosion had receded, he flew sideways for a second time. The heat and light confounded the sensors' ability to locate a target and Sergeant Vance fired on instinct. Chain gun bullets punched through the intense flames and Recker wasn't certain if they were on target.

The flames drew back, vanishing quickly and leaving a section of the spoke glowing red with the memory. The receding of the blast allowed Recker a view of the inner cube and he was impressed to find that Vance's aim was true.

"Most Daklan shuttles carry two tube soldiers, sir."

Recker grimaced. They'd killed one, he was certain. About the other, he had no idea.

"Now they've seen what we did to their shuttle, whoever's left in that cube is probably hunkered down," said Montero.

"The Daklan don't like to lay low," said Recker.

"No, sir," said Vance. "If they've got another tube in there, they'll probably wait for us to show up outside that opening."

The incision vehicle was still in the air and responding well to the controls, but Recker didn't want to test if its damaged hull could soak another Daklan rocket. Equally, he didn't want to chance a standoff either, in case another enemy shuttle made it past the *Expectation*.

"If the enemy plan to surprise us, they've got to be hiding around a corner where our chain gun can't hit them," mused Recker.

"Could be they're behind a door instead, sir," said Vance. "And opening it every few seconds to see if we've arrived."

"Let's hope they aren't doing that, Sergeant." Recker gave a tight smile. "Raimi's got a tube."

"Yes, sir."

Recker got on the comms channel. "Private Raimi, take that rocket tube up the forward exit shaft, open the hatch and be ready to fire when I give the order."

Raimi didn't hesitate. "Yes, sir. On my way."

Somehow, the soldier made it up the shaft while carrying the tube in about ten seconds.

"Ready for pressure loss, sir," he warned.

"Do it."

Pinvos had an atmosphere, though not much of one and the opening of the hatch caused the air in the deployment vessel to vanish outside in a few seconds.

"Ready whenever you are," said Raimi.

Sure enough, one of the external sensor arrays showed Private Raimi's upper body protruding through the hatch, with the dull grey rocket tube over one shoulder. Against an armoured vehicle, a degree of accuracy with placement of the missile was desirable. When the target was ground troops in an enclosed space, landing the shot somewhere in the general vicinity of the opponents was normally enough to cause widespread carnage. All Raimi had to do was get his rocket into the opening.

"I'm going to fly out from behind this support pillar," Recker advised. "At the same time, I'll switch on our lights so you can see what you're aiming at. Look for an opening, dead centre in the cube and put a rocket through it while Sergeant Vance fires the chain gun to ensure the enemy stay out of sight."

"Hell, sir, I didn't know you had the sergeant in control of the gun. He's got more chance of hitting me than that opening!"

"Private Raimi, you're walking the line," said Vance.

"Just saying."

"That's enough - we're going," said Recker.

He didn't wait any longer and took the spaceship sideways, while Vance pelted the opening with bullets. Raimi turned out to be a good shot and his shoulder-launched rocket screamed away, the sound audible through the hatch. When the missile exploded, sending a gout of flame out of the cube opening, Recker had already taken the deployment craft back into cover. He gritted his teeth in anticipation, but no Daklan missile came.

"Nice work, Private Raimi," said Vance.

"No problem, sir. Am I staying outside?"

Recker judged that he'd done everything possible to reduce the risk of a second Daklan missile attack, but it was best to remain alert. "Stay there and watch."

"Roger that, sir."

With Private Raimi acting as a one-man turret, Recker flew the spaceship out of cover and headed for the opening. Sergeant Vance didn't take chances either and he fired an extended burst from the chain gun in case the Daklan were alive and watching.

"Ammo's running low," he said, when he released the triggers.

The vessel wasn't designed for an in-combat reload, so the bullets in the magazine would have to be enough. A glance at the readout told Recker it would be touch-and-go if they encountered another enemy shuttle, though Raimi's shoulder launcher would likely tip the balance.

"Hold fire, Sergeant," he ordered. "Let's keep what we have left."

"Yes, sir."

"You'd best get out back and prepare the squad for a fast exit from the side hatch."

It was like Sergeant Vance had waited his entire life for just that order. He snatched up his gauss rifle and surged into the troop bay, shouting commands like a man who'd regained his voice after spending ten years mute.

Flying too quickly for the conditions, Recker turned the spaceship and lined it up with the opening. It took Private Montero a moment to point the sensors the right way and the auto-lock snapped everything into focus.

"A passage and an intersection," said Recker. "Anything around either of those corners would have been incinerated."

"No sign of any survivors," said Montero. "No lumps, nothing."

The Daklan didn't appear and Recker guided the spaceship towards the opening, aligning its side exit with the three-metre entrance to the inner cube. With the gentlest of thumps, contact was made.

"Sergeant Vance, time for you to move. Sweep through and clear out any Daklan. When you're done, return here and it'll be your turn at the controls."

Vance already knew what was expected and he exited the spaceship, leading his soldiers into the alien cube. Hating that he was reduced to inaction, Recker held the control sticks in a death grip while he waited for developments.

CHAPTER TWELVE

SERGEANT VANCE and his squad had proved their worth back on Oldis and Recker was sure their sharp edge hadn't turned rusty in the four weeks or so since that engagement. The squad's losses from the lightspeed missile strike on the warship *Punisher* had been replaced and Recker had learned that Vance had pulled a few strings to ensure he got the final say over the replacements. Doubtless he'd hand-picked five laconic, alien-murdering bastards to join his team.

At two hundred metres along each edge, the inner cube had the potential to be riddled with passages and rooms, offering the Daklan numerous places to hide or cause problems. Recker tried not to think too hard about it. Mutual destruction here on Pinvos would benefit neither side, but equally, it was inconceivable to allow the Daklan access to the technology in the satellite. Just thinking about them fitting core overrides onto their annihilators filled him with dread.

To Recker's great relief, Vance didn't keep him waiting.

"Sir, we've secured an area not far from the entrance. We encountered three hostiles and killed them," he said. "I can't guarantee that's all of them, but we found some consoles I thought you might want to look at. In the circumstances, maybe the enemy are secondary."

"I agree. Return to the shuttle immediately."

Within a minute, the broad figure of Sergeant Vance appeared in the tunnel and a short while after, he entered the cockpit.

"Take the controls," said Recker, standing and picking up his own gauss rifle. The metal hummed with faint vibration, reminding him of times long ago.

"Got them, sir. I'll hold steady here." Vance hesitated. "Private Raimi's inside the cube."

"Any sign he's needed there?"

"No guarantees either way, sir."

"Recall him and send him into the forward exit shaft again. It doesn't matter what happens in that cube – if we lose this incision craft, we're not getting back to the *Expectation*."

"No, sir. It's a long way down and I forgot to pack my wings."

Recker exited the cockpit and hurried along the narrow bay. A rear door gave access to the small cargo area, in which crates of guns and ammunition were fixed to the walls. The engines were below the floor and another module was beyond the rear bulkhead, which meant the sound of the gravity drive was more intrusive here than elsewhere.

Stepping quickly across the dimly lit space, Recker arrived at the side exit, which was little more than a short crawlspace leading through the armour to the currently open exit hatch. Clambering along, Recker found himself facing a metre-wide gap between the incision craft and the cube entrance, with only darkness below. He didn't stop to think and launched himself across the space, throwing his weight forward when he landed.

Private Raimi was coming the other way.

"Left at the end and first right, sir. You won't get lost."

With these briefest of instructions delivered, Raimi slid his seven-foot rocket tube lengthways into the shuttle. The soldier followed in what appeared to be a practiced dive which carried his entire body into the crawlspace and left only his feet dangling over the edge. A moment later, Raimi was gone.

Checking his helmet readout, Recker discovered that the temperature was minus ninety-five degrees Centigrade and the air composition would ensure a quick death if he tried breathing it. His spacesuit kept him protected from most naturally occurring environmental conditions and he set off for the intersection.

On the way, Recker noticed a film of char which covered every surface and a harsh, bitter stench came in through his helmet filter. The source of both char and stench had likely once been Daklan, though Recker didn't dwell on their deaths.

Vance hadn't left anything to chance and had posted Corporal Stoner Givens, Private Hunter Gantry and one of the recent additions to the squad – Private Bonnie Stevens - at the intersection. Gantry had his MG12 fleshripper set up on the floor and aimed it along the right-hand passage.

"Nothing to report, sir," said Givens, looking jumpier than normal.

Recker turned his head right and the sensor in his helmet outlined the edges of the passage in green. The corridor continued for a short distance and turned left.

"Daklan?" he asked.

"None that we've seen, sir." Givens shrugged in his crouching position.

"I don't care if you've seen them or not – do the enemy have a presence?"

"Sergeant Vance wasn't sure, sir. He left us here just in case." Givens nudged the prone Gantry with his foot. "If any of them show, we'll cut them down."

While Recker admitted the squad hadn't been given the opportunity to explore and secure the entire cube, he wasn't happy with the uncertainty. On a whim, he set off into the right-hand passage, turning his helmet flashlight on low. Ten metres along, he found another smear of char on the floor and walls. Something had disturbed the greasy coating.

"Footprints," said Recker. "Did any of you go this way?"

"No, sir."

Recker returned to the intersection. "In that case, the Daklan are still here. Get on the comms and alert Sergeant Vance."

"Yes, sir."

The discovery left Recker in a foul mood and he strode past the soldiers, heading left. This passage was a mirror of the other and it turned right twenty metres along. After that, it ended at some stairs with high risers, which Recker descended rapidly. Halfway down, he suddenly noticed how quiet the interior of the cube was, with no propulsion sound or anything else that would indicate it was operational. On balance, he'd have preferred noise over silence.

At the bottom, he came to a doorway with no sign of an associated door. He stepped across the threshold into a room about ten metres square and with a three-metre ceiling. The place was a mess of thrown about, smashed up tech, most of which had ended up against the left-hand wall. Torn cables protruded from holes in the floor and console holding brackets had been ripped away, leaving sharp edges which looked as if they could slice open a spacesuit easily enough. While Recker was sure the cube had a life support unit, it evidently wasn't up to the job of cushioning the blow from a high-speed planetary impact.

Two additional exits – both sealed and with red lights on their access panels – led to places unknown. The squad members had positioned themselves in cover and they watched the doors carefully.

Elsewhere, thick smears of frozen blood showed where the soldiers had dragged the bodies of the three Daklan they'd shot earlier. The crimson trail led to the right-hand corner nearest the entrance, and there the huge aliens had been left in a heap. The face of one was aimed Recker's way, its dark red skin visible through the clear glass of its visor and its humanlike green eyes staring in accusation.

He turned away. "Private Steigers, return to the intersection – it seems like we didn't kill all the Daklan."

Recker's words were greeted by the expected level of

cursing, while Steigers didn't delay and sprinted through the exit.

"Right, what've we got?" Recker asked. "Sergeant Vance said you'd found consoles."

"Over here, sir," said Hendrix, rising from behind a ragged sheet of alloy which was propped up against what had once been a console. "Only one survived the impact." She came around the sheet and motioned Recker towards the far corner where he found a station that was likely intended for two personnel. Debris was piled up next to it, most of which seemed to be broken pieces of a larger console, with its tightly packed innards exposed to view.

"There was some other crap on top of it when we arrived," Hendrix continued. "We cleared it away, but some of it was pretty heavy."

"Doesn't look damaged," said Recker.

"If you put your hand on the front, you can feel the power running through it, sir. We figured you'd want to check it out."

"I'll do just that," said Recker. He remembered the panel arrangement from his time on Oldis and poked a finger confidently at the button which would bring the console out of deep sleep.

For a long time, the four screens remained blank and he noticed that two of them were cracked. Just when he was ready to believe the console was out of action, the four screens lit up, awaiting input.

"Time to check this out," said Recker, calling up the top-level menu. Back on Oldis, not every console had access to the most secure functions of the tenixite converter and he worried that this one here would be on a lower security tier. "This is a maintenance console," he said.

"Is that good or bad, sir?"

"I don't know, Corporal."

As quickly as he could, Recker delved into the different menus.

"You look worried, sir," said Hendrix, attempting subtlety in her hunt for information.

Recker didn't see a requirement to keep secrets. "If I'm right, this cube was automated and what that means is that these consoles were only installed to allow the technicians to finish their sign-off checks."

"Sounds great. Right?"

"I'm not sure. Each one of these consoles should have equal access to whatever data arrays and processing cores are installed but might not actually be able to activate the hardware after it went live."

Hendrix looked like she wanted to scratch her head. "That means you can't remove the core override from our ships?"

"I'll soon find out," said Recker without looking up. "Maybe yes, maybe no."

Seeing that he was in an answering mood, Hendrix kept talking. "If this console *can* activate the hardware, all of our warships are getting out of here?"

"It's not so straightforward - there might be no facility to remotely halt the override." Recker glanced across. "Whoever designed the weapon may not have seen the need."

"Oh."

"Please - I need to think."

Hendrix closed her mouth and took a slow step backwards, giving Recker some room.

"Let's see..." he said under his breath.

The console seemingly gave him access to everything. However, that meant Recker had too much to search through - like each single element of the cube from design drawings to technical specifications was included here, along with test routines for everything. He exhaled, wondering how he could possibly wade through the overwhelming quantity of data.

After five frustrating minutes, Recker stumbled upon something unexpected. A physical toggle he hadn't noticed on the control panel switched the console from test mode into operation mode.

"That new screen looks different," Hendrix observed.

"It is, Corporal," said Recker, hardly able to believe his luck. "They installed the operation software as well as the backend test stuff."

"I thought you said this cube was automated, sir."

"It was – but the automation routines run from the same command and control software that a flesh and blood operator would use. This is how the technicians made sure everything worked."

"I'll let you get on with it."

In moments, Recker had discovered what he was looking for. "Interrogator priority list," he read.

"Interrogator?"

"That's what they called this satellite, Corporal. Anything coming near Pinvos was to be corrupted with the core override and its databanks searched for useful data."

As he dug deeper, Recker found himself going cold with fear. It turned out that the primary data the Interrogator was interested in was star charts. Whoever had built this satellite, they wanted to find out where their enemies – or maybe any species which randomly stumbled into the net – lived. Recker had been given the smallest example of what the tenixite converter network was capable of and he didn't want to see the outcome of a maximum-level depletion burst on an HPA planet.

Desperate to unearth more information, Recker hunted for an audit log of what the Interrogator had recently extracted and transmitted. He found the log, but it contained endless quantities of data and most of it was just codes that were doubtless understood by the receiver but made no sense whatsoever to the human brain.

Recker knew it was critical that he return to base with the contents of the log. He remembered his discussion following the loss of the *Barbarian* and *Claymore* and how Lieutenant Eastwood speculated that their processing cores were too slow to crack their own data arrays. One way or another, it was imperative to find out the truth.

The console had an interface port on the left and Recker instructed his suit to link. Once done, he commanded the log file to upload into his helmet databank. The interface port was narrow and the log file was huge. He let the upload continue while continuing his search for a way to deactivate the core override.

During the next few minutes, he uncovered additional information about the satellite, most of which was interesting, but not necessarily important to the current situation. The cube was fitted with a huge but apparently inefficient ternium engine, the modules of which were incorporated within the outer walls of the structure. The external pillars served several purposes. The first was to detect warships in local space and the second was to target them with core overrides. Other functions related to comms and sensors.

"Hmm," said Recker. "I've found a reference to a *Purge* option."

"That's what took out our destroyers?"

"Seems likely. It's offline – must have been damaged in the impact."

"Shame – maybe you could steal the plans they used to build it, sir."

I'm already uploading other data, Corporal and I'd guess my suit databank will be full when it's done.

"The databank in my suit isn't holding much, sir. Photos, mostly." Hendrix smiled and Recker could see it was an effort. "From better times."

He nodded and met her gaze. "I appreciate the suggestion, but everything is taking a long time through this interface pipe."

"We could find a wider interface, sir, and there's a portable data cube on the deployment craft. We could probably pull everything out of this satellite and take it home."

Privately, Recker didn't think that the portable cube had a fraction of the necessary capacity. "I'll think on it, Corporal. Truth is, my priority is to get our warships back into the air. Once that's accomplished, we'll have plenty of time to empty the Interrogator's data arrays."

A minute later, he found what he was looking for.

"Core override command menu," he read.

The software was filled with options and Recker quickly gathered that the override itself could be tweaked in dozens of ways, depending on requirements. To his surprise, he discovered that it wasn't merely software either – the override weapon fired a beam which contained not only the code, but something else, which was capable of burning out certain kinds of data arrays and maybe even processing cores.

For now, the details were peripheral and he accessed the discharge log for the core override. A list appeared, along with a sub-menu to allow manipulation of the weapon's effect. Inside that menu was a *delete* option, which Recker believed would return a selected spaceship to its previous state.

Despite this apparently momentous discovery, Recker wasn't happy and he swore loudly.

"Sir?" asked Hendrix.

"I've located an option to delete the override from the affected ships. However, the Interrogator has assigned each target a numerical code, with no other identifier."

"Which means we don't know which code relates to which spaceship?"

"Exactly. We've got seven active core overrides running, four of which relate to HPA warships and three others which are assigned to the Daklan heavies."

"Four against three. Easy," Hendrix said the words lightly, but her expression indicated she knew the truth – an engagement would be too close to call.

While he considered the options, Recker scrolled through the list, to find out how many other warships the Interrogator had encountered. The satellite had been busy during its operational period, though he had no way to determine how long ago these other warships had stumbled into the trap.

The more Recker discovered about this distant war, the greater he understood the monumental scale of it and he suspected it made the conflict between the HPA and the Daklan appear little more than a playground fight in comparison.

"I'm missing something," he said, tapping his knuckles gently on the console.

"Sir?"

"This number here..."

The longer he stared at one of the entries lower down the list, the more he became sure he was on the verge of understanding. Then, the pieces began falling into place.

"The identifier used by the Interrogator for this warship here," he pointed, "I saw that number on the *Vengeance*."

Understanding came. The *Vengeance*'s processing core identifier number was mixed up with the code assigned by the Interrogator. He accessed the entry and was confronted by a file containing nothing but numbers. These numbers likely had significance, though he didn't know what it was just by looking.

The data download which Recker had started earlier was finished and his suit storage was almost full. This additional file wasn't too large and it fitted easily into the remaining space.

This diversion held him up for less than five seconds and when he was done, Recker scrolled once more to the top of the core override list.

"I know the core identifier for the *Expectation*," he said, his eyes fixed on the top seven ships. "With a bit of time, I'll be able to pick out the other ships in our fleet as well."

"That's great news, sir," said Hendrix.

Recker spotted the core override entry for the *Expectation*. This level of the menu offered no obvious way to interact with the weapon, but he had no doubt he could soon locate what he was looking for. He didn't get the chance. Suddenly, a new entry appeared next to each of the top seven designated numerical codes.

Core Override: Withdraw.

The moment he read the words, Recker knew it was time to act.

"Move!" he yelled. "Back to the spaceship!"

With the squad following close behind, Recker sprinted from the room.

CHAPTER THIRTEEN

"SIR, WHAT'S HAPPENING?" asked Hendrix as the squad dashed up the stairs.

"The Daklan inside this cube accessed the core override from another console and they've issued the command to withdraw the code from all seven warships. They're happy to engage our forces with their three desolators."

"Maybe you should leave the squad behind to flush out the Daklan soldiers, sir."

Recker had already considered it. "Negative, soldier. Whatever happens, the side which thinks it's about to lose will destroy the Interrogator rather than let it fall into their opponent's hands."

"Damn."

They came to the top of the stairs and Recker found the stationed soldiers ready to move.

"Into the spaceship," he barked. "Go!"

One-by-one, the soldiers threw themselves over the

gap and into the open hatch leading to the deployment vehicle's interior. Those waiting their turn shifted nervously and kept their guns aimed at the intersection in case the Daklan chose this moment to attack.

"How long will the core override take to shut down, sir?" asked Sergeant Vance on the comms.

"I have no idea," said Recker. "We might already be too late, in which case it's going to be a matter of luck whether our deployment craft can escape from the conflict without getting shot down."

"There's nothing on the comms yet," said Montero.

"Even a warship comms won't penetrate the walls of this cube, Private. The core overrides could be gone and they wouldn't be able to tell us about it."

When his turn came, Recker scrambled through the hatch and into the bay, ignoring everything else as he made his way along the narrow aisle to the cockpit. Sergeant Vance had already made room and Recker took the middle seat.

"That's the last one in, sir," said Montero. "Hatch closed, we're good to go."

Recker fed in the power and the incision craft pulled strongly away from the inner cube. The support pillars appeared to have doubled in number and he snarled in frustration as he guided the spaceship above one and beneath the next.

"The steps!" said Montero.

"I see them."

Flying around two more of the spokes, Recker aimed the vessel's nose at the opening below. At the last moment, he rotated the hull so that it was parallel with the gap and dropped it inside.

The following seconds or minutes – Recker wasn't quite sure how long the escape took – tested his skills to the limit. He skimmed edges and walls, pulling the control sticks in every direction, constantly adjusting to save precious fractions of a second.

"Last step coming up," said Vance. His voice was dead calm and Recker had no idea if it was an act or if the man's state of mind was simply immune to external influence.

The deployment vessel hit the lowest level and the underside shuddered as it scraped across uneven alloy. Dimly, Recker noticed one of the Daklan shuttles that Vance had shot down earlier and, incredibly, saw that two of the alien soldiers had somehow made it out. They had nowhere to go and fortunately, they weren't carrying a shoulder launcher.

"Lucky bastards," said Montero.

"No, Private," Vance corrected her. "They're the unlucky ones."

"Forget them. Where's the *Expectation?*" growled Recker, his eyes scanning the feeds.

"No sign of it, sir."

"Keep checking the comms!"

With fear building, Recker took the deployment craft outside under full thrust. The dust hadn't settled and he suspected it was here to stay, along with the winds which immediately buffeted the spaceship and forced Recker into an instinctive correction.

A fast-moving shape sped into the forward sensor arc, followed by a second.

"Sergeant Vance be ready!" shouted Recker.

Vance had his hands on the triggers and the gun motors whined.

"Hold fire!" yelled Montero.

The tension remained in Vance's shoulders, but he didn't unleash the destructive power of the nose gun.

"Friendlies," said Montero, panting, like she'd run a thousand metres in a full loadout. "They're shuttles from the *Shock and Awe.*"

"Tell them to return to their docks immediately!" said Recker. "And find me that destroyer!"

"There!" yelled Montero, juggling comms and the sensor controls.

A huge shape fell from the sky and Recker saw that it was the *Expectation*.

"Coming in fast," Vance observed.

The destroyer's propulsion sound engulfed the much smaller incision vehicle and the billion-ton *Expectation* decelerated like only a ternium-engined warship was capable of. About fifty metres overhead, it came to a halt and Recker mentally congratulated Aston on her judgement.

"Where's the docking bay?" he said, his eyes searching for the outline of the hatch on the destroyer's underside.

"We've got an interface with it, sir," said Montero.

An ingenious arrangement of overlapping alloy plates retracted into the *Expectation*'s hull in a way which had always reminded Recker of a kaleidoscope.

Without warning, a comms channel opened.

"It's Lieutenant Burner, sir," said Montero.

Recker's full focus was on bringing the deployment

vessel into the bay. "Has the core override ended?" he managed to ask.

"Lieutenant Burner doesn't know what's happening, sir." Montero went quiet, listening. "The crew have regained control over some of the onboard systems."

Once the incision craft was lined up with the bay, Recker prepared to activate the gravity chains on the internal clamps, which were designed to pull the deployment craft into docking position. Before he could do so, the overwhelming howl of the destroyer's propulsion abruptly cut out and the *Expectation* dropped lower. It collided with the deployment craft, producing a hollow boom.

Aston reacted quickly and steadied the destroyer once more. The incident could have delayed the docking procedure but instead it brought the incision craft right alongside the clamps. A console light went green and Recker stabbed the button to dock.

"What happened?" asked Vance loudly over the clunk of the gravity clamps engaging.

"The *Expectation*'s propulsion just went out of overstress, Sergeant, which means the core override is either purged or nearly purged."

The moment a second green light – *docking successful* – appeared, Recker sprang from his seat. He wasn't even out of the cockpit when he heard the destroyer's engines, this time without overstress, rise again and he experienced a sense of acceleration which told him Aston was going somewhere fast.

Recker was first through the exit hatch and he dashed across the *Expectation*'s bay, speaking on the internal comms to Lieutenant Burner. In short sentences, Recker explained what he'd found on the Interrogator and made sure his crew was aware of the significance.

When Recker was done, Lieutenant Burner filled him in on the destroyer's as-yet incomplete recovery from the core override.

"Almost everything's responding, sir. The core override is still affecting some of our systems, but we're heading back to normal."

"What about the other ships in the fleet?" asked Recker, charging along a corridor which seemed to stretch on forever.

"They're not yet on the comms, sir. One of the desolators lifted off about five seconds ago and disappeared into the dust."

All the signs of early-combat chaos were present and Recker hated that he wasn't yet able to stamp his mark on the situation. At last, he made it to the bridge and threw himself into his chair.

"Welcome back, sir," said Aston. She didn't look over and her expression was set in absolute determination. "The controls are all yours."

"Thanks, I've got them."

Recker's brain absorbed information from numerous different sources. The sensors were online, he could see that from the way Burner was updating the view on the bulkhead screen, though the feed was glitchy and lower resolution than usual.

Aston had kept the *Expectation* within the dust storm at a low altitude and the closest HPA warship – the *Trojan* battleship – was twenty kilometres south. Other than that, the view was of swirling red particles and faintly discerned shapes which could be anything.

"We're heading around in support of our fleet," said Recker, bringing the destroyer into a tight arc. "Where's that desolator?"

"Nothing on the sensors, sir."

"I doubt it ran for the hills."

"No, sir. I'll find it."

"Still waiting for full control over several of our subsystems," said Eastwood. "I shut down this overstress device the moment I could access the propulsion. The box produced a bunch of errors and I don't know if it's going to work again."

"Weapons are apparently online, sir, but the targeting systems aren't responding," said Aston. "Our missiles won't lock."

"Is it something you can fix?"

"I'm trying, sir. This is a lingering result from the core override – I think we'll have to wait for it to clear."

"It needs to happen soon. We're going to find those desolators and put a couple of Hellburners through their armour."

"I'll do what I can, sir."

"The *Trojan*'s comms came online!" said Burner. "I've got a channel."

"Fill them in."

"Yes, sir." Burner made a surprised sound. "Captain Eden Melody is in charge."

"What happened to Admiral Fraser?"

"He's no longer on the battleship, sir."

Recker had no doubt there was a tale to hear regarding

Admiral Fraser's departure from the *Trojan*, though it wasn't a good moment to press for the gory details. "Is Captain Melody planning to join the battle?"

"She is intending – and I quote – to *kick some ass*, sir. She's the most senior officer in the arena and we're ordered to assist."

"Gladly," said Recker.

"Still nothing from the targeting systems, sir."

"We've got to locate those desolators first," said Recker. "One took off, that leaves two others. If they're grounded, we can hit them from short range, with or without a target lock."

"Yes, sir."

"The *Trojan* is off the ground, sir, and we're joining a battle network," said Burner.

One green dot – the battleship – appeared on the sensors and was closely followed by two others, the furthest being forty kilometres from the *Expectation*. "The *Shock and Awe* is with us," said Recker, his hopes of a successful mission climbing for the first time since the *Expectation* exited lightspeed twenty million kilometres off target.

"The *Harken* is still on the ground, sir. They're reporting engine problems."

Recker's newfound hopes faded as quickly as they'd arrived. "Can they resolve?"

"Early indications point to a *maybe*."

"Damnit, this is our opportunity to strike!" Recker calmed himself. "Anything from the *Titan*?"

"No, sir – still offline."

"It's a difficult thing to say, but I don't think the lifter's crew made it," said Eastwood. "I hope I'm wrong."

Recker hoped so too, though he couldn't allow himself to think about it.

"We're about five klicks from the expected position of the second desolator," said Burner. "Our sensors aren't responding correctly, sir. At first I thought it was a calibration issue, but now I'm beginning to wonder if the core override did some lasting damage – it's like the array processing units are at ten percent even though the status monitor says they're running normally."

Not only was the feed quality terrible, Recker also wondered if the dust had thickened during the time he'd been inside the Interrogator. The storm seemed concentrated within the impact craters, making them a potential hiding place for the Daklan heavy cruisers. With the sensors operating at reduced efficiency, Recker was doubly worried about his warship taking a Terrus cannon hit from out of nowhere.

Maybe every warship is affected, not just the Expectation.

"Lieutenant Burner – check in with the other spaceships and find out if they're suffering the same limitations as we are."

In the few seconds it took Burner to obtain a response, Recker piloted the *Expectation* low towards a ridge which had been formed by the multiple impacts with Pinvos.

"Every ship has a problem, sir. Mostly sensors and targeting like ours."

"We're going to need a complete strip-down once we return to base," said Eastwood angrily.

Recker didn't get a chance to respond. Suddenly the forward feed was obscured by an explosion of dust and rock. It cleared in moments, leaving him staring at an enormous hole in the ridge, like a god's fist had punched clean through.

Not a fist. A Terrus cannon.

Even as the thought formed, Recker banked the *Expectation* away from its previous course. The Daklan had got a sight of his warship and the fact that they'd missed with their first effort suggested they were having the same issues with sensors and targeting.

Facing nine billion tons of Daklan metal, Recker knew he'd need plenty of backup.

CHAPTER FOURTEEN

WITH HIS WARSHIP at full thrust, Recker clenched his jaw and waited for the missiles to come. A flash lit up the rear feed, the plasma light turning quickly to grey as the storm shrouded the flames. At the same time, an explosion of rock fountained from the floor of the impact crater below and stones like hard missiles clattered against the underside plating.

"There goes their second Terrus cannon," said Aston. "Shame they've got a quick reload."

"We need a sensor lock," said Recker. "Otherwise this is going to be the shortest engagement of the war."

"Working on it, sir."

"And where's our backup?"

A red dot flickered on the tactical, hardly more than fifty kilometres from the *Expectation*. The dot vanished and reappeared at ninety kilometres on a different vector. It vanished again and another dot appeared, this time at 120 kilometres.

"Are those ghosts or enemy warships?" Recker asked.

"I don't know, sir. The storm is screwing with our sensor lock. Gut feel is the Daklan have two desolators in the air, not three."

Recker was furious to have missed the opportunity to get the first strike at the enemy and he desperately hoped one of the Daklan heavies was still on the ground.

"I trust your instinct, Lieutenant Burner - there are two desolators in the air. That leaves one down and I want you to figure out where it is."

"Yes, sir. I've got fifty-fifty coordinates."

In the circumstances, Recker was happy with a fifty-fifty. "I'll take us low into this next impact crater to cut out the firing angle of the Terrus cannons," he said. "We need to blanket those coordinates with missiles."

This was one of the times when a good comms officer could prove his or her worth, and Burner was up there with the best. Rather than acting as a dumb relay of information between the HPA warships, he could read the situation by watching the sensors and listening to the other officers, allowing him to act and react quicker than an officer who relied on direct instruction for everything.

"Yes, sir. I've made the *Trojan* aware. They're going to saturate the area with plasma warheads."

Between them, the *Trojan* and the *Shock and Awe* were packing enough missile clusters to lay waste to a city in a single combined launch. It wasn't necessary to have a weapons lock to hit an unmoving target and a few seconds after Recker passed on his recommendation, hundreds of missiles plunged into one of the impact craters. Such was the intensity, the dust storm was unable to completely obscure the view and it seemed as though the burning horizon gave warning of the brutality to come.

As if fate had chosen to mock this effort to destroy the Daklan heavy cruiser, three red dots appeared on the tactical, each one solid and travelling along its own vector within the dust storm. The closest was at 150 kilometres and the furthest at 200 kilometres. Then, the flickering resumed and all three of the desolators vanished completely.

"Gone to ground," said Aston. "Sneaky bastards."

"They're within fifty klicks of the Interrogator," said Burner. "It's like they're staking out their claim."

"The Daklan aren't ready to give it up yet," said Recker.

If the enemy felt obliged to protect the alien cube, it was a constraint on their action, though maybe not a significant one.

"Pass on my recommendation to Captain Melody that the satellite should not be given any consideration."

"Yes, sir. I've already made the *Trojan* aware of the data you extracted."

"Commander Aston, think you can get off an Ilstrom launch with the guidance systems disabled?"

"Yes, sir, but the chance of scoring a hit is slim at best – that flickering on the tactical means the target could be hundreds of metres away from its apparent position. If the enemy detect us from our launch, they'll retaliate and they might be luckier than we are."

The HPA military taught its officers how to fight in limited visibility situations, but the simulator could never be a perfect copy of the real thing. It offered a glimpse of the endless variables and a hint at the difficulties. What the simulator absolutely couldn't do was prepare an officer for the stress of an engagement like this one. Recker had experience, but that didn't make it easy for him.

A red dot appeared on the tactical and another two Terrus slugs crashed into the side of the impact crater, only a few hundred metres from the *Expectation*. Recker swore at the speed of the attack. The curse had barely left his tongue when one of the flickering red dots on the tactical jumped about thirty kilometres from its previous position.

He cursed again and banked the *Expectation* deeper into the impact crater. This one had been created by the *Shock and Awe* and pieces of debris - recognizable as armour plates - were scattered everywhere, suggesting the cruiser had taken significant damage.

"The enemy are staying low in the Interrogator's impact crater," Recker guessed. "And only putting their heads up long enough to fire at us."

"What do they have to gain from that, sir?" asked Eastwood.

"This is how they think they can beat us, Lieutenant."

Recker tried to figure out the permutations. When it came to an engagement between opposing warships, altitude wasn't necessarily an advantage. What mattered most was a combination of outright firepower and – though the manuals rarely talked about it in such honest terms – outguessing the opponent. Right now, the Daklan believed they could win by staying out of the *Trojan's* charge cannon firing arc, while relying on the much higher velocity of the Terrus slugs to do some damage to the HPA spaceships.

"The *Harken* is unable to get into the air, sir," said Burner. "They're thirty klicks north in the next crater." He cleared his throat. "Captain Melody is concerned the enemy will locate the cruiser and destroy it before those technical issues are overcome."

"Time for the fireworks," said Aston, understanding the meaning.

"We're instructed to treat the Interrogator as a secondary mission goal, sir," Burner finished. "A *nice to have*. However, we are to take whatever action is required to protect the *Harken*."

"What about our weapons? Are we to hold fire when there's a risk of hitting the Interrogator?"

"Captain Melody is assured that the cube is robust enough to withstand a certain amount of punishment, sir. Just not the level of punishment that would result from deployment of one of the devastator bombs the *Trojan* is carrying in its hold."

The answer left Recker no clearer as to how much of the destroyer's weaponry he was permitted to deploy – without active targeting, the warship's missiles might easily strike the Interrogator. Luckily, Captain Melody didn't leave him guessing for long.

"The *Trojan* suggests we halt our progress towards the cube," said Burner. "They're about to set that area of Pinvos on fire."

The words were a trigger, not only for the HPA fleet, but also to the Daklan. Recker's tactical became speckled in flickering, fast-moving objects in both red and green.

Through the dust clouds above, a ball of pure, deep blue energy with a 200-metre diameter streaked across the sky.

"Charge cannon bolt, heading straight into the Interrogator's crater. So much for *nice to have*," said Aston.

A second glowing sphere went after the first, racing by just as the first detonated in a vivid flash which turned everything white, highlighting the dust particles as tiny dots which appeared like static on the feed.

In between the first charge cannon explosion and the second, Recker saw a line of orange race into the sky, closely followed by another, this time from a different source.

"Daklan incendiaries," said Burner. "Target location currently unknown."

Feilar missiles suddenly exploded all around the *Expectation*, in such quantities that the entire slope behind the warship became covered in plasma, and rock was ejected from dozens of new craters. It took Recker a moment to realize that one of the Daklan warheads had struck the *Expectation* and the rumble of the blast made the control bars shake beneath his palms.

"Damage report," he growled, giving the propulsion maximum as he aimed the destroyer for the opposite side of the crater. The slope that way wasn't steep, but it would offer cover if the desolator targeting them was at a low altitude.

"No breach, sir," said Eastwood. "Didn't even break through the plating."

It sounded to Recker like the new angled armour had done its job, though he wasn't planning to let it suffer any more impacts than necessary. He brought the *Expectation* to the slope of the crater and banked to follow the perimeter, while staying two thousand metres below the planet's original surface level.

A red dot appeared on the tactical, its altitude increasing rapidly. Twin Terrus impacts on the floor of the crater followed and then the desolator vanished into the Interrogator's crater again. Too late, missiles from the *Trojan* and *Shock and Awe* flew in answer.

A third bolt from the *Trojan*'s charge cannon went overheard, along with the burning lines of Ilstrom propulsions. Feilars went the other way and Recker was beginning to feel like an insect, creeping along the skirting board and hoping to reach a place of safety before the underside of a boot descended upon him.

The taunting thoughts of his mind made him purse his lips in tense frustration. He knew the *Expectation*'s Hellburners could do some damage, but only if he landed them on target.

"Where are those incendiaries coming down, Lieutenant?" asked Recker.

"I've just put the overlay on the tactical, sir."

The projected detonation area for the Daklan explosives was several hundred square kilometres, concentrated on the *Trojan*'s position.

"All of this dust is going to burn up, sir," said Aston.

"Those charge cannon blasts will have done the same to the vicinity of the Interrogator," said Recker. "We just have to get close enough to take advantage."

He pictured the combat arena in his mind. The Interrogator was 120 kilometres north and the *Expectation* was still in the overlapping crater made by the *Shock and Awe*.

To the west was the adjoining crater where the *Harken* had come down.

Recker didn't want to go west in case it drew the Daklan's attention to the HPA cruiser. Instead, he went east, towards the place where the heavy lifter *Titan* had crashed. From memory, he reckoned it should be possible to approach the site of the Interrogator and maybe get a couple of Hellburners into one of the desolators.

"I've detected another incendiary launch, sir. It's too early to predict the target area," said Burner. "Charge cannon plasma ball coming in response."

The blast from the charge cannon had a radius of ten kilometres which should have been exceptionally effective in the current engagement, but somehow Recker didn't think the Daklan were likely be sucker-punched. The way the three heavy cruisers were operating made him think their commanding officers had plenty of experience.

A flash lit up the dust-heavy sky on the edge of the central crater, interspersed with smaller flickers from a huge cluster of Ilstroms. Simultaneously, the first and second wave of multi-warhead Daklan incendiaries landed on Pinvos, way in the distance where the *Trojan* had been only seconds earlier. Harsh light came and lingered for long seconds. A charge cannon sphere went by overhead and then a second wave of incendiaries detonated, these ones much closer to the *Expectation* than the first. Straight after came a third incendiary burst, this time to the east.

"We only detected two incendiary launches!" said Recker. "That third one came down right over the *Shock and Awe.*"

Incendiaries were crude weapons and in normal

circumstances, no threat to a warship. Given the low altitude of this engagement, they took on a greater significance and Recker was furious that the third launch had gone undetected.

"The last desolator must have launched without us knowing it, sir," said Burner. "I'm waiting on a damage report from the *Shock and Awe*."

The heat from the incendiaries had interfered with the battle network synchronisation and for many seconds, the *Shock and Awe* appeared to be stationary on the tactical. Recker couldn't give the cruiser too much of his attention, but he kept glancing across, hoping that the battle network would update and show him that the cruiser was still active.

The bad news kept on coming.

"That next incendiary launch is coming down right on top of the *Harken*, sir. And us if we don't get out of the way. I've detected two further launches, target areas currently unknown."

"What news from the *Harken*?"

"No guarantees of flight, sir. The *Shock and Awe* took some heat damage, along with one Terrus and two Feilar impacts when they climbed out of the flames. Their offensive capability is not significantly diminished."

Recker could read between the lines – the cruiser had taken some damage and probably lost a few missile clusters. It was weakened and it was foolish to pretend otherwise.

The engagement was rapidly heading towards an unfavourable outcome and Recker prepared to take a calculated gamble. He was beginning to understand the behaviour of the enemy warships – how they'd appear briefly to launch their weapons and then disappear, the timings not quite random but not exactly predictable either.

"Ready the Hellburners, Commander."

"Yes, sir."

"This won't be an easy shot for you."

"I'll make it."

Recker watched and waited for the moment. The opportunity wasn't long in coming – a salvo of the *Trojan*'s Ilstroms flew into the main crater. Anticipating the appearance of a desolator, Recker brought the *Expectation* higher, until it was above the rim of the crater and facing down the long slope leading to the Interrogator.

At once, he was shocked by how much of the dust had been burned up by the exchange of fire. It still swirled, yet enormous pockets of comparatively clear air had been formed by the *Trojan*'s charge cannon blasts. In the crater's centre, the Interrogator lay where it had been since impact, any sign of missile and charge cannon damage obscured by dust which remained thick around it, despite the clearer pockets elsewhere.

With his spaceship's nose aimed towards the Interrogator, Recker flew it sideways while keeping the Hellburner tubes pointed right at the cube. Almost at once, the sensors detected a grey, elongated shape lifting into sight from behind the Interrogator, showing a full broadside. For a couple of seconds, the desolator climbed strongly and Recker adjusted the orientation of his warship.

"Hellburners away," said Aston, firing just as the heavy cruiser slowed.

Twin igniting Hellburner propulsions created low-bass thumps, audible through many metres of solid alloy. Bright orange circles appeared on the forward feed and then they were gone.

"Enemy launch detected, sir," said Burner.

With the Hellburners fired, Recker dumped the *Expectation* towards the cover offered by the slope of this linked crater, hoping he was quick enough to escape the retaliation.

The Hellburners crossed the short distance in the blinking of an eye. One flew wide of its target, while the second hit the desolator five hundred metres from its nose section. The blast hid the front third of the Daklan warship, but with the *Expectation* dropping towards the crater, Recker knew he wouldn't have time to judge the damage caused by the explosion.

A colossal impact against the *Expectation*'s upper section sent a shockwave through the bridge, making Recker's ears ring. He groaned in pain and it took all the focus could muster to maintain control of the destroyer and get it into the crater, out of sight of the enemy warships.

"We took a Terrus shot, sir," said Eastwood, the loudness of his voice indicating he had some problems with his hearing after the soundwave.

"What damage?"

"We lost some plating and our topside is burning hot."

One of the sensor feeds gave Recker a partial view of the damage. The force of the Terrus strike had torn away several plates in their entirety and buckled several others, leaving a rough furrow. Heat generated by the crushing blow left traces of red which outlined the damaged area and once again Recker noticed that the slug had been deflected by the sloped edges of the armour.

"And I thought I fired a good shot," said Aston ruefully. "That alien bastard got us right between the eyes."

Recker wasn't sure who had the bigger hammer and he put his faith in the HPA Hellburner tech to have caused the Daklan a few problems.

Unwilling to stay in one place, he flew around the crater's inner perimeter, a thousand metres below surface level. The *Titan* heavy lifter was about twenty kilometres to the south-east and dimly visible through a gap where two craters joined.

"Find out if the *Trojan* or the *Shock and Awe* have a damage estimate for our Hellburner strike," said Recker.

"On it, sir."

With reluctance, Recker turned his eyes to one of the feeds showing the *Titan*. Like he'd feared, the lifter was crushed beyond recognition and the force of its impact with Pinvos had compacted its hull to less than half of its usual height. It didn't matter how much reinforcement the engineers added – a hollow spaceship could never withstand such a collision in the same way as a solid one could.

He turned away and checked the reload timer for the Hellburners. In a few seconds, the destroyer would be ready for another shot.

"Incendiary detonation in five seconds," Burner announced.

The brief intensity of the engagement with the desolator had taken Recker's attention away from the coming sea of plasma fire. The *Expectation* was out of the target area, but the *Harken* was not. At the predicted moment, the incendiaries went off, burning the air, thinning the dust and engulfing the HPA cruiser in a heat which its armour couldn't withstand.

Confronted by the destruction of another warship from the Pinvos task force, Recker closed his eyes for the shortest of moments, before opening them again, his body pumping enough adrenaline to make him nauseous and his thoughts filled with determination and a craving for revenge.

CHAPTER FIFTEEN

IT TURNED out Recker wasn't the only officer who could read a situation and act accordingly. Captain Melody had seen enough to conclude that the chance of victory was slipping away, and with it the opportunity to recover the Interrogator.

"She's going to execute a high-speed flyover and drop a devastator bomb, sir," said Burner. "The intention is to take out the cube and the desolators at the same time. We're to retreat to a safe distance and prepare for the aftermath."

"Easy as that," said Recker, his mind already working out an escape route.

"They could drop that bomb from space," said Eastwood.

"High speed and low altitude is the only way to ensure it lands, Commander," said Recker. "An orbital deployment would leave the devastator vulnerable to the Daklan

Graler turrets. They could aim manually and still take it out."

"That bomb's going to make a big bang," Aston said. She grinned. "A *real* big bang."

Recker drummed his fingers. "The Daklan aren't stupid. The moment they detect the *Trojan* coming in so fast, they'll scatter."

"And we'll punch them in the face as they run towards us, sir," said Burner. "Metaphorically speaking, of course."

What had, at first, sounded like a simple, straightforward plan lacking in nuance and forethought, suddenly seemed more layered than Recker had initially thought. "It might just work," he said. "Insane, but maybe that's what we need."

"Shame about the Interrogator," said Eastwood. He gave a snort of humourless laughter. "Having said that, I'd far rather get back home in one piece, carrying that data we extracted from it."

Recker didn't like to lose, even when the odds against victory were stacked so high he couldn't see the summit. In this instance, he fully agreed with Eastwood's words. Above all else, the HPA needed to find out what data the Interrogator had transmitted from its encounter with the fleet.

Keeping his warship low out of the enemy firing arc, Recker watched as the *Trojan* rose from its own impact crater and accelerated across the planet's surface, heading directly away from the Interrogator.

"Right into the thickest part of the remaining dust," said Burner. "And at a two hundred metre altitude."

"The longer Captain Melody keeps out of sight, the greater the chance of pulling this off," said Aston.

"Two hundred metres is low for the approach – they'll be travelling too fast to correct any errors in flight," said Recker, trying to calculate the velocity at which Melody would deploy the bomb.

"Our Hellburners are reloaded," said Aston. "We're ready anytime."

Five hundred kilometres from the Interrogator, the *Trojan* slowed and turned. Captain Melody delayed a few seconds, during which Burner reported the launch of more Daklan incendiaries. One of the desolators appeared on the sensors and fired a thick wave of Feilars, then a second appeared and did likewise.

"Some of those were aimed towards the *Trojan*'s last known position," said Burner.

Recker held his breath, hoping the enemy wouldn't realise the battleship was elsewhere. The desolators had only emerged from cover for a short moment – long enough to hunt for a target and then drop out of sight when they failed to detect one.

"It's likely the enemy comms officers will examine the recorded sensor data more closely now that they're back in cover, sir," said Burner.

"Damnit," said Recker. His eyes returned to the green dot representing the battleship on his tactical. It wasn't moving. "What's keeping them?" he muttered.

The answer was: nothing.

Captain Melody gave the order and the *Trojan* thundered across the sky, gathering speed at a rate which put anything else in the HPA fleet to shame. At four thousand metres and 35 billion tons, it was the pinnacle of the HPA's weapons and engineering expertise. It would need to be, if it were to resist the incoming fire from three desolators for more than a few seconds.

"The devastator bomb," said Eastwood, reminding himself of the facts. "A ternium-accelerated plasma cannister with an armoured shell and twin boosters, designed to blow the crap out of absolutely anything it lands on."

"Don't forget to mention the blast radius," Aston reminded him.

"Everything within two hundred kilometres of the initial blast will be incinerated. The sides of the crater should limit much of the expansion."

Recker wasn't keen to find out exactly how much containment the Interrogator's impact crater would offer his warship. He watched for a moment and the instant he saw three red dots appear on the tactical, he flew the destroyer backwards, gaining altitude at the same time. The engines roared and the warship's nose pointed straight at the enemy.

The velocity gauge surged upwards and Recker kept his eyes on the sensors, searching for the best target. He chose one - a shape flying amongst the confusion of flames and dust that engulfed this area of Pinvos.

"Give them some missiles, Commander."

"Firing forward clusters #1 and #2."

Twenty Ilstroms raced away into the gloom. Without targeting, they had little chance of hitting the enemy, but Recker hoped they might provide a distraction.

"*Trojan* at two hundred klicks from deployment area," said Burner. "Their comms team reports heavy incoming fire."

One of the sensor arrays was locked on the battleship and, though the image was far from clear, Recker's eyes picked out a series of faint grey trails which seemed to be following the *Trojan*'s progress.

Plasma fires, he thought.

A sphere of blue appeared underneath the battleship's nose and then accelerated towards the Daklan positions. The desolators scattered and the charge cannon bolt exploded in a flash on the rim of the Interrogator's crater. When the feed cleared, the three enemy warships were still in the air, one of them with its rear half alight.

"Come on," urged Burner. "Break up, you asshole."

The desolator didn't break up, though the flames didn't burn out. Recker guessed the heavy cruiser might fail eventually, but it wasn't happening quickly enough.

As he watched events play out, Recker's grip on the controls tightened until his knuckles ached. He hated being relegated to the position of spectator. He couldn't approach the bomb deployment zone and he couldn't order the launch of the Hellburner missiles – it would require a miracle to hit the enemy from this range. Fifty klicks east, the *Shock and Awe* was similarly constrained and reduced to firing a smattering of Ilstroms, rather than waste its own Hellburners on a fire and hope launch that would leave its missile tubes mid-reload if the Daklan changed tack.

At three hundred kilometres from the planned blast zone, Recker slowed the destroyer and flew it unpredictably from side to side. The Daklan didn't seem interested in either the *Expectation* or the *Shock and Awe*, having evidently concluded that the *Trojan* was the main threat to their victory on Pinvos. Recker took little consolation from the lack of inbound missiles – the *Expectation*'s front armour was particularly thick and he would have happily used it to soak some of the heat directed at the *Trojan*.

The approach of the battleship allowed Burner to improve the feed quality and what Recker saw made him sick to his stomach. Instead of individual plasma fires burning on its hull, the *Trojan* had become a fireball of vivid white, which left a thick grey smear for a dozen kilometres in its wake.

"Why isn't Captain Melody taking evasive action?" said Aston.

"She is, Commander," said Recker, coming to a sudden realization. "The weapons targeting is active on at least one of those desolators."

"You're right, sir!" said Burner. "The sensors didn't pick it up until you said it. Some of those Daklan missiles are veering onto target!"

"Which means the Terrus cannons will be on target as well," said Eastwood.

"Our own weapons lock is still unavailable," said Aston miserably. "I can't even access the configuration menu."

"We've got to do something," said Recker.

It was easily said, but he didn't know what the hell he could do about the unfolding tragedy. One of the three desolators was showing a broadside to the *Trojan*, which meant that was the warship with the functioning targeting systems. Unfortunately, the Daklan rarely let down their guard and the heavy cruiser was flying up, down, left and right to evade the *Trojan*'s own – unguided - inbound missiles.

"The *Trojan* has lost its front charge cannon," said Burner. "Half of its forward missile clusters are out of action."

"It's not coming through this," said Aston softly.

Recker didn't say anything. The *Trojan* looked as if it was on the verge of breaking up, though its velocity was undiminished.

"Nearly there," he said.

"The desolators are heading for the stars," said Burner. "They've guessed the plan."

While two the Daklan heavies accelerated vertically and one went sideways, the *Trojan*'s stern drifted wide and Recker knew warship's control systems were failing. With her battleship on the brink, Captain Melody took the only available course of action and detonated the devastator bomb while it was still in the hold.

A shocking flash of black-specked blue-white appeared where the *Trojan* had once been. With tremendous speed, the blast sphere expanded, hitting its peak diameter of four hundred kilometres in less five seconds and making the bridge feed so bright that Recker was forced to squint. Somewhere amongst it, the desolators were lost from sight.

The blast wave struck the *Expectation*, sending a

dozen electronic needles jumping, and agitating the surrounding dust clouds enough to make them briefly impenetrable to the sensors. With the blast wave, came heat enough to fuse the airborne dust into hailstones of glass and set off the destroyer's hull temperature alarms.

"Here come the Daklan incendiaries," said Burner.

The last of the previously launched warheads crashed into the surface in an overlap to the recent devastator blast. More flames – an ocean of them – came and lit up this distant world.

Recker sat it out, his expression fixed. The bomb blast receded quickly and, for long seconds, that area of Pinvos was clear of dust – an oasis in this ruined desert. Soon, the incendiaries dwindled on the uncaring stone, the winds blew and the dust swept in once more.

Then, something – a desolator - rose from beneath the rim of the *Harken's* impact crater. Every inch of the heavy cruiser glowed in patches of white, orange and red, while semiliquid sections of its plating tumbled away like an alloy rain. Slowly and with an apparently monumental effort, the Daklan cruiser rotated and climbed, as if it were desperately seeking whatever had inflicted this damage upon it.

How this opponent had survived the devastator bomb, Recker had no idea and he guided the *Expectation* towards the enemy ship. On the *Shock and Awe*, Captain Hutton did likewise. An injured beast could lash out unpredictably and Recker flew erratically in case of incoming fire.

"How the hell is it still operational?" said Eastwood in disbelief.

A piece of the rear section – a billion tons or more - snapped free and fell into the crater, yet still the heavy cruiser remained in the air, firing nothing, but still searching.

"Give it the Hellburners," said Recker.

At a range of twenty kilometres, Aston fired and the twin warheads thundered into the stricken desolator, producing gouts of flame from the huge openings they created in the armour. A moment after, four more Hellburners, this time from the *Shock and Awe*, crashed into the enemy ship.

Six Hellburners were more than enough. The desolator's resistance was over and the heavy cruiser broke into pieces, which hung briefly in the air before plummeting down. Once again, Pinvos was struck a series of massive blows as the debris crashed into the Interrogator's heatscarred crater.

"I've got Captain Hutton on the comms, sir," said Burner.

It was the first time since the beginning of the mission that Recker had spoken directly to his opposite number on the *Shock and Awe*.

"Bring him through on the open channel," he said, piloting the *Expectation* towards the place where the Interrogator hit the surface. It seemed best to check on the satellite's condition.

Captain Jack Hutton had a deep voice and an accent that was probably from somewhere on Earth. He provided a concise summary of the mission so far. "What a heap of shit."

Recker couldn't bring himself to smile. "It's not over

yet," he said. "Ten days to base and then a week explaining what happened. We lost some good officers here."

"You extracted some intel, Captain Recker."

"For all the good it'll do us against the Daklan. The best outcome is that an unknown alien species doesn't know where our home worlds are located."

"One way or another, we've got to be sure."

"I've got no arguments with that."

Recker was exhausted. It felt like he'd been fighting nonstop for weeks and now the prize at the end of it might be no more than early warning about a coming attack from an unknown species. On the other hand, that species might be long dead, or no longer interested in data from the Interrogator. Whatever the truth, humanity – already pushed to the limit – was about to find itself with a whole bunch of additional worries and no easy way to deal with them.

Putting the distraction aside, Recker flew the *Expectation* over the edge of the largest crater, the sides of which were now completely glassy and with an unhealthy red sheen.

Much of the alien cube was spread across the crater, in melted pieces and pools of hardening alloy, but the devastator bomb hadn't entirely finished the job. In the centre of the crater, a much larger section of the Interrogator remained. Three of the cube's faces were missing and its interior was open to the elements. Without proper support, the remaining two vertical walls sagged and leaned, and the inner area had suffered so much damage that Recker struggled to connect its current appearance with what he'd seen before.

"Anything we can salvage?" asked Hutton on the comms, his warship stationary and twenty kilometres east.

"There's plenty of debris," said Recker. "I guess if this was an easy operation, high command would be interested."

"What I'm asking is whether we need to shoot it some more."

Recker slowly shook his head, aware the other man couldn't see him doing so. "We could unload everything we have and still be asking that same question." He held in a sigh. "We've done enough."

Evidently unconvinced, Hutton piloted his warship closer. The comms channel stayed open, though neither man spoke for a while.

"Let's go," said Hutton eventually.

"I'll have my comms man send you a synch code," said Recker eventually. "It's time we returned to base."

"You're forgetting something, Captain Recker."

The words left Recker puzzled. "What's that?"

"Before we leave, it's our duty to locate Admiral Fraser. He's on a shuttle somewhere." Hutton's voice was scrupulously neutral.

The reminder of Fraser's actions left Recker angry once again. Still, he couldn't abandon the man, no matter how tempting it might be.

"Then let's find him and get back to base," he growled.

At that moment, Aston made a discovery. "Our weapons targeting system just came back online," she said.

"You've got to be shitting us?" said Eastwood.

Aston wasn't shitting them and Recker experienced a brief wave of giddiness in the way he usually did when it seemed like the entire damned universe was conspiring against him. He ground his teeth and guided the *Expectation* away from the surface.

CHAPTER SIXTEEN

THE TEN-DAY FLIGHT home passed quickly and gave Recker an opportunity to reflect upon the mixed fortunes of both the HPA and the personnel fighting this war. Captain Eden Melody – an officer whom Recker had never met - had proven resourceful in the engagement at Pinvos and had offered the ultimate sacrifice to ensure a mission outcome that, while not exactly successful, was more in favour of the HPA than the Daklan.

In contrast, Admiral Fraser had offered no gratitude – at least as far as Recker was aware – for the rescue which had delayed the start of the return journey by thirty-six hours. Not only that, but Fraser had quickly started pointing the finger of blame in every direction – from the personnel who'd drawn up the mission briefing to the people who had died. Nobody was spared in the man's efforts to justify his craven act of cowardice in abandoning the *Trojan*.

And that justification was so weak as to be laughable,

were there any humour whatsoever to be found in events at Pinvos. Every time Recker played the words through in his mind, he felt his piss boiling and his hands clenched unconsciously into fists.

I decided the mission was best served by putting myself into a risk-laden position from which I could observe matters and report them in the event our assets and resources were neutralised.

Warships, people, death, reduced to spreadsheet terms, like it was a game of numbers to be played late evening over a glass of Cognac. The disconnect between the man and reality was beyond Recker's comprehension.

After coming out with that one, Fraser had then gone on the offensive, creating as much of a smoke screen as possible to hide his own failings and magnify those of others. The man even had the insolence to suggest that the comparative lack of damage suffered by the *Expectation* was a direct result of Recker's reluctance to engage with the desolators and thereby ensure the destruction of the *Trojan*.

The mental pursuit of justice gave Recker no satisfaction and, with an effort, he made himself concentrate only on the day-to-day activities required to keep the destroyer running smoothly. Whatever would happen once the mission reports were in would happen, though shit had a strange way of sliding off Fleet Admiral Solan's cohort of friends and sympathisers.

At last, the *Expectation* broke out of lightspeed, five million kilometres from Lustre. When creating the synch code, Lieutenant Eastwood had detached the overstress box in order that the lightspeed calculations could be performed normally. Even so, it was a relief when the destroyer arrived on target, though none of the crew mentioned it.

"The *Shock and Awe* just entered local space, a hundred thousand klicks away."

"Home, safe and sound," said Aston with unusual rancour.

"Let's hope the repercussions are aimed at the right people," added Eastwood.

Recker felt his blood pressure rising, so he didn't encourage the conversation. Instead he fed power into the engines and set the warship on a trajectory leading to the Adamantine base, which was currently on the visible side of the planet. With the sensors on maximum zoom, planet Lustre lived up to its name, with the orange-tinged light from its sun making the blue oceans glisten with a beautiful, shimmering pattern reminiscent of scales from a mythical dragon.

The wonder of it wasn't lost on Recker, but he took no comfort from the sight – not now. This return to base may herald the HPA's entry into a new period of fear and uncertainty and he was the one bearing the news.

Lasting a little more than an hour, the approach should have been easy to cope with. To Recker's chagrin, it dragged interminably for thirty minutes, at which point Admiral Telar requested a comms channel. The discussion which followed was brief and only touched on some of the mission details, with Telar being uninterested in much of it. Recker wasn't fooled – the admiral had his reasons for asking the questions he did, though it left him with no reassurance as to which way the wind was blowing.

Recker had put his faith in high command before. It had bitten him on the ass and then come back for the other buttock. That faith wasn't yet nearly restored.

"We've received a request from the Adamantine flight control mainframe, sir," said Burner. "It wants to bring us in."

"Fine," said Recker, reaching out and selecting an option on his console to accept the request. "I've handed over the controls."

After that, it was a case of sitting back and letting it happen. The flight controller was programmed with multiple layers of caution, so the eagerness with which the velocity gauge climbed came as something of a surprise.

"It's in a hurry," said Eastwood. "I wonder if Admiral Telar had the protocols updated."

"That would make sense," said Recker. "The mainframe has plenty of processing grunt to make sure nothing hits anything else."

The *Expectation* plunged through a thin layer of high clouds and the base appeared far below. Still the flight controller hardly slowed and the construction trenches became visible as diagonal gouges across one side of the base, like a clawed hand had ripped through the concrete.

"Looks like you were right about the planetary dredger making trenches, sir," said Eastwood. "Two new ones, both seven klicks long and wider than the others. What the hell are they going to build in those?"

Recker wasn't aware of plans to build spaceships larger than the current battleship design, but he didn't get to hear everything about what was happening in the military. "Maybe they're going to build two cruisers in each trench," he said. "Or half a dozen riots."

Burner switched between sensor feeds and settled on one he liked. The chosen array was locked on one of the newer trenches, which was a place of intense activity. Shuttles flew in great numbers, most of them carrying huge slabs of alloy. Around the sides, gravity cranes – one of which was about the size of a riot class – manoeuvred the slabs into position, while an army of other machinery sealed the joins and smoothed the surfaces. In addition, a swarm of much smaller vehicles sped here and there, bringing personnel in and out of the construction site.

"Twenty-two days is a long time, huh?" said Aston. "Another five days and they'll be finished with that trench and ready to lay down the first hull."

It was a similar story with the second new trench – endless resources being poured into the war effort. In a way, Recker felt proud to witness what the HPA could achieve when it needed to. That pride was tempered by his fear that this was all coming far too late.

"They've already started bringing in the engine modules for whatever they're about to build," said Recker, gazing at the stack of eight huge grey blocks near the end trench.

"And there's a new battleship in trench one," said Burner. "A second in trench two."

The two warships weren't near completion – the underside plates of both were in position, along with some of the smaller propulsion blocks. At one time, Recker would have vaguely guessed that twelve months would be needed to bring these warships into service. With endless funding and extra personnel, he was sure Admiral Telar would not tolerate a construction plan that lasted a full year.

As the descent continued, Recker's eye was drawn to the landing strip. It appeared no different to how he remembered it – a couple of riots and a cruiser were on the ground in the middle of a re-arm and a check-over by the maintenance teams. Once the fleet numbers were bolstered by the dozens of new-planned warships, he was sure the landing strip would be far more crowded than this.

And then something else caught his eye, on the western fringe of the landing strip.

"They took down that wall around the *Vengeance*," he said.

The alien spaceship was parked up, far from the closest HPA warship. The sensor feed was clear enough that Recker could see a couple of tanks, some troop transports and a few maintenance vehicles in the vicinity, but other than that, it seemed as though the warship had been forgotten.

"Maybe Admiral Telar has given up on it," said Aston.

"Maybe," said Recker, unsure exactly what he thought. Sometimes he had to remind himself that the *Vengeance* was only one ship and at some point, the HPA might have to accept it held no worthwhile secrets.

A minute later, the flight controller set the *Expectation* down next to one of the other riots. Immediately, the maintenance crews moved in.

"We're going to require trench work," said Eastwood.

"They can't patch up that Terrus damage from the ground and they certainly can't let this ship fly until they've run a thorough audit to find out exactly what happened during the core override."

"They'll find nothing," said Recker. "The technicians found no lasting effects on the *Vengeance* and I'm sure they'll find the same thing with the *Expectation*."

He stood and rolled his shoulders to alleviate the aches which had crept up on him. His muscles still felt tight and he knew it was a result of far more than sleeping on a thin foam mattress for so long.

"Let's get out of here," he said.

Recker led his crew towards the forward boarding ramp. Muggy air greeted them as they climbed towards the gathering mix of personnel on the ground below. Halfway down, the communicator in Recker's pocket buzzed and he withdrew it. He hadn't charged the device since the beginning of the trip and the battery was at one percent. It lasted long enough for him to read the message.

"I've been *invited* to a meeting with Admiral Telar," he said.

"No surprise there," said Aston. "At least he isn't keeping you waiting."

It wasn't such a small mercy and Recker was glad that his debriefing would begin at once.

"What about us, sir?" asked Burner, vigorously scratching at his unruly hair.

"No specific orders. Until I hear otherwise, you're still on my crew, so don't get lost."

"I need a bath," said Burner.

"You sure do," said Aston, crinkling her nose like she'd

just noticed a terrible stench coming from somewhere close by.

Recker didn't hang around to listen to the outcome of the conversation and forged through the incoming soldiers and maintenance teams. Someone had parked a common-or-garden gravity car adjacent to one of the personnel cabins which dotted the landing strip. Recker commandeered the vehicle without guilt and ordered it to transport him to building Outer Admin 7. The car chattered away, offering up snippets from the military's extensive collection of rules and regulations. Smiling inwardly, Recker guessed that some bright spark had decided that the thousands of newly conscripted former civilians on Adamantine might well benefit from these little reminders.

At last, following an uneventful journey through a base on obvious high alert, Recker was deposited at his destination. A short time later, he arrived at the door to Admiral Telar's subterranean office, having noticed that the confusion apparent during his last visit was now replaced by an air of organized calm. The soldiers, however, remained, though it seemed like Recker's arrival had been telegraphed and he was only stopped once.

In the intervening time, the security systems had been updated and the outer door to Telar's office opened automatically, a feat copied by the inner door.

"Carl," Telar greeted him. The atmosphere was distinctly frosty and it was nothing to do with the air conditioning.

Recker strode into the office and stopped in front of the other man's desk, studiously ignoring the two chairs.

"Sir," he said.

Telar's usually ordered desk was covered in paperwork, most of it contained in folders with the contents half-spilled until none of the rich wood of the desk was visible beneath the chaotic piles of reports. If Recker was any judge, the uncontrolled mess would likely be grinding Telar's gears.

"Sit," said Telar using one hand to indicate the left-hand chair.

Recker saw it now – Telar was furious. "I've been sitting for most of the last twenty days, sir. Have you spoken to Admiral Fraser?"

Telar's eyes glittered, but he didn't answer the question directly. "You gathered data from an artifact known as the Interrogator."

"I did, sir. I had my comms man send the files to the Adamantine base on the way in."

"I've seen those files, Captain. Numbers. Lots of numbers."

"We'll need to set a cruncher on them. Find out if they can be tallied with our own star charts."

"You believe these files are relevant?"

The question caught Recker off-guard. "The Interrogator didn't want to know who we were, but it certainly wanted to know where we came from."

Telar tried to pin him with his gaze, but Recker didn't waver. After a long moment, Telar sighed and some of the tension fell from his shoulders.

"I've spoken to Admiral Fraser. He was very keen to tell me all about the mission to Pinvos and the performance of the officers I chose to accompany him. I am sure mine aren't the only ears to have heard his verbal report."

"Admiral Fraser spent most of his time in a shuttle, sir, denying him the opportunity to witness the bravery of his officers. Captain Melody in particular was…"

"Enough, Carl. There is no need for you to defend the actions of Captain Melody – her sacrifice is apparent and I will not permit the truth of what happened to be corrupted by the lies of an officer who has failed in his duty at every level."

That was when Recker understood – Telar was raging, but it wasn't at him, or at the outcome of the mission. The target of the anger was Admiral Fraser and for Telar to outright accuse another senior officer of lying made Recker think that high command was teetering on the brink of a major upheaval. Which way that would end, he didn't want to guess.

Telar picked a folder from his desk and lifted it so the words were visible. *Recker, Carl. Final Report: Pinvos.*

"I see you composed a comprehensive report during your ten-day return flight. I have skimmed the contents and will give it my full attention once this meeting is over."

"Do you wish to discuss it now, sir?"

Telar raised an eyebrow. "Is there something missing which I should know about?"

"No, sir. The report is a thorough and honest account of the mission."

"I'm sure it is." Telar leaned back and his chair creaked. "The *Vengeance*," he said, leaving the words hanging.

"I saw it on the way in, sir. You had the barriers removed."

"Our investigation of the warship has come to an end, Captain."

Recker hid his disappointment. "Did you find anything while I was at Pinvos?"

A hint of a smile played on the corner of Telar's mouth. "As it happens, we now have more questions than we did when you first landed the warship here on Adamantine."

"You're hiding something, sir."

"I'd say I'm drawing out the disclosure." This time a trace of humour was evident in Telar's eyes. "We *did* find something." For a second time, he gestured towards the two chairs. "Sit."

Recker sat.

CHAPTER SEVENTEEN

TELAR GOT ON WITH IT.

"You're aware the *Vengeance* has tied itself to your biometrics, Carl."

"Yes, sir."

"And you're also aware that you were unable to access the weapons systems, indicating that the warship's systems are subject to tiered security."

"It's not just the weapons, sir. On our way back from Oldis, Lieutenant Eastwood became certain the propulsion was underperforming."

"We have tried everything to uncover the secrets of this alien warship."

"Did you succeed?"

"No."

Recker's expression showed his confusion. "You told me the technicians found something."

"They did. Not weapons, not something new and destructive that we can copy and use against the Daklan."

This time Recker's disappointment was far greater and he wondered why Telar was stringing him along. "Then what?"

"A comms ping."

The disappointment faded and was replaced by the beginnings of excitement. The only reason he was hearing this was because Telar had plans.

"What data did the ping contain?"

"An identification code – the warship equivalent of name and rank."

"Did you find where the ping is aimed?"

"We'll get to that."

Telar let the silence hang for a moment. Then, he leaned sideways to pick something from the floor. When Telar straightened, he was holding a cup of coffee, rather than a folder containing a mission briefing.

"No room on my desk for the simple pleasures," he said, taking a measured sip. Then, he leaned again and set down the cup with the utmost care. "You look like you wish to strangle something, Captain."

"Not something, sir. *Someone.*"

Telar proceeded like he hadn't heard. "There's something inside the *Vengeance*, Carl. Alien technology that we cannot access."

"I thought you found nothing except the ping, sir."

"Call this a hunch. I know that an admiral isn't meant to be influenced by anything other than cold, hard logic, but there it is. I have a *hunch* that the *Vengeance* contains technology we might benefit from."

"Then why not dismantle it in the shipyard, sir? Pull it to pieces and find out what's inside."

"Have you heard about the golden goose, Carl?"

"Of course I have, sir, but we're talking about a space-ship here."

"What would happen if the Daklan salvaged one of our warships and took it apart?"

Recker understood at once and immediately felt fool-ish. "If they didn't know exactly what they were doing, they'd sever the security tie-ins between the different modules and once that happened, they'd never get any of it working again."

"And that's why I haven't taken the *Vengeance* to pieces, Carl. If we did so and there was technology to be found, I'm certain we'd disable it, however carefully we approach the task."

"So this ping, sir?"

"It was aimed at a solar system a long way from here. Because of the distances involved, Deep Space Quad 1 has been unable to narrow the destination to a single planet. At least not in the time I was able to utilise its resources without drawing undue attention."

There it was – another suggestion of division in high command. Recker didn't press for details.

"You want me to investigate," he said.

"That's right, Captain. I can't allow a hunch to draw valuable resources from the war effort, so this mission will involve only the *Vengeance*. Since the warship is seemingly useless to us, I can justify treating it with reckless abandon."

"I found some data relating to the *Vengeance* on the Interrogator's core override menu, sir," said Recker. "I have a feeling the warship is well-known to its enemies."

"It may be that you extracted something useful about the *Vengeance*, but I won't allow that to alter the plans I have drawn up."

"What do you hope to achieve, sir?"

"I believe – it is an idea I cannot get out of my head - that this ping is aimed at the spaceship's home base, or a similar facility. It may be that if the *Vengeance* returns to this facility, any additional hardware will be automatically unlocked."

"That's how it happens with our warships," nodded Recker. "If one of our security systems detects or suspects interference, it will disable much of the hardware functionality until the vessel returns to base."

"There are parallels," Telar agreed. "And I'm hoping that is how this unknown alien species configured the warships in its fleet."

"I am keen to begin, sir," said Recker, understating the reality.

"You had sufficient rest during your long return journey from Pinvos?"

"Yes, sir."

Telar laid his hands palm down on the desk. "This mission accomplishes two of my goals, and I would like it to commence at once."

The first goal was already discussed and it didn't take a great leap of Recker's imagination for him to guess at the second. "You want me out of the way."

"Well spotted, Carl. Yes, it would be convenient if you were elsewhere until the fallout from Pinvos settles."

"Will I be returning to a court martial, sir?"

"I don't know. I will do everything I can to prevent injustice."

"Perhaps this is a battle I should fight at home, sir. Not just for me, but for the other officers at Pinvos. Those who died do not have a voice and if I returned to news that the truth had been altered in order that a coward might be treated as a hero, I don't know what action I would feel obliged to take, sir."

"I will be their voice, Captain. Until this is resolved, your presence will do nothing more than inflame the situation. As it stands, Admiral Fraser's friends are reluctant to become involved - they are well-aware that his star is falling. However, I am not certain they would stand idle while you speak your own version of events."

"I can keep my mouth shut, sir."

"No you can't, Carl. If there's a truth, you will speak it, however uncomfortable it might be for the listeners to hear. I need you elsewhere – out of sight and out of mind."

"I don't like it, sir."

"You want the mission."

"I do."

"Then accept what I've told you. The *Vengeance* is ready to fly, and I want you gone from Adamantine today."

Recker understood that Telar had done him a great favour. "I'll recall my crew and soldiers. I'm sure they'll appreciate the news."

"I've arranged to have something taken onboard, to show the military's appreciation for recent performances at Pinvos."

"I'm sure everyone will be happy when they find out

what it is, sir," said Recker. The meeting was drawing to a close and he prepared to be dismissed.

"Go," said Telar. "Find a way to unlock the potential of the *Vengeance*. Failing that, bring back something we can use against the Daklan."

"I'll do what I can."

With that, Admiral Telar turned his attention to the paperwork on his desk. Recker took the hint and exited the office without another word.

Outside in the corridor, his pocket communicator had already been recharged to full by some magic of wireless technology which kept every battery-powered object on the base topped up. He made several calls while striding through the groups of personnel who now occupied this area of the base. Recker's expression sent people scattering out his way and when he snapped the communicator shut, he wasn't far from the Outer Admin 7 exit.

The gravity car which had brought him here hadn't yet been claimed and Recker climbed inside. He gave it an order and it pulled out into traffic. Evening approached, but the base never slept – not anymore – and a column of tanks slowed the car's progress.

All the while, the vehicle's computer talked. It no longer regaled Recker with details of randomly selected rules and regulations. This time, it wanted to be his analyst and asked him numerous questions about his feelings and emotions. Recker's answers left the computer in absolutely no doubt about his state of mind and his opinion of its efforts to take him back to his childhood in order to discover the root of his adult fears.

When the car stopped, Recker climbed out into the

warm air. The sky was darkening to the west, but the artificial lights of the base segued in to ensure personnel could work comfortably. To Recker's eyes, those lights illuminated the *Vengeance* in a way which made him think of an object in a museum, rather than a fighting ship.

He cast his gaze along the hull, with its projectile scarring and speckling of high-speed particle impacts. The *Vengeance* wasn't by any stretch the largest spaceship in the HPA fleet, but it had an air of calm certainty – like it had no fear of anything. Recker shook away the thought, aware that he was still applying human emotions to the tools he was given. He guessed he'd never stop doing so.

Two Puncher medium tanks – broad-shouldered and angular vehicles with enormous-calibre gauss guns protruding from their turrets – hovered one to each side of the *Vengeance*'s forward boarding ramp, their propulsions drowned out by the oppressive bass which beat down from the warship looming overhead.

A soldier approached, bringing two others from the squad of fifteen nearest the ramp.

"Sergeant Tracker," Recker said. "Seems like you're on permanent assignment to guard my warships."

The man gave a salute. "Captain Recker. The *Vengeance* is clear of personnel and the technicians' report is all green lights."

"Thank you. Have you heard from my crew or Sergeant Vance?"

"On their way, sir. You got here first."

Recker approached the boarding ramp and Sergeant Tracker fell in step, though he didn't say anything until he was a few paces from his squad.

"Good luck, sir."

Tracker gave another salute and returned to his soldiers, while Recker climbed the steps on the boarding ramp. It seemed like an age since he'd been on the *Vengeance* and he braced himself for the attack on his senses.

Inside the compact airlock, he paused in the cold blue light and breathed in the scent of metal – it was an odour similar to that on every other HPA fleet warship, yet magnified here on the *Vengeance*, like the warship had been constructed from materials a billion years older.

Once through the inner door, Recker followed the corridors leading to the bridge. The closeness of the walls, the bass pressure from the engines and the feeling of enormous weight pushing in from every side made him feel like he was deep underground or inside an ancient submarine. He reached out and tapped his knuckles against the side wall – an act which was in danger of becoming superstition – and the action produced no sound at all.

Feels like I'm home.

The bridge hadn't changed much – it was the same confined space with its five stations and blue lights. The maintenance team had bolted a storage locker to the rear bulkhead and fitted a small food replicator nearby. A couple of diagnostic tablets left on the edge of the command console suggested that the technicians had moved out in a hurry.

Next to the tablets, a stoppered glass bottle of golden liquid invited further investigation. Recker picked it up and, though he didn't recognize the vintage, he was sure Admiral Telar wouldn't have bothered sending a bottle he'd picked up from an off-base convenience store with the original intention of serving it to his mother-in-law.

Recker put the bottle aside and picked up the tablets. In a shocking breach of security protocols, the last technician to use one of the two had left himself logged in, though the device was ten seconds from automatically shutting down. Recker didn't generally pry but his eyes automatically read some of the text and he pursed his lips.

The tablet logged itself out and Recker opened the locker, where he found gauss rifles, ammo, a medical box and four replacement spacesuits. He placed the tablets inside and closed the door.

He took his seat at the central console and began pre-flight checks. The technicians had left everything powered up and the *Vengeance* was ready to fly immediately. Since his crew hadn't arrived, Recker used the time to dig deeper into the alien control software, finding its use came naturally to him. Five minutes was all it took for him to be sure the HPA technicians hadn't installed or removed anything he wasn't expecting.

Once he'd finished checking the hardware status, Recker's attention was drawn to a mission briefing file which arrived via the comms system. The document was notable only for its brevity and he scanned the contents quickly.

Behind him, the bridge door opened with a quiet rumble.

"Sir."

Recker turned. "Commander Aston."

The next person through the doorway was Lieutenant

Burner. "I promised myself a real burger when the Pinvos mission was over. I didn't get the chance."

"Life sucks," said Lieutenant Eastwood, coming last. "And then you die in the fiery agony of a corrosive plasma explosion."

"Seats, please," said Recker.

"Let me guess – we're in a hurry," said Aston.

"Admiral Telar is always in a hurry, Commander. I thought you'd have learned that by now."

Aston took her seat and stared at the console. "I take it you're keeping the mission details to yourself, sir?"

"Not this time. We're taking the *Vengeance* to an alien facility in the hope of activating its weapons and any other tech it might be carrying. Weapons and tech that might not, in fact, exist beyond the missiles and countermeasures we already know about."

"We're going alone?"

"Yes. Save the questions for later, folks."

"Sergeant Vance just came onboard, sir," said Burner. "We've got twenty minutes left on our departure window."

"Speak to Sergeant Tracker. Tell him to move away."

"Done."

Two minutes later, the ground outside was clear and Recker declared he was ready to depart. With a deep breath and adrenaline gnawing at his belly, he took hold of the controls.

CHAPTER EIGHTEEN

THE *VENGEANCE* HAD NOT FLOWN since the time
Recker and his crew had brought it back from Tanril, with
military politics ensuring the warship remained firmly on
the ground until this moment.

"Here we go," said Recker.

He drew the controls towards him, compensating for
the extra resistance as they slid along their guide slots. The
propulsion note increased in volume and, though it
sounded almost indistinguishable from an HPA ternium
drive, Recker detected underlying nuances that made it
seem like an entirely different animal.

As he fed in more power, the differences increased
and it was this which made him certain the *Vengeance* had
plenty to give, but that he was unable to access the
warship's reserves because it was running in some kind of
safe mode after its recovery from the core override which
caused it to crash into Tanril.

Without drama, the spaceship rose from the ground

and its landing legs groaned as the immense strain was relieved. Recker's eyes darted across the instrumentation, hunting for signs of failure. He found none and so he gave his attention to the sensor feeds, where his eyes lingered on the part-built hulls in the construction trenches.

Limitations on his permitted velocity ensured that many seconds passed before the whole of Adamantine became visible on a single array and the rapidly approaching night made the facility appear like a gaudily lit patch on an area of gathering dusk.

"Approaching the upper atmosphere," said Burner. "Twenty seconds until the first limit on acceleration expires."

The *Vengeance* passed the distance threshold and Recker fed in more power and then again once the final acceleration distance limit was behind them. The alien warship hit 1450 kilometres per second and went no higher, though the propulsion took on a strange lumpiness as if it were cutting out and then resuming.

"Nothing's changed," he said. "It still feels like something's holding it back."

"Maybe we'll find out what," said Aston.

The moment he was outside the lightspeed exclusion zone around Lustre, Recker brought the *Vengeance* to a halt.

"Lieutenant Eastwood, you've got access to the destination coordinates. Plug them in and let's go."

"Coordinates entered. Fifteen days? Damn."

"We're going somewhere unknown to the HPA, Lieutenant. That means a long journey."

Eastwood didn't mention it again, while Aston and

Burner read the mood well enough to keep their own mouths shut.

"Eight minutes for ternium drive warmup, sir," said Eastwood.

"Quicker than anything in the HPA fleet," said Burner. "The *Vengeance* is fitted with a fast core."

"Or more efficient algorithms," Eastwood reminded him.

The *Vengeance's* lightspeed drive grumbled and everything shook. When Recker touched his console, he could feel the vibration in his fingertips and again he was left with the impression that the warmup was being deliberately constrained.

At exactly eight minutes, the ternium drive activated and the *Vengeance* accelerated to a lightspeed multiple similar to that attainable by a fleet battleship. The transition was rougher than he remembered from Tanril and he guessed that last time he must have had too much on his plate to worry about minor issues like moderate physical pain.

Nobody said much during the following ten minutes as they maintained a vigil over their consoles in case anything went south. Nothing did.

"Fifteen days," said Aston. "Time for you to spill the beans, sir," she continued with a disarming smile.

"For once, there are no beans to spill, Commander. Admiral Telar wants me out of the way while he handles the post-mission repercussions from our recent journey to Pinvos. Other than that, I already gave you the outline. The *Vengeance* sent out a ping to a distant world and our technicians intercepted it. We're going to find whatever it is that we find."

"That's it?" said Burner.

"I thought you'd appreciate the straightforward nature of the briefing, Lieutenant."

"What more were you expecting?" said Aston curiously.

"I don't know – maybe it's just that the crumbling supports propping up my illusions that military planners are somehow much cleverer than me just got knocked out with a fifteen-pound sledgehammer."

Recker laughed. "Is that your play for a transfer to ground duties, Lieutenant?"

"Hell no, sir. Hand me a food replicator and a headset and I'll give you the universe."

"I'm glad your enthusiasm remains undiminished," said Recker. "And I hope that remains true at the end of a fifteen day lightspeed voyage."

"Where did this ping come from, sir?" asked Burner, his expression becoming serious. "And did we learn anything else from it?"

"The transmission source is somewhere deep in the hull and that's about the extent of our knowledge," said Recker, repeating what he'd read in the mission briefing document.

"Is the *Vengeance* still sending pings?" Burner persisted.

"I don't know. Admiral Telar only mentioned one ping. It didn't contain positional data for the *Vengeance*, if that's what you're asking."

"That's what I was wondering," Burner confirmed.

"It's usually impossible to reverse-trace an inbound comms – assuming it doesn't contain the relevant source data – but we don't know what kind of tech the receiver might contain."

"Or even if the receiver still exists," said Aston.

"That's a good point, Commander."

"We're dealing with plenty of unknowns, Lieutenant," said Recker. "I intend to find some answers."

Burner gave a nod of acceptance and turned back to his console.

"Is there anything we need to know about the *Vengeance*?" asked Eastwood. "Maybe something the technicians discovered or changed while we were at Pinvos?"

After landing the warship at Adamantine, Recker's crew had been denied access to the ongoing research into the alien vessel's capabilities, though not Recker himself. Since they had a stake in this, he made sure they heard most of what was going on, even if that amounted effectively to nothing.

"As far as I'm aware, we know little beyond what we found on the return trip from Tanril, Lieutenant. The *Vengeance* is a little faster than we'd expect given the ratio between mass and its assumed ternium drive output. At 2.7 billion tons, it's also approximately thirty percent heavier than its overall volume would suggest."

"Hold up, sir. That's a new one on me," said Eastwood.

"And on me – I only found out because one of the technicians left themselves signed into a tablet and forgot to bring it with them when they exited the ship."

"Ternium is already enormously dense and the alloys

we use to construct our plating likewise," said Eastwood, his interest clearly piqued. "Did the technicians have any theories?"

"I didn't get a chance to find out – the tablet shut itself down."

"Damn."

"It'll give you something to think about, Lieutenant."

"You're about to remind me that I've got fifteen days to come up with some ideas."

"I'd prefer to find out by unlocking the *Vengeance*'s security systems," said Recker.

"I think that's the captain's blessing for you to spend two weeks scratching your ass, Ken," said Burner.

Eastwood snorted. "Chance would be a fine thing - I've got my hands full looking after you and picking up your empty coffee cups."

Recker smiled to himself and let them talk. Like Burner had said on his entrance to the bridge – it didn't seem as if their feet had a chance to touch the ground. Not that Recker had any complaints, and, though he missed his family, he recognized that wars were won by the side giving maximum commitment. His parents understood, though a whispering voice reminded him that maybe he should have spoken to them by FTL comm back on Lustre, just so they knew their boy was safe. Recker felt himself unexpectedly choking up and he took a deep breath.

"Commander Aston," he said, rising. "You've got the controls – I'm going to speak with Sergeant Vance. He and his men deserve the courtesy."

Aston didn't miss much and she looked at him closely.

"Yes, sir," was all she said.

"Sir, before you go?" said Burner.

"Lieutenant?"

"Someone left a bottle next to your console."

"A gift from Admiral Telar. For Pinvos. Whisky. We'll try it later."

Recker left the bridge and went to find Vance and whoever else was with him in the mess area. The *Vengeance* may have been constructed by an alien species, but it had much in common with an HPA warship. Not that any of the few internal rooms had been fitted with beds when Recker and the others found the warship on Tanril, but the Adamantine ground crews had installed enough bunks for the soldiers, as well as tables, benches and a second replicator in the designated mess room.

The mess area was a little larger than the equivalent on a fleet destroyer and almost every bench was occupied. Each soldier was dressed in a combat suit and though nobody wore a helmet, they were close at hand.

"Sergeant Vance," said Recker, stopping at one of the tables.

"Sir," said Vance, turning from his conversation with Corporal Hendrix and Private Montero.

"I hoped you and your squad would have an opportunity to put your feet up on Lustre."

"We had a couple of hours, sir," said Hendrix with a dazzling smile. "Me? I call that a win."

Recker glanced over his shoulder. "At least they provided a new-model replicator. And Admiral Telar informs me he sent you all a token of his appreciation."

"That he did, sir. Eighteen whole crates of appreciation."

"We've got a fifteen-day trip ahead of us – make sure it's gone before we arrive."

"Yes, sir." Vance indicated an empty space next to Corporal Hendrix. "Please."

Recker sat and told Vance what was happening. As he spoke, the other soldiers drifted closer so they could hear the words first-hand. The telling didn't take long and at the end, Recker got the reaction he expected – a mixture of resigned acceptance and a few wisecracks.

"Well, Sergeant?" he asked once the soldiers lost interest and wandered off. "Feel like you've been dealt a good hand or a bad one?"

Vance pondered his response. "I've spent what seems like my whole life fighting on the ground. It's something I'm good at and I know how it works. Warships? I never understood them, except as big lumps of metal filled with missiles and other crap meant to turn me and my squad into atoms. The ship captains I've served with – at least the ones who spoke to me - said you get this *feel* for the hardware." He paused, still thinking. "I never did."

"And now?" asked Recker, interested at this glimpse into Vance's mind.

"The *Vengeance* is special, sir. You might think that sounds stupid coming from a man who says he knows nothing about spaceships, but maybe it means that this ship is so different that even someone like me can tell it."

"What do you think Corporal Hendrix?" asked Recker.

She stared at him long and hard. "Like Sergeant Vance

said - the *Vengeance* is special, sir. This war is going badly and I wouldn't trust anyone other than the Sergeant and these other lowlife scumbags," she gestured at the other soldiers in the room, "to do the dirty work." Hendrix smiled again and Recker was struck by what a difference it made.

Recker smiled in return. "Then let's find out exactly what makes it so special and bring it home in one piece."

He rose and left them to it. A brief circuit of the *Vengeance* reminded him of what he already knew – that the spaceship's internal space was even more restrictive than it was on an HPA warship. It lacked an underside bay and the hardware modules were completely inaccessible without specialised tools and facilities. Recker didn't mind – it only reinforced his impression that the *Vengeance* was designed and constructed for the sole purpose of winning wars.

With his inspection complete, Recker returned to the bridge and prepared himself for fifteen days of speculation and anticipation.

CHAPTER NINETEEN

"TEN MINUTES TO RE-ENTRY!" said Eastwood, the words heralding the end of what had been a tedious journey for everyone.

"Acknowledged," said Recker, feeling his skin tighten with an adrenaline surge.

"All systems green," said Eastwood.

Recker didn't need to ask if his crew was ready – they'd been desperate for the coming moments since the *Vengeance* first lifted off the Adamantine airfield. He ran briefly through the mission outline, to reinforce the details.

"We're arriving at the Filos-R system," he said. "The star is comparatively large, but of no real interest to our mission. We're expecting to find fifteen or more planets and DS-Quad1's arrays discovered the *Vengeance*'s outward ping was aimed at a place between one and three hundred million klicks from the surface of Filos-R. We don't know what we're looking for – the receptor could be a planet or it could be another satellite like the Interrogator."

"Once we arrive, Lieutenant Burner and I will work on the sensors to locate the target," said Aston. "Let's hope we find something early, so we don't have to go off exploring."

Recker leaned back in his chair. For the last fifteen days he'd tried not to overthink the coming mission, aware that guessing would lead nowhere. With re-entry to local space imminent, he allowed himself to wonder what might be in store for the spaceship and its crew. The previous few weeks had demonstrated how limited was humanity's understanding of the universe. Different species existed – friend or foe, nobody knew - and the *Vengeance* was heading straight for a facility created by one of these alien races. One way or another, Recker was determined to find out more about them.

"Two minutes!"

"Everyone at your stations."

With the journey being so long, Recker would not usually have been surprised if the lightspeed calculations were many seconds out. He watched the countdown timer and, the moment it hit zero, the *Vengeance*'s hull grated and shook. The sensors remained offline for less than a second and then they displayed their feeds of dark space.

Unsure if the arrival point was safe or not, Recker threw the controls forward and gritted his teeth at the nausea from re-entry and the lurch of acceleration which the life support module didn't fully suppress.

"Local scan underway," said Burner. "We arrived pretty much dead on target."

"Two hundred million klicks from Filos-R," said Eastwood. "No hardware errors to report."

"I'm trying to pinpoint the nearest planets," said Aston.

"Local scan clear," said Burner. "Expanding the search sphere."

The following two minutes were tense and Recker flew erratically until he was certain the *Vengeance* wasn't in immediate danger. When the tactical remained empty and Burner located nothing in the vicinity, Recker slowed the warship and flew it in a wide circle to give his officers time to complete their initial scans.

"I've located two planets, sir," said Aston. "DS-Quad1 already identified them and named them Uboran and Vitran. The monitoring station's long-range sensor data suggests these may be planets three and four, but with a strong likelihood of error."

"Uboran is 210 million klicks out from the star and Vitran 290 million," added Burner. "We're closest to Uboran at 30 million klicks and it's drifting away from us at twelve klicks per second."

Burner had put the Filos-R sun onto one of the bulkhead screens and Recker stared at the shimmering sphere of red. The *Vengeance*'s sensor capabilities were approximately equivalent to those on an HPA battleship – something it accomplished with far fewer sensor arrays – but at this distance, the star's surface variations were hard to distinguish.

"There could be a half dozen other planets blind side that fall within the expected range of Filos-R," said

Recker. "Admiral Telar only had limited time with DS-Quad1."

"I notice that the guys who detected the outward ping attempted to tally its lightspeed velocity with the orbital period of Uboran and Vitran," said Burner. "That was a good idea, but they weren't able to produce a definitive conclusion."

"Have you located any other planets?" asked Recker.

"Kilatas and Zarkus," said Burner. "Those are way outside our search distance. One's a gas giant and the other is covered in ice."

"Ignore them for the moment," said Recker. "We'll check out the closer planets. Bring Uboran up on the screen."

"Here it is," said Burner. "Diameter: eleven thousand klicks. Not much else to say about it."

"Rocks and shit," said Eastwood.

"What about Vitran?" asked Recker.

"It's 120 million klicks from us," said Burner. "Let's see how much enhancement I can wring out of these arrays." He swore under his breath. "Hell, I was not expecting that."

The planet's image came up on the screen, a fist-sized circle of grey mingled with dark green.

"Are those what I think they are?" said Recker.

"If you thought you were looking at clouds and forests, then yes," said Burner.

"Life," said Aston.

Recker and his crew knew the significance. For all its centuries of space exploration, the HPA had only ever discovered a handful of habitable worlds and the best estimates suggested the Daklan had populated a similar number. And here, out in Filos-R, was another.

"That's got to be the place," said Aston.

"Maybe," said Recker. "Anything else we can learn without having to make a lightspeed jump to get closer?"

"Not much, sir. I could probably guess at the atmospheric composition, but with all those trees, the answer isn't going to come as much of a surprise. And we've got zero chance of locating an alien installation if there's one down there."

"YOU'VE GOT ten minutes to check out Uboran," said Recker. "After that, we're heading for Vitran."

He dropped back into his seat and scratched at the stubble covering his chin. While space technology meant that installations could be established in the most hostile places, the presence of a life-bearing planet was too much like coincidence and Recker dearly wanted to know if Vitran was home to only trees, or whether a potentially hostile alien species also lived there. Perhaps with a fleet of advanced warships.

"Nothing of note on the visible side of Uboran," said Burner when his ten minutes were up. "I've identified a couple of areas where I'd prefer a close-range sweep and then there's the entire blind side to check out."

"I'm willing to discount Uboran for the moment," said Recker.

"Leaving us with Vitran," said Aston.

"A life bearing planet with plenty of unknowns," mused Recker. "Especially since the evidence suggests another alien species got here first."

"We can't risk a lightspeed approach, sir," said Eastwood. "It's much harder to sneak up on a populated world than a planet with a single installation guarded by a warship or two."

"The journey on sub-light engines is approximately twenty-three hours," said Burner.

"We've come this far, I don't see why we should rush the final and most important part of the mission," said Aston.

"I agree," said Recker. He fed power into the warship's engines and aimed it towards Vitran. "Let's get going while we think about the possibilities."

"If the species who built the *Vengeance* live on Vitran, they might send out a welcoming committee," said Eastwood. "And politely request the return of their spaceship."

"They might," said Recker. The enormity of the situation was sinking in – the crew of the *Vengeance* could well be on the brink of making contact with a hitherto undiscovered alien species, with all the uncertainty that entailed. "Does anyone remember much about their alien contact training?" he asked.

"I keep a copy under my pillow, sir," said Burner.

"I thought you had other kinds of reading material under there," said Eastwood. "The kind that has more pictures than writing."

"Enough," warned Recker.

"Sorry, sir," said Eastwood. "I can't recall any of that

contact training, since it was about twenty years ago and lasted an hour."

"The HPA didn't expect this to happen," said Burner. "We're so tied up fighting the Daklan that nobody really thinks too hard about other species. Not anymore."

"We can have a post-mortem later, folks," said Recker. "I'm going to keep us headed for Vitran until we're close enough that the sensors might pick up something useful."

Thirty minutes passed, during which Aston and Burner gathered information about the planet ahead. At this early stage, there wasn't much the sensors could provide.

"Definitely trees," said Burner. "Lots of clouds. I can't find any sign of oceans, so the facing side of the planet might be watered by rivers and small lakes. Really, I'm pulling ideas out of my ass to fill the time until we're close enough for the sensors to detect useful stuff."

"I understand, Lieutenant. Keep doing what you're doing."

Time went on and the distance to Vitran fell below a hundred million kilometres. The automatic shift scheduler ensured the crew were fully rested at the end of the fifteen-day inbound journey, but Recker was aware that eventually, they'd need to sleep again and he didn't want that to happen with the spaceship still hurtling towards the planet. Eventually, he'd have to slow things down so that everyone could sleep. Either that or insist they took boosters, though his experience told him it was usually best to keep those for the moments when there was absolutely no alternative.

At ninety-five million kilometres, Burner made a startled noise which got Recker's attention at once.

"Sir, you need to look at this."

Recker was at the comms station in three strides. "Show me."

A single line of text glowed orange on the central comms screen.

> *Crew of terminator class warship: Vengeance. Meklon station Excon-18 welcomes your arrival.*

"Meklon? Is that the alien name for the planet?" said Burner. "Want me to respond to the message?"

"Not yet. Can you locate the source of the broadcast?" asked Recker.

"Negative, sir. I'm still denied access to some of the deep comms functionality, including the ability to read the encrypted sub-data on this transmission. Uh-oh."

"Uh-oh what?" snapped Recker.

"The *Vengeance* just sent a response, sir."

"Shit. What did it say?"

"I don't know. Our return transmission came from a part of the comms system I can't access. Maybe the same piece of hardware that sent the ping which brought us here in the first place."

Recker watched the comms screen. Either the two-way comms was sub-light, ensuring a delay between responses, or the receiving station had nothing else to say beyond its initial greeting.

Abruptly, a second line of text appeared beneath the first.

> *Crew of terminator class warship: Vengeance. Secu-*

rity Tier 1 biometric authorisation detected. Unattended approach: approval not granted.

"What the hell does that mean?" asked Burner. "Is that a polite way of telling us to piss off?"

"I think it's a polite way of telling us we're in the crap," said Aston.

Recker had an idea what was coming. He threw himself into his seat, grabbed the controls and hauled on them to make the *Vengeance* bank away from Vitran. To his dismay, the spaceship remained on its existing course.

"The Excon-18 flight control system has taken over," he said. "The controls aren't responding."

"Can you override?" said Aston.

Recker tried everything he could think of, but nothing worked. He resisted the urge to crash his fist against the command console, aware it wouldn't do any good.

"Lieutenant Burner, have we received any further communication from the ground station?"

"No, sir."

"We're slowing," said Recker.

"Our processing core has received a new instruction," said Eastwood. "It's loading up for a lightspeed jump."

With Recker unable to stop it, the *Vengeance* came to a halt, while the lightspeed calculations burned the core.

"Can you find out where we're going, Lieutenant Eastwood? As if I couldn't guess."

"We're heading for Vitran, sir. I estimate we'll re-enter local space at an altitude of fifty thousand klicks."

"Well, we wanted to find some answers," said Recker. "And now it seems we're on our way to do just that."

As the eight minutes counted down, he was torn

between alarm at the possible danger, and relief that a long and tense sub-light journey had been avoided. Underlying both was an excitement which Recker couldn't deny – an excitement at the mysteries of the universe.

At exactly the predicted moment, the *Vengeance* entered lightspeed.

CHAPTER TWENTY

HAVING BRACED himself for the double pain of an in-out transition, Recker was not badly debilitated. Even before his vision cleared, he tested the controls to find out if the ground station had relinquished its command of the warship. It had not.

"We're stationary," he said. "Give me a sensor report before we start moving again."

"We're at a fifty thousand klick altitude," said Burner. "Putting the feed up."

Viewed from this much closer distance, the *Vengeance*'s sensors left few details unrevealed. Much of the planet's surface was obscured by dense grey clouds, but many areas were exposed. Beneath the clouds, everything was trees, covering millions of square kilometres in different shades of green, with no expanses of water amongst them.

Above the equator, Recker noticed dark grey shapes protruding from between the trees and he peered at them.

"Zoom this area," he said.

The sensor array magnified and Recker understood what he was looking at.

"Structures," he said.

What may have once been a city covered an extensive area and, rather than sprawling like the human equivalent, it appeared to be contained within the bounds of an imaginary square, with sides a hundred kilometres long. None of the buildings were particularly tall, such that the trees towered above many, concealing the shapes and functions.

"Is that a city or a military facility?" asked Eastwood. "I can't make it out."

"I don't know," said Recker. "Any sign of life?"

"The sensors are reading no movement of any kind and no significant sources of heat, sir."

"A mystery," said Recker.

A change in propulsion note brought his attention to the command console, where he discovered the *Vengeance* was once again accelerating.

"Find out where we're going," he said. "Do it quickly."

"Got it, sir," said Burner. "I'll circle the place on the feed."

A red ring appeared around an area of the planet about a thousand kilometres from the city. Here, the trees were not so thickly clustered, though the angle meant that Recker couldn't clearly see what they were approaching. He studied the feed closely and thought he made out two square buildings and not much else.

"Any idea what we're heading into?" he asked.

"Whatever it is, it's got to be military," said Aston.

"The ground controller isn't saying anything, sir," added Burner.

"I don't think it needs to, Lieutenant. The *Vengeance* has reported that its crew aren't on the correct security tier, so it's bringing us in for investigation."

"Who's going to ask the questions?" said Eastwood. "It's like the planet is deserted."

"There's still nothing in the air, sir," said Burner. "And the sensors should detect ground traffic from here as well – if there was any to find."

"The planet can't be dead," said Recker.

"We know about the existence of a war," said Aston. "Maybe something happened here."

Recker didn't like it and he experienced a feeling of creeping dread. Vitran had once held life and now there was seemingly none – except for the trees - with only the ground station giving indication that the planet still had power.

"Ten minutes and we'll be at the predicted landing site," said Burner. "I'll have a better idea what we're heading into before then."

The *Vengeance* continued its approach, while Recker scraped his teeth in frustration. He hated being a passenger and worse – he had no idea what the outcome would be once the warship landed, assuming that was the intention of the ground station. Added to that, he suspected he might never regain control, since he and his crew were effectively intruders on what he felt sure was a high-grade military vessel. What the punishment would be, he didn't want to guess.

Inexorably, the control station brought the *Vengeance*

towards the landing site. The warship plunged through clouds and into a deluge of pelting rain, which added a gloominess to the vibrant greens of the foliage. By this point, Recker had a clear view of the target area, which was directly between two square structures made of stone and metal. Trees filled the space between the buildings and the visible patches of ground were paved in light-coloured alloy. How the trees had found room to grow, Recker had no idea.

"The distance from one building to the other is a thousand metres, sir," said Burner. "This must be a landing field, though it's not much bigger than the *Vengeance*. The alloy is covered in holes."

"We're rotating," said Recker. "Coming in for landing."

"I don't know if the ground will support us, sir," said Burner.

"We'll soon find out."

Smoothly and accurately, the ground station aligned the *Vengeance* and held it briefly stationary. At eight hundred metres up, the crew were given an excellent view of the multitude of craters which covered the landing area. From each hole a tree grew; sometimes more than one.

Then, the warship descended vertically, straight onto the trees. The sound of cracking and splintering didn't penetrate the hull, but Recker could see the damage well enough on the sensor feeds. The trees were strong and proud, and no match for the 2.7 billion tons of warship landing on top of them.

"Ready," said Recker.

The *Vengeance*'s landing legs touched the ground. Or

rather, most of them did – others came down over craters and the warship lurched. The landing legs groaned and Recker heard the blunted sound of a metallic crack, which must have been incredibly loud to reach the bridge. Instrumentation on the command console indicated the *Vengeance* was slowly sliding at a diagonal. Another crack came and then the sliding stopped.

Recker held his breath and everything remained steady. He glanced at the port and starboard feeds. Through gaps in the smashed trees, he saw the vertical facing walls of the flanking buildings.

"We're down," he said.

"There's a new message on the comms, sir," said Burner.

Recker wanted to see it first-hand and he climbed from his seat.

> *Crew of terminator class warship: Vengeance. Biometric update required.*

"What does that mean?" said Burner.

"If I'm right, it's both good and bad news," said Recker slowly.

"Can we start with the positive?" said Eastwood.

"We speculated that the core override the *Vengeance* suffered wiped the spaceship back to a new state, like it had just come out of the construction yard."

"I remember," said Aston.

"That meant I could imprint my biological signature and from there I could give you all access to run your specific functions on the warship," Recker continued. "If I'm right, access to the *Vengeance*'s offensive and defensive systems is only granted once approval is given from two sources – the warship itself and also by a military facility like this one."

He looked at Aston and her eyes were wide. "I want to believe," she said. "Why do you think a ground station would complete the security setup instead of treating this as a security breach?"

"Because the *Vengeance* has completed the first half. That might make the ground station trust me as the designated command officer for the warship."

"That's totally different to the way it happens in our military," said Eastwood.

"This isn't the HPA, Lieutenant," said Aston.

"I have to find out. Not that we have a choice," said Recker. "The *Vengeance* saw duty in a war that was fought using weapons beyond our technological capabilities and it came through with no more than hull scarring. Just think what humanity will gain if we unlock those secrets and use them against the Daklan."

"We might end up facing more than just the Daklan, sir," said Eastwood. He looked troubled and with good reason.

Recker's suit helmet was next to his console and he put it on. "Commander Aston, I'm the only one who can do this. The bridge is yours, for what good it'll do. Lieutenant Burner – have Sergeant Vance and nine of his squad assemble at the forward boarding ramp." He opened the bridge locker and pulled out a gauss rifle and spare magazines.

"What about the other five soldiers, sir?" asked Burner.

Aston understood. "In case anyone from the ground station tries to come onboard."

"That's right."

Recker was desperate to find out if his theory about the *Vengeance*'s onboard security was correct and he hurried from the bridge. His steps quickened and soon he was as close to a run as the narrow passages allowed.

He was first to the airlock since the soldiers had further to travel and because the order to mobilise had come without notice. Recker waited impatiently, unwilling to activate the ramp without backup.

Next to arrive was Corporal Hendrix,

"Sir," she said. Hendrix was lugging her heavy med-box, so Recker had no idea how she made it before the others.

"Corporal," Recker greeted her.

"What shit are we in now?"

"What makes you think we landed in shit?"

"The day the ramp opens and I step out onto a pink-iced cake with a cherry on top, is the day I'll know I've gone insane."

"We'll brief once the others are here."

Sergeant Vance and the rest of the chosen soldiers weren't far behind and Recker filled them in on the scant details.

"This is important, isn't it?" said Raimi. Like the others, he understood the ramifications.

"It might be the most important thing any of us has ever done," Recker confirmed. "Are you ready for it?"

"Hell, yes!"

"Born ready, sir."

Recker thudded his palm against the square blue button which controlled the boarding ramp. With a crunch of overused gears, a section of the floor detached and dropped towards the ground below. The outside air came in and Recker's environmental sensor told him it was hot, humid and breathable.

With a second crunch, the ramp contacted the ground and the slight angle reminded Recker that the *Vengeance* wasn't on stable footing. The sound of rain – heavy, unrelenting rain – came to him and he experienced a fleeting memory of home.

"Let's move," said Recker.

Pride was not a consideration and he allowed Vance to take the lead. Following in the middle of the line, Recker descended to the surface of this alien world.

From the light, he guessed it was late afternoon and he cast his gaze around at the broken trees and the strangely circular craters from which they sprang. Several of the *Vengeance*'s landing feet had settled in or near to these holes and the spaceship's weight had produced countless stress lines in the weakened surface. Above the subdued engine note, Recker heard a slow, inexorable scraping that made him wonder how long it would be before the *Vengeance* tipped further.

While Recker absorbed the details, Vance and the squad spread out, clambering across leafy branches and bright shards of severed wood as they watched for anything which might constitute a threat.

"Which way, sir?" asked Vance. "We've got structures east and west."

"That one," said Recker, pointing at the east building, the path to which seemed a little easier.

Under Vance's command, the squad headed warily across the grey alloy surface, still beneath the shelter offered by the warship's enormous hull. It was impossible to move silently and every footstep produced a crack or a rustling of disturbed leaves. That same foliage reduced visibility and the rain shrouded everything in a shifting cloak of refracted light.

Gradually, as Recker approached the edge of the warship's cover, the spatter of raindrops came much louder over the grumbling propulsion and no sooner had he stepped out from beneath the *Vengeance* than the outer layer of his suit was drenched. He could feel each droplet striking him and they produced tiny explosions of water everywhere he looked.

"Move," said Vance.

The squad headed for the target and those soldiers further than a few metres away became no more than grey shapes, the details seemingly washed away in the torrent. Recker skirted one of the craters – this one ten metres across - and glanced inside. It was much deeper than he expected and went a long way down.

Soon, they arrived at the facing wall of the building and the soldiers stood guard while Vance gestured towards a door.

Recker hurried over. The structure was larger than he'd imagined and it towered windowless over him, a flat-faced and functional example of the architect's hand. He noted that the stone cladding was smooth and with an ageless appearance, defying his attempts to guess how long ago the place was built.

"This door, sir," said Vance, knocking on its unblemished metal surface with gloved knuckles. He lowered his hand and pointed at a hand-sized panel flush to the wall adjacent. "Access panel there."

Recker glanced at the soldiers nearby. They hardly moved such that he got the impression they were statues from a museum dedicated to war. Only the faces behind the visors – wide eyes and flared nostrils – spoiled the illusion of their permanency.

"Get it open, Sergeant."

"With pleasure."

Vance spun neatly on his heel and planted his hand on the panel. A row of red lights flashed once and the door stayed shut.

"Nice work, Sergeant," said Steigers.

"Let me try," said Recker.

He placed his own hand on the access panel and felt a buzzing vibration through the material of his glove. No lights appeared and the door slid open with a whine. Beyond the opening, a short passage led to an inner door.

A feeling of strangeness took hold of Recker. While he'd always embraced the emptiness of space, abandoned places like this had an utterly different feeling about them. The ceaseless rain and the sense of loneliness combined to make this part of the adventure seem overwhelmingly strange.

Recker took a deep breath. "In," he said.

CHAPTER TWENTY-ONE

A SECOND ACCESS panel controlled the inner door and Recker waited until Vance nodded to indicate the squad was ready. He readied his gun and activated the panel. The door opened as readily as the previous one and Recker stared into a space hardly lit by the wan light coming from outside. He saw shapes around the edges of what he guessed was a large room.

Vance didn't require prompting. He switched on his helmet light and darted into the room, with the other members of the squad behind. Recker stayed by the door and within a few seconds it was clear the room held no direct threats.

He turned on his own head torch and entered. The dancing beams from the flashlights illuminated a fifteen-metre-square room, with alien consoles along the left and right walls. A flight of metal steps led up through the opposite wall, their destination unclear from Recker's current position. Gantry and Drawl were already cautiously ascending and Vance ordered two other soldiers to provide cover from the bottom.

"The equipment looks powered off, sir," said Vance.

"It's in deep sleep, Sergeant. Or most of it is. The flight controller which brought us here must be in an always-on state."

Recker approached one of the wall consoles at random since they all seemed identical or near enough. This blocky piece of tech was fitted with four screens, along with levers, switches and buttons, giving a sense of age that he'd noticed before on the tenixite converter. He knew instinctively how to turn the console on and he flicked the right switch first time.

"It's powering up," he said, turning his head to see if he'd missed anything obviously useful on the other consoles.

"Sergeant, you might want to come check this out," said Gantry on the open comms.

Vance disappeared up the stairwell like a man who'd been told his house was on fire. A moment later, he suggested Recker might be interested in what lay at the top.

"On my way."

Recker abandoned the console, dashed up the steps and emerged into a huge, unlit space which occupied much of the building's interior. The flashlights weren't nearly powerful enough to dispel the darkness and Recker spent a moment aiming the beam into the corners to find out what details he could.

The walls were clad in a black, nonreflective substance, with unevenly spaced consoles here and there.

A fifteen-metre diameter cylinder made from the same material as the walls rose from the floor and connected with the ceiling way overhead. The cylinder's base was ringed by another console and the panel lights indicated the hardware was powered up.

"This might be the place," said Recker.

"What's that cylinder, sir?" asked Gantry.

"It's the transmission tower for the flight controller, Private. That's what brought us in."

"We need some more light," said Vance, calling for another three soldiers to come up the stairs.

Recker didn't pay attention and he stopped in front of the circular console. Each of the numerous top-mounted screens contained a prompt for input. He called up the control software, which he noted contained many similarities to that on the *Vengeance* and notable differences to that on the tenixite converter.

"Meklon station – Excon-18," he read from the top banner. Recker was becoming increasingly certain that *Meklon* was how this alien species referred to either themselves or their civilisation.

He dug further into the menu, dimly aware of Sergeant Vance directing the squad to explore and secure the area. Recker believed there was a way to upgrade his security clearance for the *Vengeance*, though nothing jumped out at him. What he did find was extensive records of other warships which had come to this planet, including the *Vengeance* on at least eight previous occasions.

"Have you found what we came for, sir?" asked Vance.

"Not yet." Recker swore under his breath. "What I

would give to spend a day here without pressure, finding out what happened to the inhabitants of this planet."

He located the security menu, where he found time-stamped records of communication between the *Vengeance* and Excon-18. The files were all ones and zeroes. Even so, Recker felt he was on the right track and his heart jumped when he located a menu titled *Biometric Approval.* Upon accessing the menu, he was presented with a single option.

> *Terminator class warship: Vengeance. Request approval?*

With a trembling finger, Recker touched the screen.

> *Request submitted. Awaiting response.*

With no idea where the request was submitted to and how long it would take to obtain a response, Recker called up the software on an adjacent screen, where he searched for clues as to how the process worked. He soon discovered that Excon-18 had sent an FTL comm to another facility, called Excon-1.

He beckoned Sergeant Vance across and explained the situation.

"Even an FTL comm might take days to reach its destination," said Vance.

"It might. We don't know what kind of lightspeed multiplier these Meklon can push their comms transmissions up to."

The expression on Vance's face indicated his thoughts on the matter and he went back to his slow-paced patrol around the transmission cylinder.

Although he wasn't happy at the delay, Recker told

himself to make best use of the time he'd been granted. After a few minutes, he discovered that the Excon-18 software maintained audit records of numerous incidents and Recker scrolled through them. Most of the events were assigned a specific code that likely meant something to a trained operator, but not so much to a passing member of the Human Planetary Alliance. Reluctant to miss an opportunity, Recker downloaded the files into his suit, hoping one of the analyst teams ▌Lustre would find a way to understand.

A new line of text appeared on the screen from which his security approval request had been sent and Recker snapped his head towards it.

> *Transmission uncertainty threshold breached. Alert. Receptor failure. Receptor unknown. Excon-18 approval tier increased [temporary]. Update biometric security?*

"Damn right!" said Recker, accepting the prompt.

> *Biometric security updating. Re-writing data blocks: terminator class warship: Vengeance. Core override: software defence reconfiguration. Mesh deflector: updates in progress. Replicator: updates in progress.*

A progress bar appeared and began its long journey from left to right on the screen. Recker's heart thudded painfully and his breathing deepened.

"We're on our way, Sergeant Vance," he said.

Vance appeared at his side and leaned closer to the screen. "Replicator updates?"

"Interested in the new menu?"

"The Adamantine technicians put tape over the *Vengeance*'s original replicators, but someone in the squad pulled it off." Vance contrived to look ignorant of the culprit and innocent at the same time. "A few of us have been experimenting with alien chow, sir."

In spite of the situation, Recker couldn't help but ask. "And?"

"The meat stew isn't bad." Vance straightened. "How long for these updates?"

"See that progress bar? That's how long."

"Hmm."

Vance resumed his patrol and Recker gave Aston an update on the comms. With that done, he turned once more to the console and resumed his poking around. Inside the transmission, log he found something which made his blood run cold.

"Shit," he said.

Vance was there in an instant. "What's wrong, sir?"

Recker pointed. "See this list of past transmissions?"

"The most recent ones say receptor failure," said Vance, his brow furrowed.

"Those aren't the ones I'm worried about – it's these ones which say receptor unknown. The same message came up when I requested a biometric security update. I didn't recognize the significance until now."

Vance was one of those people who, when he didn't know something, generally shied away from guesswork. "I don't understand, sir."

"These transmissions have been split between two receptors, Sergeant. An unknown receptor should not be one of them."

"An interception?" said Vance, realization dawning. "I don't know much about comms, sir, but isn't it almost impossible to randomly intercept military transmissions?"

"The key word is *randomly*. With the right know-how and the right equipment, you might be able to do it." Recker looked frantically around the room as the feeling of horror grew. "Or if you'd installed some additional hardware into an abandoned facility in order to duplicate every broadcast and use the antenna to send the copy to a place of your choice."

Vance got onto the comms. "Listen up – the comms security in this facility might have been compromised. I want everyone to check for something which looks out of place – maybe a box wired into a place you wouldn't expect."

"Hell, Sergeant, that's vague," said Hendrix.

"I don't care – get on it."

"It won't matter, Sergeant," said Recker. "If there's something listening in, we're already too late."

A glance told Recker that the progress bar was at 75% and increasing steadily.

"What's the likely outcome, sir?" said Vance.

"Whoever the Meklon's enemy were, they left a warship, or maybe several warships, nearby to monitor for returning vessels - outliers of the Meklon fleet coming back to base. They've picked up my request for a security update and now they'll be on their way to investigate."

"That means we're in the shit."

The progress bar inched up another two percent and Recker was reluctant to exit the building while it was ongoing. He recalled how his initial biometric imprinting on the *Vengeance* had taken place while he was on the warship's bridge, a process which had seemingly only required his presence. Recker didn't want to leave until he was certain his security tier was updated.

"We can't leave," he said. "Not until this is done."

Vance opened his mouth, like he was about to offer an objection. In the end he just shrugged. "You know this better than I do, sir." A smile appeared. "Watch that progress bar stick at 99%."

"Don't remind me, Sergeant," said Recker. He opened a comms channel to the *Vengeance* and filled Aston in on the latest details, while pacing up and down in a fruitless effort to burn off some of his nervous energy.

"There's nothing on our comms, sir. Did you analyse the FTL comm multiplier to obtain an estimate of the distance to this unknown receptor?"

"No, Commander - there are too many unknowns to make the exercise a useful one."

"Okay - I just thought I'd mention it. Is there anything else we can make use of from that facility?"

"Given time we no longer have, I could build a picture of the military activity on this planet."

"Any idea what caused the inhabitants to leave, sir?"

"I didn't find anything," Recker's frustration was chewing at his insides. "Another missed opportunity."

"Maybe we'll find something in the *Vengeance*'s data-banks once you return."

It was a hope that Recker clung onto. "Once we're away from here."

He closed out of the channel and stopped pacing. The progress bar had sped to 98% and stalled, showing its final incomplete task.

> *Replicator: updates in progress.*

"I hope that meat stew was worth it, Sergeant."

Recker had no idea why the replicator software was included in the overall update process and he couldn't see any reason why he needed to stick around while it uploaded.

"Sergeant Vance, we're leaving."

Vance had already made preparations. Half of the squad were in the room below and the rest were gathered at the top of the steps.

"Soldiers – get your asses back to that warship," barked Vance.

Recker deliberately slowed his first few strides in order that he could watch the progress bar. It hung at 98% and then the figure changed to 100%. As soon as he saw it happen, he sprinted hard for the steps and descended two at a time.

The rest of the squad were already out of the building, except for Vance who allowed Recker to exit before him.

"Any change on the bridge, Commander?" asked Recker on the comms, as he crashed through the broken branches and the teeming rain.

"Negative, sir - the flight controller's still in charge," said Aston.

The shelter of the *Vengeance* provided relief from the rain, but the branches made the going tough. Spears of wood jabbed into Recker's legs and thighs, their efforts to pierce his skin defeated by the advanced polymers in his combat suit. Angrily, he brushed through leaves and twigs, and crushed smaller branches underfoot.

At last, he came to the ramp and he charged upwards,

checking once over his shoulder to make sure Sergeant Vance was still with him.

Inside the airlock, Hendrix was waiting at the ramp activation switch, while the other soldiers had proceeded into the ship so that they wouldn't crowd the space.

"Do it!" ordered Vance.

Recker didn't stay around to watch the ramp closing and he continued his sprint, his breathing loud and his heart rate elevated.

"Any change?" he repeated on his comm channel to the bridge.

The same question got the same answer.

"Negative, sir."

Aston went quiet for a second and this time when she spoke it was with the news Recker had feared.

"Lieutenant Eastwood has detected the presence of a ternium cloud, at fifty thousand klicks altitude and a quarter turn around the planet."

With the arrival of a presumed hostile warship, Recker knew the success of the mission hung by a thread. Hoping his return to the bridge wouldn't be too late, he ran.

CHAPTER TWENTY-TWO

RECKER THREW himself into his seat and immediately, he spotted several additional options on his command menu.

"Report!" he shouted, accessing the security menu in order to update the access level of the crew.

"A single ship, sir," said Burner. "A big one. It arrived and is currently out of sensor sight."

"Must be confident they can take out whatever turns up at Vitran," said Eastwood.

"Let's prove them wrong," said Recker, his hands on the controls. "Is everyone's security tier updated?"

"Yes, sir," said Burner.

"Looks like," added Eastwood. "We've got a switchable two-mode propulsion. I'll check it out."

"Whoa, plenty on my weapons panel now," said Aston. "We've got missiles, interceptors, an energy weapon of some kind and a mesh deflector, whatever the hell that is."

"How many in the magazines?"

"They're almost full, sir. The *Vengeance* must have been brought down not long after it was rearmed."

While he talked and listened, Recker fed power into the propulsion and brought the *Vengeance* away from the ground in a diagonal that would put maximum distance between it and the anticipated position of the recently arrived vessel. With a surge of acceleration, the warship leapt into the air, the resonance from the engines sweeping the fallen trees in every direction.

"Red dot on your tactical, sir," said Burner. "Shit, that's coming fast."

The first Recker saw of the enemy warship was an immense fireball streaking through the deep blue of the planet's sky at the upper extremes of the atmosphere. Dark smoke trailed hundreds of kilometres behind the incoming spaceship and he thought briefly that it must be close to burning up.

"There's an energy spike coming through their hull, sir," said Eastwood, surprise in his voice. "That's the first time our instrumentation has picked up this kind of information."

Recker heard, but his hands were full. The last thing he wanted was to confront what he assumed was a highly capable hostile opponent while his officers were still learning about the *Vengeance*'s newly unlocked abilities. From the corner of his eye, he'd spotted another such ability, accessible only on the command console. It was called *Fracture* and a warning light indicated the existence of a system problem he had no time to investigate.

Keeping the *Vengeance* at a low altitude, Recker

banked east on a diverging course from the enemy craft. He figured that the best way to avoid notice was to circle the planet and then run for space once the moment was right. As soon as Recker changed course, the approaching ship did likewise by turning sharply to follow.

"Looks like we've got a fight on our hands, folks."

The *Vengeance*'s nose already burned hot and its own trail appeared on the rear sensors. On the ground beneath, the trees blurred into a green carpet as the warship raced for the horizon.

Several events happened at once and all Recker's experience wasn't enough for him to immediately separate the strands.

"The energy spike has dissipated from the enemy hull," said Eastwood.

At that precise moment, the *Vengeance* became surrounded in a cage made from countless lines of blue energy, with no pattern to them, like random sword cuts made by sweeping blades. The instrumentation went crazy and Eastwood swore.

Recker got a sense that the ground itself had erupted. It happened too quickly for his eyes to follow and then the sensors went dark, while the propulsion gauge fell and the controls felt suddenly unresponsive, like a giant hand was holding onto the spaceship. Automatically, he increased power to compensate, while his brain fought for understanding. As he fought to maintain control, the bridge became filled with a thousand distant thumping sounds of impacts against the exterior plating.

Understanding came. The *Vengeance* had been hit by an energy weapon and the status display indicated that the mesh deflector had activated, diverting the enemy attack into the planet's surface and causing it to explode into the air with such violent energy that the entire warship was caught in a maelstrom of earth and stone.

With a roar of engines, the *Vengeance* burst free from an immense fountain of rock, much of which was still on an upward trajectory. The enormity of the weapon's attack began to sink in – the entire horizon behind the *Vengeance* was erupting towards space and amongst it, Recker saw dull reds and bright oranges which made him think the planet's crust had been ruptured by the attack, casting the hot rocks of the upper mantle into the sky.

"The mesh deflector went offline, sir," said Aston. "It's either failed or there's a cooldown period."

"Find out which."

"Yes, sir."

"And where's that enemy ship?" asked Recker angrily.

"I'm looking, sir," said Burner. "I can't see anything through all this rock."

Recker didn't have time to stare but his eyes kept jumping to the rear feed. The flight of the *Vengeance* was carrying it further from the eruption, which only served to allow a more expansive view of the devastation.

To Recker, it seemed like he was staring at a sheer wall of fragmenting stone, from which immense boulders tore themselves free as they raced for the heavens, whilst others were travelling so quickly they overtook the *Vengeance*, giving the illusion that the warship was amongst a storm of fiery missiles.

The tactical computer tracked the highest threat objects and marked them as orange squares on the screen. Every second or two, one of those missiles impacted the rear plating with enough force that the sound of it was audible over everything else happening on the bridge.

"That's going to be one hell of a crater," said Eastwood.

"I don't much care about the crater just now, Lieutenant. I care about the warship which is trying to kill us."

The rock explosion had blocked the sensor view of the enemy craft, but the tactical displayed the vessel's assumed course. It was difficult to be certain with so much happening, but Recker thought his opponent should be visible already. The fact that it wasn't made him think it had changed heading.

"Maybe they think we're dead," said Aston.

"They must know about this mesh deflector we're carrying," said Recker.

"And if it's got a cooldown period, they'll know about that as well, sir."

Recker bared his teeth. "Then why haven't they taken advantage?" His brain served up a possible answer to his own question. "Whatever they used against us, it can't be a rapid-fire weapon. Not with that much destructive power."

"I've been checking out the energy readings from their hull, sir," said Eastwood, talking quickly to get his message across. "It's almost the same as what I saw on the cylinder back on Oldis."

"That warship is carrying a portable tenixite converter?" asked Recker in disbelief.

"Looks like."

"The effect was different," said Burner. "On Oldis, the Daklan warships disintegrated."

"We don't know what effect the mesh deflector has on the discharge," said Eastwood. "Maybe it converts the depletion burst into a different kind of energy."

"However it works, our opponent must be using tenixite they're carrying onboard," said Aston. "Otherwise the weapon would be useless without a nearby source of ternium ore."

"It was a big craft," said Burner. "Hard to be sure on the numbers, but I reckon we're facing something of a similar size and mass to one of our battleships. They could be carrying a few billion tons in their hold if that's how it was designed."

Another check of the rear feed informed Recker that the *Vengeance* was far enough ahead of the stone eruption for him to bank east without the warship's flank being exposed to projectile impacts. Still the wall of rock hadn't fallen, like it was suspended in defiance of gravity. Recker knew that it was a trick caused by the distance and the magnitude. While a few trillion tons of ejected rock had likely made it into orbit, the rest of it was only going in one direction and once it was over, Vitran would never be the same again.

"I've detected the enemy!" said Burner. "They're heading the wrong way!"

A red dot appeared on the tactical - amongst the thousands of orange targets - high and five hundred kilometres behind. On the sensor feed, the enemy craft and its trailing smoke was partly obscured by debris, preventing Recker from obtaining a good view of his target. He preferred to see what he was fighting and he growled in irritation at being denied this simple satisfaction.

However, from the enemy's trajectory, Recker could see they'd tried to anticipate the *Vengeance*'s course and got it wrong. At the same moment, he realized that his opponent didn't know that he and his crew were inexperienced with this alien tech – the enemy was treating the *Vengeance* like it was fully battle-ready and with a crew who knew how to operate it at maximum efficiency.

"They're banking towards us," said Recker.

"Mesh deflector still offline," said Aston. "Our missiles are locked – I can't recommend firing them until they have a clearer path to target."

"I agree, hold fire. Any readings from the enemy hull, Lieutenant Eastwood?"

"I'm not sure, sir – too many obstacles between us and them."

"Commander Aston, you mentioned we're fitted with an energy weapon."

"Yes, sir. It's called *Executor* and it has a narrow front-firing arc. It's tied into the propulsion and is currently showing offline."

"Damnit," Recker swore. "We need an hour to pick this apart and find out how everything works. As it stands, we're an easy target."

"I'm detecting a missile launch from the enemy ship," said Aston. "Interceptors launched. Uh interceptor *storm* activated."

Everything happened so fast that Recker's brain struggled to keep up. Dozens of red dots – enemy missiles - appeared on the tactical and many of them detonated fruitlessly against the intervening debris. From the size of the plasma blasts it was apparent the warheads carried a massive payload.

At the same time, a thunderous boom of several hundred propulsions igniting came to the bridge and tiny missiles burst from concealed launch tubes positioned around the *Vengeance*'s hull. Green dots met red dots on the tactical and the enemy missiles were destroyed by the agile interceptors sent against them.

"That was close," said Aston.

"We've got to give them something back," said Recker, wondering how he was going to achieve it. The *Vengeance* was travelling low and fast and he banked again, aiming to skirt around the still-hidden crater formed by the tenixite converter weapon. By now he could clearly see the shower of rocks was coming down rather than going up and countless fragments punched into the sea of green below, crushing the trees and leaving huge gaps in the canopy.

"The crater's got a 220-klick diameter," said Burner, when the path of the *Vengeance* brought it close enough for the ground to be seen over the planet's curvature.

"I'm detecting a second missile launch," said Aston. "Interceptors away."

For the second time, many of the enemy warheads crashed into flying debris and those which made it through were knocked out by the *Vengeance*'s interceptor storm. Meanwhile, the opposing spaceship increased its altitude further in order to maintain a constant visual lock and Recker couldn't do much to counter the move.

"Our nose section's getting hot," Eastwood reminded him. "Much more and the plates will soften."

It was just one concern amongst a dozen which competed for Recker's attention. Every one of his crew was in the same position – they were being asked to familiarise themselves with new weapons and tech whilst under the greatest of pressure.

"Executor still offline," said Aston. "It's not getting enough supply to activate."

"You said it taps into the propulsion."

"It does and the link is open. Still not enough."

The time for timidity was over. "Hit that bastard with missiles," said Recker. "I don't care if there's too much debris – I want to give them something to think about."

Way overhead and far behind, the fireball which was the enemy warship accelerated higher still, now on a course that would carry it directly over the *Vengeance*. Recker adjusted his own heading, aiming to cut across the edge of the crater and lose his warship amongst the rocks. Once the enemy's sensor lock was broken, he intended to make a run for it to buy some time for him and his crew to figure things out.

"The mesh deflector came back online, sir," said Aston.

"I'm detecting an energy build up on the enemy hull again, sir," said Eastwood.

The first thought that jumped into Recker's head was *depletion burst* and he prepared himself for a second expulsion of the planet's surface.

"Sir – it's a core override!" said Eastwood. "They're about to fire!"

Not exactly sure why he did it, Recker banked again and this time he aimed the *Vengeance* directly at the centre of the newly formed crater in the planet's surface. No longer did he see the sheer cliff of an unimaginable mountain – now gravity had asserted itself, turning the mountain into a deluge of boulders raining upon the ground.

"Core override discharged."

The needles on Recker's console jumped and swung, while the bridge light flickered and the onboard systems went offline one after another. A message appeared on his screen.

> *Core Override detected. Configuration: total shutdown.*

A second later, the propulsion stuttered and then fell to idle. The last thing Recker saw before the sensor feed went out was the rock-shattered forest coming up fast to meet the warship, while the hard rain of stone continued to fall.

CHAPTER TWENTY-THREE

THE SOUND of impacts against the hull was deafening and the controls juddered in Recker's hands. He felt the *Vengeance* hit the ground – the impact should have killed him and the crew, but then he noticed that the life support modules hadn't gone offline. In fact, a few of the monitoring gauges were still receiving input, though he didn't like what they were telling him.

Long before the spaceship's momentum had run out, Recker's eye fell on a single line of text which appeared on his left-hand screen.

> *Core override: backup restore in progress.*

"I've got access to the weapons again!" said Aston, shouting over the sound of the rocks hitting the warship's armour.

Recker hadn't let go of the controls and they weren't responsive. "Nothing here," he said.

"Propulsion still not available!" said Eastwood. "How

long until those alien bastards locate us amongst all this crap?"

"I'm not planning to guess," said Recker. He winced at the solidity of a thud on the plating, which he felt through the padding of his seat. He'd taken a gamble on hiding the *Vengeance* amongst the falling stone, but it would only pay off if the spaceship wasn't completely crushed.

We're solid alloy and ternium. No amount of rock is going to hurt us.

Even as the thought appeared, Recker knew it wasn't quite true. He clenched his jaw and hoped the *Vengeance* would resist the weight piling on top of it.

"Propulsion online!" said Eastwood. "Whatever modifications we received at Excon-18, they're purging the core override!"

"Sensors back!" yelled Burner excitedly.

The feeds reappeared simultaneously, though they didn't have much to display other than the mountain of rocks piled up on the warship. On the forward feed, the hull plates were still glowing and the rock there was already melting into a glutinous sludge.

The status display on Recker's console updated.

> *Core override. Restore complete. Adaptation partially complete.*

"We're getting out of here," said Recker.

"Where to, sir?" asked Aston.

"Away from this mound of stone, Commander. Ready on the weapons."

He increased power to the engines and the warship strained against the weight holding it down. Recker gave it yet more power and suddenly the *Vengeance* surged upwards, like it was completely unencumbered.

In a new explosion of rock, the warship escaped from the ever-increasing pile that was forming on the surface of Vitran. Once free, the vessel's hull was again subject to a bombardment of missiles coming from above and the sensor feeds were a chaos of shapes and movement, with patches of sky and ground only glimpsed in the most fleeting of moments.

"I can't see the enemy, sir," said Burner. "Visibility is poor."

The clattering on the hull didn't reduce at all and Recker was amazed at the aftereffects of the depletion burst's discharge. He peered ahead, accelerating steadily. Having eyes on the enemy would be a big advantage if they were to get through this.

"There's not much more to come down, sir," said Burner. "So if you were hoping to play hide and seek..."

An immense falling boulder, which Recker had already noticed a few kilometres ahead of the *Vengeance*, suddenly exploded into a shower of fragments. Recker got a sense of a huge, white-hot projectile blur past the port-side sensor feeds. A moment later, he watched a diagonal line of other, smaller rocks detonate into pieces as a second projectile from the enemy warship smashed through the debris. Somehow the superheated gauss slug missed the *Vengeance* by a hair and Recker could only imagine that it had been deflected by its path through the falling rocks.

"I've detected a missile launch, sir," said Burner. His voice climbed an octave. "There's the enemy! From their course, I'd say they've completed a half-circuit of the crater. They're at a three hundred klick altitude and west of our position."

"Launching interceptors."

A series of plasma explosions went off all around the *Vengeance*, some within touching distance. Recker banked, still accelerating, and then the spaceship was through the blasts, its hull scarcely licked by the intense heat.

"Missiles incoming," said Aston. "They're not holding back any longer." She cursed. "Our interceptors haven't reloaded!"

Recker banked again, instinctively, just as a third gauss projectile crashed through the thinning rocks. He had no idea how it missed the *Vengeance*, but he didn't think the enemy missiles would do the same - they filled the tactical and the falling rocks were too few to thin their numbers significantly.

A cage of blue energy sword cuts sprang into being around the *Vengeance*. The barrier held for several long seconds, while plasma missiles exploded against it. Just before it winked out of existence, Recker saw a gauss slug strike the mesh and flatten into a brightly glowing disc which slipped away as the shield faded.

"Automatic activation?" asked Recker, hardly able to believe he was still alive.

"Manual control," said Aston.

"Good timing. *Damn* good timing."

"And now the mesh deflector's back on cooldown."

The *Vengeance* emerged from the fringes of those tumbling rocks which were last to escape the heavens, and the warship was already travelling fast enough that its nose glowed anew. Overhead, the enemy warship hadn't slowed and the pattern of its trailing smoke in the now-clear skies made it easy to read the vessel's path.

"Missiles locked and launched," said Aston.

The missiles streaked through the air – forty-eight pinpoints of orange from the spaceship's upper four clusters. A split-second later, a hundred or more lines of white light sprang from the centre of the fireball which still concealed the details of the opposing warship.

"Interceptors," said Aston.

"Let's hope we get a few hits," said Burner.

The *Vengeance*'s missiles were rapid and they packed a real punch. Several flashes of white plasma appeared in the midst of the blazing fireball of atmospheric friction. Recker had no idea if the damage was significant and his thoughts were still on escape. He mentally plotted a course away from the enemy spaceship which would also allow the rear clusters to launch. The propulsion rumbled and the *Vengeance* thundered for the horizon.

"Engine mode 2 is a controlled overstress," said Eastwood, from out of nowhere, and calmly like he'd been poring over a technical magazine while drinking a cup of coffee. "Maybe not exactly the same, but that's the best way I can think to describe it."

"Switch us over, Lieutenant," said Recker without hesitation. "I'll take all the extra power that's available."

"Sir, I also found out that the Executor is tied in to mode 2," said Eastwood. "Once we're switched over, it should become available."

"Do it."

"I already did, sir."

Unlike the overstress mode on an HPA warship, which made the propulsion howl like banshee, the *Vengeance*'s second engine mode only straightened out the lumpiness which Recker had often noticed. He checked the monitoring gauges – their needles hadn't shifted, but the scales had updated and the numbers were bigger. Much bigger. At the same time, one of the previously dead buttons on the left control bar lit up, with no clear indication what it was for.

He tested the controls and discovered a step change in the *Vengeance*'s acceleration. It almost leapt into the distance, catching Recker by surprise and setting off a series of temperature alerts for the hull.

"As Lieutenant Eastwood said, the Executor is now available," said Aston.

"What does it do?" said Recker.

"Blows shit up I hope," offered Burner.

"I don't have precise details, but I think Lieutenant Burner's assessment is correct." Aston spotted an inbound missile attack from the enemy warship. "Interceptors launched. Rear clusters one and two fired in response."

"I'm reading another energy surge from their hull, sir," said Eastwood. "The tenixite converter!"

"The mesh deflector is on cooldown," said Aston.

In a split-second, Recker evaluated the possible outcomes of another discharge from the tenixite weapon. Without the mesh deflector, the *Vengeance* was going to be destroyed and everyone onboard killed.

"Ready the Executor," he said, cutting power to the forward propulsion and giving extra to the rear modules. The *Vengeance* spun wildly, crazily, and the sensors feeds were of greens, browns and greys, the details moving too fast for the human brain to register.

Timing it as best he could, Recker brought the warship from its 180-degree turn and the nose was pointing almost towards the enemy spaceship.

"Fire!" he ordered.

From the corner of his eye, Recker watched Aston plant a finger on one of her console buttons and hold it there for a long second. The Executor fired and, at first, Recker wasn't sure if anything had happened. Then, a bass note of such depth and intensity crashed through him that it made him groan with the pain and he felt like his bones were being ground into powder within his body.

In a flash of bottomless darkness which filled a sphere two thousand metres in diameter, the enemy ship exploded into countless pieces. Alloys, still burning from atmospheric friction, were sent in every direction at tremendous speed and Recker could only stare in wonder at the complete and utter destruction of his enemy.

"Done." Recker couldn't think of much else to say.

"As easy as that," said Eastwood numbly. "The Executor kicked us out of mode 2," he said, recovering enough to provide a status update.

"The weapon has gone offline," Aston confirmed. "One shot and no more."

"How soon before we can switch back to mode 2?" asked Recker.

"No idea, sir," said Eastwood. "I'm sure there's a way to find out and I'll tell you when I've figured out the method."

"That's fine, Lieutenant. We're all learning."

This victory – which he attributed more to luck than anything else – left him feeling empty and he didn't want to look at the pieces of the enemy warship, many of which had already crashed into the trees. He turned the *Vengeance* away and accelerated for orbit. The forest receded rapidly and the sky darkened as the planet's atmosphere transitioned to vacuum.

"We're leaving here," said Recker.

"I'll pass on the good news to Sergeant Vance, sir," said Burner. "After that, I'll send an FTL comm to Adamantine – in case something happens to us and we don't get home."

"Shame Excon-18 got caught up in the tenixite blast," said Aston. "Else we could have taken down a data extractor and recovered what was available."

Recker shook his head. "We've found the biggest prize, Commander, and I wouldn't have risked a return to the planet. We came through an encounter with one enemy ship – next time it might be five. Or a dozen."

She smiled tiredly. "Home it is, then."

After five minutes at maximum sub-light speed, the planet was far behind, though the crater made by the depletion burst was clearly visible. Lieutenant Burner scanned it and confirmed his earlier assertion that the hole was 220 kilometres in diameter and more than 120 kilometres deep, even if the falling earth and stone made it impossible for him to be certain about the latter figure.

A minute later, Lieutenant Eastwood declared that engine mode 2 was again available.

"Want me to switch over so we can put in some extra distance, sir?"

"We don't know if overuse causes additional stress on the warship, Lieutenant."

"That's true, sir." Eastwood had something else to say. "I found a mode 3, sir," he said. "It appeared while mode 2 was in operation."

Recker turned. "What would be the results of activating this new mode?"

"I don't know, sir - I was denied access. Since I didn't have the required security level, that leaves you as the only one with authority to access mode 3."

Recker felt troubled at the words. On the surface, a propulsion switch shouldn't require the approval of a commanding officer to activate. The fact that this one did made him ask what he was missing. It didn't matter yet – this was the time to return home, not to experiment.

"One of the control buttons lit up during mode 2," he said eventually. "I didn't get a chance to see what it was for."

"There was plenty going on, sir."

For a full hour, Recker flew directly away from Vitran and then he brought the *Vengeance* to a halt. "Five-point-two million klicks is enough," he said. "Lieutenant Eastwood, we're going to Lustre."

"Yes, sir. Course set. Lightspeed drive activation in six minutes."

"Where'd the two-minute reduction come from?" asked Recker.

"Some extra cycles on the processing core became available when you returned to the ship, sir," said Eastwood. "With everything that was happening, I didn't have time to mention it." He looked closely at his console. "And

ANTHONY JAMES

the expected duration just came through – we're down to twelve days for the return journey, so our lightspeed multiplier went up as well."

Recker had plenty to talk about, but he couldn't bring himself to speak. He waited with one eye on the timer and, at six minutes, the *Vengeance* transitioned into lightspeed.

CHAPTER TWENTY-FOUR

THE CREW WERE EXHAUSTED and Recker likewise. In order to prevent mistakes resulting from tiredness, he called a halt to any investigation work on the *Vengeance's* unlocked systems until everyone was sufficiently rested. The crew was accustomed to short rest breaks taken at inconsistent times and it didn't require longer than a day for them to recover to full alertness.

From that moment, they devoted themselves to uncovering as much as possible about the alien warship, to ensure they wouldn't be disadvantaged next time trouble showed up. Some secrets were easily dug out of their hiding places, others were more reluctant.

"We know the Executor is linked to propulsion mode two," said Aston. "And when I fired it, the *Vengeance* was forced into mode one again."

"For five minutes," said Eastwood.

"I checked the logs for the mesh deflector and that was

on a five-minute cooldown as well," said Aston. "I don't know the cause of the limitation."

"I also checked those logs," said Eastwood. "And I reckon the mesh deflector hardware contains its own power source. I can't find the schematics, so I don't know where it's located in the hull."

"I noticed that the deflector acted automatically against the tenixite weapon," said Recker.

"Yes, sir," said Aston. "And then I activated it manually against those incoming missiles."

"The obvious conclusion is that the mesh was actually designed to combat depletion bursts, yet with the additional function of being able to block pretty much anything else, but at the operator's discretion."

"We've seen the cylinder network and we've discussed what might happen if someone decided to aim a full-charge depletion burst at a planet," said Eastwood. "It makes sense that if you were on the opposing side, you'd want to develop a way to counter the effects."

"I wonder if all those holes covering Vitran were a result of other depletion bursts blocked by a mesh higher in the atmosphere," said Recker, rubbing his chin in thought. "Maybe the two sides – the Meklon and whoever else – fought over the planet for so long that eventually the Meklon were forced to abandon the place."

"We might find answers in the *Vengeance*'s audit logs," said Eastwood. "When you moved me to a new security tier, I found a whole bunch of them which I hadn't seen before."

"Same with the comms logs, sir. I've had a look through some, but mostly it's just checking in with bases and the automated replies. I'm sure I'll find more interesting stuff if I keep looking."

"Do you have access to any new hardware functions on the comms and sensors, Lieutenant?"

"There's a distress beacon walled off from the rest of the comms system, where a core override can't reach it. Other than that, I've got some extra processing cycles that will help with sensor work." Burner sighed. "Weapons and engines. Those guys get the exciting stuff. I get extra filters on the sensor arrays."

"You love it really," said Aston, grinning broadly.

"A warship's comms station is always the closest one to the replicator," Eastwood observed. "There's a degree of cold calculation behind his chosen specialisation."

Burner let it slide off him. "So when we boil this down, once every five minutes, the *Vengeance* is a match for almost anything. Then for the next five minutes, it's an easy target."

"Not exactly," said Aston. "That interceptor storm was remarkably effective." She cleared her throat and a hint of pinkness appeared in her cheeks. "We've got gauss repeater turrets as well. I didn't find them in time to use them against the enemy missiles."

"No shame in that, Commander - we were all fighting to stay afloat. Next time you'll know."

"Yes, sir. Anyway, those missiles we fired were faster than anything in the HPA. I haven't located their maximum lock range, or most of the other technical details, but I'm sure our weapons labs can learn something from the hardware."

"It's the unlocking of the mesh deflector we should be

celebrating most," said Recker. "If the Daklan don't already have a tenixite converter in their possession, then they're actively seeking to obtain one. Plus, we've found proof that the species which built those weapons are still active and not far beyond the fringes of our known space."

"They might not be hostile, sir," said Burner. "They attacked us, but they must have thought we were the Meklon."

"It's wise to prepare for both war and peace at the same time," said Eastwood. "Expect the former and hope for the latter."

"A lesson the HPA has had every opportunity to learn," Recker agreed. "To conclude – in the right hands, the *Vengeance* is a match for maybe anything in the Daklan fleet, as long as we can deal with its weaknesses."

"It's not likely flying again, sir," said Aston. "As soon as Admiral Telar reads your report, he'll order this warship dismantled in order to copy the technology. With your upgraded security access to the *Vengeance*, an HPA ship-yard should be able to extract the components without breaking anything."

Hearing the words produced a sadness in Recker. He didn't for a moment believe it was his right to pursue glory in this alien warship, yet it was in HPA control because he and his crew had fought hard to recover it from Tanril. He sighed inwardly, accepting that this would be his last mission on the *Vengeance*.

"I ran some figures based on recorded data from engine mode 2," said Eastwood a few minutes later. "We'd top out at four thousand klicks per second."

"Fast," said Burner.

"More than twice the speed of an annihilator," said Aston.

"Not faster than a missile," said Eastwood. "Furthermore, I don't know what limitations there are on engine mode 2. It might automatically shut down after ten minutes or it might last forever."

"If it lasted forever, there'd be no requirement for a switchable engine mode," said Recker.

"Maybe. I can imagine a few reasons why it would be preferable to set things up like they have, sir."

"I'm curious about engine mode 3," said Aston. "More precisely, I'm curious to know what happens if the Executor is fired at the same time."

Recker felt the chill of promised death and he shivered. He'd earlier asked himself why a propulsion switch would require activation by a commanding officer and Aston had hinted at a reason. If the Executor had access to an even greater power supply, maybe it could destroy far more than a single warship.

"These alien species must have been fighting a nasty war," said Recker.

"The more desperate you become, the greater the lengths you'll go to," Eastwood replied.

Recker exhaled noisily. "If we get caught up in this old war, will be facing opponents who are geared up to eradicate anything they come across. There may be no negotiation and no chance to build trust."

"We'd better hope the Interrogator didn't find anything in the databanks of our warships," said Aston. "Otherwise we might find our planets taken out by the tenixite converter network without us being able to do a damn thing to stop it."

"It could be that we're of no interest to these two species," said Recker quietly. "Either that or they fought each other to a standstill and they lack the capability to open up a war on a new front."

"Or they pursue a war against us with enough brutality to finish it before it's even started," said Eastwood.

Recker didn't want to shut down the conversation entirely, but he needed a break from the speculation. "We're not getting anywhere with this, folks," he said. "Once we return to Lustre we'll find out if the Interrogator data produced anything to worry about. Until then, we should sit back and enjoy the ride."

"Like that's going to happen," said Burner.

"And when we arrive at Adamantine, I want us to be familiar enough with the *Vengeance*'s unlocked hardware that we can finish the debriefing as quickly as possible."

"So they can put us back on a different warship and send us to our deaths, sir?" asked Burner. "I'd rather put my feet up in a comfortable technician's office for a few months while I help our sensor designers understand all this new stuff."

"A few months?" said Aston with a raised eyebrow. "You could tell them everything about those extra lens filters in an afternoon."

"I'll draw it out as long as possible, Commander, while junior officers bring me real coffees made from real beans."

"Like hell you will," said Eastwood. "You'll document everything in the ten days we have remaining before arrival at Lustre. When we land, you'll be down one boarding ramp and up the next. If they park the ground transport close enough, your feet might not even touch the ground."

"Enough," laughed Recker. "Lieutenant Burner, I think that deep down inside, you know exactly what's going to happen."

"A man can dream, sir."

Recker stretched. "Commander Aston, you've got the controls," he said. "I'm going for a look about."

"Yes, sir."

When he left the bridge, Recker made straight for the mess area. Sergeant Vance was elsewhere, but Corporal Hendrix was killing time along with a few other members of the squad. Recker didn't stay for long – he eschewed the potential delights of the *Vengeance*'s original replicator and instead ate a plate of bland food from the HPA equivalent. When he was finished eating, he walked a circuit of the warship's interior. The break from his console made him feel better and when he returned to the bridge, Recker's brain felt clear.

"Fracture," he said, remembering something.

"Sir?"

"It's a function accessible from my console," he said. "I had a brief look after we entered lightspeed but I couldn't work out how it activates."

"Sounds interesting," said Aston.

Recker called up the function again. The amber warning light was still on and he poked around to find the cause.

"Failure in linked hardware," he muttered.

Eastwood became interested. "I can't see any of the fracture hardware modules on my console, sir. If you send me the tie-in codes, I'll check if they're linked to anything else."

"I've sent you the codes."

"Those tie ins are with the propulsion and the main processing core," said Eastwood a couple of minutes later.

"Just like most parts of a warship," said Aston. "Doesn't tell us much."

"Let me have a look at this failed module," said Recker under his breath. "Hmm. It's tied in to some different hardware."

"Send me the code, sir."

"Done."

"That links to the tactical, sir," said Eastwood. "Lieutenant Burner's probably best placed to tell you the significance."

"Already on it," said Burner. "Give me five minutes."

"Take as long as you want, Lieutenant," said Recker, hiding his impatience.

"Got it!" said Burner at last. "The failed hardware links to the tactical computer's decision-making brain. I think this *Fracture* is designed to activate automatically. Or maybe it's meant to be remotely activated. I'm not sure."

"Except it's broken."

"You can probably trigger it manually, sir. Override the automation and I guess you'll see the option to switch the entire function to manual."

It took a minute or two for Recker to figure it out.

"Done," he said. "Whatever Fracture does, I can activate it from the control panel."

"Maybe we should test it out when we arrive at Lustre," said Eastwood. "Before we hand over the *Vengeance* and never see it again."

"I'll think about it, Lieutenant."

In truth, Recker was itching to find out what would happen if he activated the Fracture command, but he didn't want to do it anywhere near a human planet in case the results were more explosive than he anticipated. Equally, he didn't want to break anything that might otherwise prove useful to the HPA. With ten days until re-entry to local space, it was an easy decision to put off.

Those ten days trickled by like sand through an hourglass. Recker knew he was just one man, but he hated being effectively out of action for so long. As each day passed, the clenched feeling in his stomach tightened a little more and he craved the end of this journey more than any other he could remember.

On the plus side, the crew used the time efficiently and as the end of the voyage approached, they'd learned much about the alien tech carried by the *Vengeance*. Armed with the knowledge, Recker felt confident that he could challenge any single Daklan warship – not that he expected to be given the opportunity.

The only certainty about time was that quick or slow, it never stopped flowing and the ten days became nothing more than memories.

"Ten minutes!" yelled Eastwood.

"Twenty-seven days away from base," said Aston. "And now we're back."

"Nervous, Commander?"

"Same as the rest of us, sir."

Recker nodded. "Part of me wishes the journey would never end."

He saw in Aston's face that she felt the same. She smiled without much conviction.

"Two minutes!" called Eastwood. "Get ready!"

Recker didn't think the *Vengeance* would re-enter local space any more than a second or two either side of the predicted arrival time. He held tightly to the controls and waited for it to happen.

CHAPTER TWENTY-FIVE

THE TRANSITION NAUSEA faded and Recker called for a status update.

"Scans underway," said Burner.

"All systems green, sir," said Eastwood.

"We're five million klicks from Lustre, sir. I've put it up on the screen." A disc representing the planet appeared on the bulkhead feed with a surprising level of detail, given the distance.

Recker didn't spare it more than a glance. "Talk to base and make them aware of what we're carrying."

"Yes, sir. Five million klicks means there's a short comms delay."

As he waited, Recker's attention returned to the feed showing Lustre. He recognized the main land belt which covered the equator. The Adamantine base was on the visible side, meaning a lesser delay when it came to setting down. A pinpoint of light appeared and vanished. Recker frowned, then swore.

"They're under attack," he said.

Burner was just learning the same thing. "Sir, the comms channels are all busy. The Daklan showed up less than an hour ago. They're bombarding our surface defences."

"What? How?" asked Eastwood.

Those were questions for later. "I need details, Lieutenant Burner," snapped Recker. "Numbers, ship types, attack patterns. Where's our fleet?"

"On it, sir," said Burner.

Recker was raging and he struggled to show outward calm. He could hear Burner talking softly and quietly into his headset, but the words were lost.

"Precise numbers unknown, sir. Adamantine estimates we're facing thirty-five ships, including two annihilators and eleven desolators. The local defence force is engaged, but they lack the numbers to prevent the Daklan striking our ground launchers."

"Casualties?"

"We've lost five warships, sir. All Teron class cruisers."

Lustre was usually defended by twenty-five warships, with a variation of two or three in either direction. Against the Daklan fleet, they were outnumbered and outclassed.

Over the next few minutes, Recker obtained a picture of events, such as they were known, and it wasn't good. The planet was ringed by a network of surface launchers that should have been tipping the tide of the conflict, but the Daklan were sitting high in a cluster and picking off the defensive installations using what were thought to be modified Odan missiles, capable of locking at a much greater range.

Soon, the surface launchers would no longer present a significant threat to the attackers, and the local fleet would be neutralised. When that moment came, the planet's fate would be in the hands of the Daklan.

"We've got to help," said Recker.

"What about the tech we're carrying, sir?" asked Aston. "Can we risk losing it?"

"Can we risk losing an entire planet, Commander?"

"I don't know, sir."

For once, Recker was confronted by a decision he didn't want to make. The local battle network showed the position of the Daklan fleet – almost a million kilometres above the planet and travelling slowly clockwise. In about twenty minutes, they'd be above the Adamantine base.

Meanwhile, the local fleet made a series of in-out strikes, before scattering in the hope of fragmenting the enemy and drawing them into range of the surface launchers. Up to now, the tactic was failing badly.

"We're nearly fifty minutes away on the sub-light engines," said Recker. "Lieutenant Eastwood, warm up the lightspeed drive – aim for 600 thousand klicks clockwise of the Daklan fleet."

"Yes, sir."

"That's just within our missile range," said Aston.

"Lieutenant Burner, you've got six minutes to get Admiral Telar on the comms. Make sure his team are aware of what the *Vengeance* represents and advise that we will join the defence of Lustre if we do not receive a direct order to the contrary."

"The Admiral is busy, sir," said Burner. It was the least surprising announcement of the mission so far.

"He needs to hear the message, Lieutenant."

"I'm awaiting confirmation, sir."

With two minutes remaining on the lightspeed timer, Admiral Telar came onto the comms.

"Captain Recker," he said, no trace of anxiety apparent in his voice.

"Sir, how are our efforts to negotiate with the enemy progressing?"

"The same as they ever do, Carl. We speak, they don't listen."

"So they're just planning to destroy us?" asked Recker bitterly. Somehow, he'd always imagined that when it came to the crunch, the Daklan wouldn't commit mass murder.

"Judge them by their actions."

Recker wished it were otherwise, but the unfolding events left little room for misunderstanding of the Daklan motives. "What about reinforcements?"

"Inbound. They won't be in time, and if we lose the entire defence force, the first wave of reinforcements might not be enough to challenge what's left of the Daklan."

"The reinforcements might have to sit off world and do nothing?"

"We'll see, Carl." A tiredness had crept into Telar's voice.

"Did you receive the details from my comms officer, sir?"

"I did. I understand the *Vengeance* is fitted with technology the HPA will benefit from."

"Yes, sir."

"Technology we can't afford to lose."

"No."

"We can't afford to lose the billions of people on Lustre either, Carl. How am I to weigh up so many unknowns and choose the path which leads to our salvation?" It seemed that Telar wasn't expecting an answer, and he continued. "Can you sway this conflict in our favour, Captain?"

Recker closed his eyes. "Yes, sir."

"Then do what you must."

"I will do what I can. Permission to act independently of the HPA fleet, sir? Our commanding officers are unaware of the *Vengeance*'s capabilities and therefore incapable of making the best decisions on its use."

"I'll take you at your word, Carl. Permission granted." Telar wasn't done. "And should we win here, this is only the beginning."

"I don't understand, sir."

"Later. Goodbye and good luck."

The channel went dead, leaving Recker staring at the timer.

"Ten seconds," said Eastwood.

Recker's grip on the controls hadn't lessened and he readied himself. "Let's give them hell."

With a shudder from its lightspeed drive, the *Vengeance* completed an in-out jump towards Lustre. Recker was prepared for the nausea and he gritted his teeth, forcing himself to ignore the pain and discomfort.

The tactical re-populated, filling with dozens of red and green dots, each with an overlay giving pertinent data. Counter-clockwise of the *Vengeance*'s position, the

Daklan fleet were at the extremes of range, while the nearest member of the HPA fleet was the battleship *Granite* – about a hundred thousand kilometres away - along with an escort of two new Teron cruisers named *Stalwart* and *Resolve*. All three had suffered minor damage without losing operational capabilities.

A glance at the bulkhead screen presented Recker with an image of Lustre that was like a perfect model – so realistic as to be indistinguishable from the real thing. On the other screens he saw darkness and unfocused feeds of enemy warships to which Burner fought to bring clarity.

"Got a sensor lock on the closest desolator, sir," said Burner. "No sign they're looking our way."

"They soon will be. Lock and fire, Commander Aston," Recker ordered.

"Missiles locked and fired," she shouted above the thumping noise of multiple propulsions.

Recker piloted the *Vengeance* in a tight circle, allowing each of the ten clusters to launch. When Aston was done, 120 missiles raced towards the desolator at a speed vastly in excess of anything possessed by the HPA.

"Eighteen thousand klicks per second," said Aston. "Thirty-three seconds travel time."

"Let's not sit around gawping," said Recker, flying the *Vengeance* away from the launch position.

"The *Granite* is moving in for an attack, sir," said Burner. "Captain Sams asks what the hell sort of missile we just fired and she's also invited us to shelter beneath her mighty wing."

"She said those exact words?" said Eastwood.

Recker had met Sams once before and she definitely

fell into the category of *eccentric*. "Pass on our thanks – we'll take her up on the offer."

He adjusted course and aimed the *Vengeance* towards the accelerating *Granite*. His eyes kept going to the tactical, where the recently launched missiles were streaking towards their target. So far, the enemy had not retaliated and continued to pelt Lustre's surface defences with Odan missiles. Something about the situation struck Recker as odd, and he couldn't immediately put his finger on what it was.

This is a limited force to send against a planet.

The ongoing demands of combat prevented him from pursuing the thought.

"The enemy have launched countermeasures against our missiles," said Aston. "That's too late, surely..."

A flash of white on the sensors indicated the desolator had taken multiple strikes from the *Vengeance*'s missiles. The warheads travelled with such velocity that Recker suspected they fooled the Daklan track-and-respond countermeasures.

"Did we score a kill?" he asked, pulling the *Vengeance* alongside the *Granite*. The battleship's flank filled the starboard feeds, like a scarred, impenetrable wall of alloy.

"Negative kill," said Burner. "No, wait! I think they're breaking apart!"

The plasma fires which gripped the heavy cruiser didn't diminish and the damaged warship split into two equal-sized pieces. The debris burned fiercely and began drifting.

Burner punched the air. "Take that, you bastards!"

"One down," said Eastwood.

Recker was glad, but it wasn't nearly enough and he hoped to send a few others the same way before this was over.

"Get me a sensor lock on one of those annihilators," he said.

The battle network data made it easier for Burner to find a target and obtain a sensor lock. "Got one, sir."

The Daklan battleship was a mean-looking craft and the sight of it reminded Recker of the annihilator which had recently pursued him across what seemed like half of the universe. Knocking this one out would be a positive development for the HPA.

The *Granite* fired its charge cannon and a sphere of blue energy rumbled through space towards the enemy. At the same time, the cruisers let their Hellburners fly, whilst launching from every available Ilstrom cluster. In a split-second, more than two hundred missiles and a charge cannon bolt were heading for the Daklan.

"Commander Aston, help them out," said Recker. "Target the annihilator."

"Forward missile tubes launched. Let's hope they're too slow this time as well."

Once again, the bridge became filled with sound, which faded rapidly as the missiles accelerated towards their target. As the tactical became busy with an ever-increasing quantity of targets, Recker thought hard about how he could maximise the impact of the *Vengeance*'s weaponry. So far, he hadn't come up with method that didn't involve suicide.

"The *Granite* and its escort are focusing on a second desolator, sir," said Aston. "They don't have the range to hit the annihilator. Looks like the enemy were prepared for the charge cannon attack – they're accelerating away from it."

Recker swore, though he was aware of the charge cannon limitations. The weapon had its uses, but at long range and against an opponent who was expecting the attack, the energy spheres were easily avoided.

"Waiting for enemy retaliation," said Aston.

Although the Daklan were dividing their firepower between surface targets and the defence fleet, the aliens weren't stupid enough to allow the *Granite* to approach unopposed. In response, the ships on the edge of the cluster fired dozens of Feilar missiles and when Recker turned to the starboard feed, he saw a huge furrow suddenly appear in the *Granite*'s flank. A moment later, a second one appeared above it, already glowing from the impact heat.

"Terrus cannons," Recker said. He was gambling that the Daklan would think of the *Vengeance* as a lesser target and thereby concentrate their firepower on the *Granite*. Judging from the tactical, the enemy were only too happy to aim their missiles at the battleship. However, the *Vengeance* hadn't entirely escaped notice.

"I'm tracking twelve Feilars heading our way," said Aston.

The seconds counted down and Captain Sams held the *Granite* on course. Recker understood what she hoped to achieve – to keep the enemy's eyes on the HPA ship best equipped to defend itself. Unfortunately, a battleship and two cruisers weren't packing enough countermeasures to destroy everything the Daklan had launched at them.

"Five seconds to Feilar impact," said Aston.

"Ready our countermeasures."

"Gauss turrets already locked. Switching to auto."

It was the first time any of them had heard the *Vengeance*'s chain guns fire and the metallic savagery was enough to raise the hairs on Recker's neck.

"Interceptors away," said Aston loudly.

Suddenly, it was as if the *Vengeance* was in the centre of a lightshow made from lines of white and orange, each one beautifully etched into the purity of the void's darkness. The *Granite*'s Railers spewed out hundreds of thousands of rounds, and interceptor missiles left curving trails of red as they burst from their launchers. The cruisers unloaded their own defences into space, to join with the chaos of warfare.

Anxiously, Recker watched the tactical. The *Vengeance*'s chain guns scored numerous hits and the interceptor storm wiped out dozens of Feilars. Dozens more were destroyed by the HPA countermeasures. Against the quantity of warheads inbound, it wasn't enough and Recker watched two detonations against the *Granite*'s nose section and a third went off against the *Stalwart*, producing a crater deep enough to expose the duller ternium engine module underneath.

"A few of the *Granite*'s missiles hit the desolator, sir," said Aston. "I've only received one successful detonation code from our own missiles."

"Better than nothing."

"Not much."

"The *Granite* is breaking off," said Burner.

Recker banked to follow, unwilling to expose his

warship to concentrated enemy fire. "This is hit-and-run, Lieutenant and all it's going to do is delay the inevitable. We haven't even seen their lightspeed missiles yet."

"Maybe these annihilators aren't carrying them," said Burner hopefully. "Why hang on to them?"

"I don't have an answer for you, Lieutenant. With or without lightspeed missiles, we're not going to win this one."

Only a fool would think the engagement was going to end in anything other than defeat for the HPA, though Recker couldn't criticise the tactics too heavily. A frontal attack would also fail – it would just come sooner.

I told Admiral Telar the Vengeance *could swing this. I promised and he believed.*

He zoomed the tactical all the way out. Elsewhere, other HPA warships were attacking the Daklan from different directions. Recker could sense the futility of it – the Daklan were too strong and the HPA lacked a means to turn the battle around. As it stood, the defence fleet might as well have been building a wall of sand in front of the rising tide.

"Their Odans just took out our ground launchers four hundred klicks west of Adamantine, sir," said Burner. "Projections indicate they'll hit the base defences soon."

"What about the base itself?" asked Eastwood. "Will they take it out as well?"

"We don't know what they're here for, Lieutenant," said Recker. He cast a quick look at the sensor feed of Lustre. "They've neutralised the defences around three major cities so far but haven't targeted our civilians."

"It would require hundreds of Odans to level a city,"

said Aston. "Why waste so many warheads when a couple of incendiaries would do the same job?"

"I wish I knew what the Daklan were planning, Commander."

No sooner had the words left Recker's mouth than the *Granite* was struck by several lightspeed missiles. The armour-piercing warheads buried themselves deep and the explosions which followed were catastrophic. Slabs of armour and whole engine modules were thrown violently into space and Recker instinctively threw the *Vengeance* down and away, to avoid the largest pieces of debris.

Seconds later, another two lightspeed missiles hit the *Granite* and the job was done. Thirty-five billion tons of HPA battleship was ripped apart, its crew incinerated or thrown into the vacuum. It was a loss which Recker had hoped never to witness and he shouted in cold, blind fury at his distant enemy.

CHAPTER TWENTY-SIX

THROUGH HIS ANGER, Recker gave an order.

"Lieutenant Burner, activate engine mode 2."

"Engine mode 2 activated."

Instantly, the grumbling edge of the propulsion became smooth and the *Vengeance* reacted so quickly to Recker's input it was like the warship was anticipating his thoughts and acting upon them before he could translate them into movements of the controls. He gave the engines maximum and the warship's velocity gauge climbed like it would never stop.

"Two thousand klicks per second," said Eastwood. "Two-thousand five hundred."

"The enemy have launched Feilars, as well as twenty Odans from the warships on the far side of the cluster." said Aston. "Targeting us, the *Stalwart* and the *Resolve.* Holy crap, we've got some real heat coming our way – it's like we've suddenly become the number one target."

The tactical offered up the bad news in all its glory,

with the battle computer counting a total of 54 missiles heading for the *Vengeance*. They were a concern, but Recker had even bigger things to worry about.

"Lieutenant Burner, way back on Oldis when that annihilator hit us with a lightspeed missile, you detected the launch. I would like some advance warning next time they deploy."

"I remember that, sir. I got lucky." Burner's voice strengthened. "I'll do what I can."

Recker continued banking away from the Daklan fleet and the *Vengeance* was accelerating so hard that the cruisers were already far behind. The Feilars were locked and launched, so it was too late to outrange them and the *Vengeance* wasn't going to outrun them, even if it maxed out at four thousand klicks per second like Lieutenant Eastwood predicted.

"Are those missiles too much for the interceptors and the chain guns, Commander?" he asked.

"My gut feeling doesn't want to commit to an answer, sir. I don't know the *Vengeance* well enough."

"Ready the mesh deflector."

"Yes, sir."

Recker picked up the doubt in Aston's voice and he turned. "Worried you won't time it right?"

"Yes, sir."

"I'm not."

"We just lost the *Opposing Force*, sir," said Burner. "The *Monarch* took some damage and it's breaking off."

The tactical – seemingly little more than a scattering of moving dots and overlays – told Recker everything he needed. With each passing moment, the superiority of the

Daklan forces became more apparent. Soon, the tipping point would come, where resistance would falter and the engagement become a rout.

Recker had never accepted inevitability. Until defeat became a tangible thing, he'd keep fighting. As it always did in these most terrible of moments, his anger fell away, shed like an unwanted skin. The biological limitations of his mind were lessened, allowing him to focus without distraction.

Sometimes, he feared it happening, like his humanity in these moments was crushed and he became more computer than living, breathing entity. His brain turned, like the cycles of a processing core as it sought a way to do something – anything – that would fix what was happening here at Lustre.

"Mesh deflector activated," said Aston.

The cage of sword cuts wrapped the *Vengeance* and the inbound Odan missiles detonated against the shield, their huge payloads turning every feed white.

"Interceptors released to mop up the last Feilars," said Aston. "Chain guns targeting."

A combination of sounds threatened to overwhelm Recker's senses. He blocked them out and banked the *Vengeance* at the last possible moment. The warship was agile even when travelling at four thousand kilometres per second, and those Feilars which evaded the countermeasures overshot and were taken out by the forward chain guns.

"Sir, you don't want to hear this," said Eastwood. "I'm reading a series of ternium waves at a quarter of a million klicks."

"You're right, Lieutenant. I didn't want to hear it."

"Particle wave modelling suggests we've got three more annihilators inbound, sir. Plus eight or ten smaller warships."

"We've still got a target lock on one of the existing annihilators," said Recker. "We're going to take it out with the Executor."

"Sir, it's over," said Aston. "This battle is lost – we should take the *Vengeance* elsewhere so the HPA can benefit from its tech later in the war."

"It is not over!" Recker shouted.

"Lightspeed missile launch detected," said Burner. "Target: unknown."

"Interceptors launched," said Aston. "For what good they'll do."

"The *Stalwart* has taken a hit from a lightspeed missile, sir," said Burner.

The cruiser was on one of the feeds and Recker didn't need a damage report to understand that the warship was in a bad way – the missile had opened an enormous crater in its rear plating and fires blazed across much of its stern.

"Ready the Executor!" ordered Recker, adjusting the *Vengeance* so that the annihilator was in the weapon's firing arc.

"Yes, sir," said Aston. She sounded deflated in a way that Recker hadn't heard before. "Range to target: 400 thousand klicks. Executor range: 100 thousand klicks. Odan launch detected."

"The battleship *Divergence* has been struck by a lightspeed missile, sir," said Burner.

"Three annihilators have entered local space," Eastwood intoned. "Plus three desolators and seven ravager class destroyers."

"Multiple lightspeed missile launches detected," Burner continued. "The enemy have had enough of waiting."

"I'm reading another particle wave," said Eastwood. "Bigger than the last one and at five million klicks. Either these warships missed the target or they want to sit back and enjoy the show."

"Odan bombardment of Adamantine defensive launchers underway," said Burner.

The updates rolled in, like a hurricane of Recker's worst fears. He stood firm for as long as he could manage. Suddenly, it struck him like a Daklan punch to the temple. He could deny inevitability as much as he liked, and maybe he could even fool himself. With the greatest of shame, Recker realized he was fooling others as well and even worse, he was using their belief to bring them to their deaths. They deserved better.

Maybe I convinced myself I'm invulnerable. Recker the machine. Recker the man who always pulls victory from the jaws of defeat. This is about more than just me.

"Feilars incoming," said Aston.

"I've detected another lightspeed missile launch," said Burner. The artificial calm in his voice was a cheap veneer. "I think this one's got our name on it."

Recker's intended words – *we're getting out of here folks* – died on his lips. The mesh deflector was on cooldown and the *Vengeance* wasn't getting away from a lightspeed missile. Two softly glowing lights on the top of his control bar caught his eye. The first button would switch the engines to mode 3, while the second was something different.

Fracture.

He pressed the button to switch the engines to mode 3. Recker heard a whoosh like air being sucked into a combustion engine and the sensor feeds went blank. A counter appeared on one of his console screens, the digits rising in a blur. A split second later, he released the button and the feeds resumed.

The *Vengeance* was elsewhere.

In front of Recker's eyes, the tactical populated with red dots representing Daklan warships. On his console, the power needles were high and falling fast, while the propulsion was back in mode 1, with mode 2 locked out.

"The enemy," was all Burner managed to say.

Recker understood. Activating the third engine mode had cast the *Vengeance* into a short, low-multiple light-speed jump. Unfortunately, it had carried the warship directly into the centre of the newly arrived additions to the Daklan assault fleet and left its velocity at zero. He saw annihilators, desolators and ravager destroyers in quantities that told him everything about the enemy's commitment to this attack on Lustre.

Less than five kilometres starboard, a Daklan battleship was stationary, its turrets, domes, chain guns and cannons revealed in perfect detail - killing technology seen from up close.

These moments of realization were the longest of Recker's life, as though the activation of mode 3 had enabled his mind to operate outside the bounds of normal time.

He activated the Fracture.

A cracking sound like a mountain snapping in two came from somewhere inside the *Vengeance* and the sensors registered the emanation of an energy wave. On the forward feed, Recker half-imagined he saw a rippling, which distorted the background of stars and continued until it was lost from the array's focus.

At first, it seemed as though nothing had happened and Recker opened his mouth to order the discharge of the Executor. Then, he noticed a change on the hull of the nearest annihilator. Recker watched and saw cracks appear in the battleship's plating. At first, these cracks were narrow but quickly they widened until they were dozens of meters across. Almost at once, new, smaller fissures formed on the undamaged areas of plating and spread like the onset of age.

"What the hell?"

Lieutenant Burner focused the other arrays and each feed told the same story. Widening patterns of cracks appeared on every Daklan warship within this newly arrived fleet – patterns which made Recker think of old oil paintings which had decayed with the passing of the centuries.

"Shit," said Aston, her eyes wide. "What did we do?"

Recker's grip on the controls loosened and his hands threatened to slip free. He tightened his fingers and forced himself to pilot his warship through the enemy fleet. The Daklan warships were gone – destroyed – he knew instinctively and not a single one fired at the *Vengeance*.

"They're falling apart," said Eastwood, his voice faltering.

Like windblown sand, the enemy fleet crumbled, creating trails of thick dust through the space behind. Where a ship had been stationary, its edges became first blurred and then ephemeral, like the particles had been given hardly any impetus by the fracturing.

For twenty seconds – though it seemed longer – the crew of the *Vengeance* could only stare at the damage they had inflicted. This was like a graveyard of ships, where the decay had been accelerated by a hundred billion years and the effects played out in a betrayal of their sanctity.

"We should return to the conflict," said Recker.

I can't watch this.

Recker's hands were shaking as he guided the *Vengeance* through the dead fleet. The warship emerged from the furthest edge of the cluster, travelling close to its maximum velocity. However much he tried to rein in the fevered thoughts in his head, Recker couldn't focus on a plan.

Thousands dead, as easy as that.

"The Daklan are still attacking Lustre, sir," said Burner.

"Do they realize what happened?" asked Eastwood in disbelief.

"They've still got the upper hand," said Aston. Once again, she fixed Recker with a stare. "Captain?"

"Fracture is offline," said Recker. "For how long, I don't know."

"That wasn't what I was asking, sir."

"I know. Status updates! I need to think."

"We can't switch back into engine mode 2," said Eastwood.

"Mesh deflector now available, sir."

Recker tensed the muscles in his arms and shoulders, and bared his teeth at the decision he faced. He didn't know how long the Fracture would be offline and he didn't want to challenge the Daklan fleet without the weapon. As he agonised, another HPA cruiser was turned into flaming wreckage by a salvo of alien missiles.

At that moment, the most unexpected of events took him along an entirely new path.

"Sir?" said Burner. "I've had a request to open a comms channel from the Daklan annihilator *Ixoler*. I've got Admiral Ivinstol for you."

With a deep breath, Recker ordered Burner to open the channel.

CHAPTER TWENTY-SEVEN

ADMIRAL IVINSTOL'S voice was so harsh that he was difficult to understand, even with the language module rounding off the roughest edges.

"You are Captain Recker."

"That's right, Admiral. Why have you attacked our planet?"

"This is war, human. In a war, two sides traditionally fight each other."

Recker wasn't sure if the Daklan had a sense of humour or if this was the kind of human-alien misinterpretation he was meant to be aware of.

"I have destroyed many of your warships, Admiral."

"You have. The remainder of my fleet is strong enough to pacify your planet and destroy its manufacturing capabilities. I have ordered a hold on the attack while we speak, though we will defend ourselves."

Muting the comms, Recker turned to Lieutenant Burner. "Make sure Admiral Telar is aware."

"Sir."

Recker took the comms off mute. "Your gesture is appreciated, though I do not understand your motives."

"You have the Meklon warship."

There seemed no point in lying about it. "Yes."

"And you have circumvented its security. You control its weaponry."

The Daklan was guessing about how Recker had gained that access, but it didn't seem like a good time to discuss the minutiae. "Yes. The *Vengeance* contains powerful technology. You have seen the effects. I would like you to call off the attack on Lustre."

"That is how you name this planet?" The Daklan made a noise in his throat, the meaning of which Recker didn't understand. "Tell me, Captain Recker - were you involved in the mission to capture the Lavorix Interrogator?"

"Lavorix?"

"You do not recognize the name?"

"No." Recker took a guess. "They were at war with the Meklon?"

"Not *were,* human."

"What do you know about their conflict?"

"Some and not nearly enough."

"No need for either the HPA or the Daklan to become involved," said Recker.

"It is already too late for that, wouldn't you say?"

"At this precise moment, Admiral, I don't know what the hell I should be saying. You've attacked our planet and I guess most people in the HPA wish we'd never started fighting. Maybe you're the same, or maybe this is what the Daklan live for."

"We do not live for death, Captain Recker. However, that is a discussion for another day. Did you claim data from the Interrogator, human?"

Recker wasn't sure where this was heading, but he sensed this was a pivotal moment in the HPA's existence. "Yes."

"What did the Interrogator extract from your warships?"

"I don't know."

"Do your superiors know?"

"I have just returned from a long mission, Admiral. I have not yet been debriefed."

"The Daklan have known tragedy, human. Soon, you will know the same."

"I don't understand."

"The Meklon and Lavorix fight with weapons of unimaginable destruction, designed to bring about the extinction of their opponents. Both the Daklan and your HPA are now involved, however remotely. Should this distant war end, perhaps the victors will come hunting for those they have recently become aware of."

"We are not looking for an extension to our war, Admiral Ivinstol."

"The choice is no longer yours, human. As I told you - the Daklan have known tragedy. Five days ago, we lost a planet. Billions killed. An attack from a place unknown."

"You blame us?"

"At first, we believed you had accessed the network of tenixite converters and used a depletion burst to kill our people. Then, we recovered a shuttle from a distant world – a world into which the Lavorix Interrogator crashed. The personnel on this shuttle survived the engagement with your forces and they had also recovered data from the cube."

Recker knew the Daklan were resourceful and this was another example of it. "And in that data, you found coordinates of your destroyed world."

"That is so. At that moment, we knew the HPA could not be blamed."

"And here you are, attempting to destroy our planet."

"No human – we came here to finish the war between us, so that we can focus our efforts elsewhere."

"You're trying to neutralise us?" asked Recker in disbelief.

"Your fleet is already depleted. Our war council decided it best if we reduced your warship numbers as soon as possible. After that?" Admiral Ivinstal made a sound that might have been dismissive, like the decision would then no longer be important.

The logic sort of worked, in a kind of strange manner that Recker would have never himself considered. Perhaps if you were a warlike alien, it made perfect sense.

"Your plans have changed," said Recker.

"You have the Meklon ship and this introduces a significant anomaly into the war council's projections. In order to consider, I will withdraw my fleet from your planet. Should it be required, I will return."

"How did you find Lustre?" asked Recker, desperately trying to find some answers. "Was it in the Interrogator data?"

"No, Captain Recker – we discovered this planet months ago."

"Then why now?"

"Because that is how it was decided," said Ivinstol, like it was the most obvious reason imaginable. "I have given the order for our ternium drives to activate. Once again, we will defend ourselves from attack."

With that, the comms channel went dead.

"I'm detecting huge energy waves coming from the Daklan hulls," said Eastwood. "I'd say they're as good as their word."

"Lieutenant Burner, I need to speak to Admiral Telar – immediately."

"Yes, sir. I'll do what I can."

Recker was coiled up and the adrenaline was pumping. Neither was lessened by the entrance of Telar into the open comms channel.

"Captain Recker, what just happened?"

"Sir, we can't talk about it now! Did we pull anything out of the Interrogator's files?"

Telar understood immediately. "The coordinates of Fortune. They were amongst the transmitted data."

"We lost the planet?"

"No, Carl. The planet has not been destroyed by a tenixite converter – I am looking at a list of comms received in the last five minutes." Telar took a deep breath and suddenly it sounded like he had the weight of the universe on his shoulders. "Before you engaged with the Daklan fleet, I told you this is only the beginning. I recommended the planet be evacuated."

"And?"

"I was told it was a step too far. That we lacked the resources required to accomplish such a feat."

Recker closed his eyes. "I spoke to a Daklan officer – Admiral Ivinstol – and he told me one of their planets was destroyed."

"We have no defence against those tenixite converters, Captain. If these distant species decide to aim a depletion burst at Fortune, there is nothing we can do to stop it."

"Yes there is, sir." Recker muted the comms. "Lieutenant Eastwood – warm up the ternium drive. Target planet Fortune. Half a million klicks out."

"Half a million klicks it is."

With the comms off mute, Recker filled Admiral Telar in with as much detail as six minutes would allow. As the timer counted down, he felt a terror building within him.

"I hope you're wrong, Captain," said Telar.

Those were the admiral's last words before the ternium drive activated and the *Vengeance* entered lightspeed.

"It's a six-hour journey to Fortune, sir," said Eastwood, when the spaceship had settled after the transition. "A hell of a lot quicker that it would have been on another warship."

"That's six hours too long," said Recker.

"You think the planet will be attacked?" said Aston. "It hasn't happened yet."

"The Daklan lost one of theirs, Commander."

"I know, but..."

Aston looked close to tears and Recker could tell she didn't want to consider the possibility of such a catastrophic loss.

"It's only six hours," said Recker, pretending sudden optimism. "The Daklan lost their planet days ago and nothing happened to Fortune yet – Admiral Telar was still receiving comms."

"What's the plan, sir?" asked Burner. "When we get there, I mean."

"We're going to park the *Vengeance* at a low altitude and leave it there. If the Lavorix target the planet with a depletion burst, the mesh deflector should activate automatically."

It was a tenuous chance and Recker knew it. So many unknowns still surrounded the *Vengeance* and he dearly wished to have a stack of specification sheets that he could read through, which would tell him the technical details and limitations on the warship's capabilities. Without them, he was left guessing.

"What did you make of that Daklan admiral?" asked Eastwood.

"I don't know, Lieutenant. He talked sense, but I don't have a point of reference."

"The Daklan took a hit and they thought the best course of action was to attack one of our planets," said Burner. "I can't understand it."

"They wanted to knock us out of the war so they could focus on a new one," said Eastwood. "At least that's what I took from the conversation."

"Change is coming, folks," said Recker.

"It's always bad change."

Recker didn't mention it, but he privately thought that the HPA was about to enter a new age of turmoil and bloodshed, even before the previous one was finished.

Humanity had already been stretched near to breaking point and it didn't seem like things were going to improve anytime soon.

"It's been a long shift," said Burner.

"You ready for sleep, Lieutenant?"

Burner lifted a cup. The contents weren't visible, but Recker had a good idea of what they were. "I'll stick with this for now, sir."

The hours passed and all Recker could do was watch the timer. Eventually, Eastwood shouted out the ten-minute warning and the crew straightened in readiness for their arrival at Fortune.

"Anyone got relatives here?" said Recker belatedly.

"No, sir."

"Corporal Hendrix does. Maybe a couple of the other squad members do as well," said Recker, trying to remember snippets of conversations he'd picked up.

"This isn't really about to happen is it?" said Eastwood.

"We're going to be dragged into another alien war, Lieutenant. No matter what happens at Fortune, it's coming."

"I hope you're wrong, sir."

Recker did too. More than anything. "That makes both of us, Lieutenant."

"Two minutes."

The timer reached zero and the *Vengeance* entered local space.

FORTUNE

The planet was gone. Even though he'd mentally prepared himself for the possibility, Recker couldn't at first allow himself to believe it. He ordered Lieutenant Eastwood to confirm the lightspeed calculations were free from error, but the sensor feeds told the undeniable truth.

"Dust, sir," said Burner. "The planet got turned to dust."

Where Fortune had once been – a home to twelve billion souls – now there was only a rapidly dissipating cloud of dust, as if the planet had been so comprehensively unmade that nothing more than particles remained.

"We got here too late," said Aston. A single tear rolled down her cheek.

For a long time, all Recker could do was stare. The dust was thickest near to where the planet's core had been and even now, it retained enough heat to glow with a diffuse redness that faded with each passing moment. The cold of the vacuum would claim it all, eventually.

A few vessels – shuttles, mostly, and a couple of riot class warships – had been far enough away to outrange the depletion burst. The passengers and crews of those craft were as shellshocked as Recker felt and he got no real sense out of any of them. He didn't push, lacking the physical and mental energy to do so.

After an hour, the FTL comms arrived in a rush and Recker gathered what little strength he had in order to deal with the questions. Already, the finger pointing had started. From the depths of calamity, it seemed there was always somebody wanting to blame someone else. He ordered Burner to block any further comms, except those which came directly from Admiral Telar.

"What now, sir?" Aston had found some resolve, pulled it from deep inside.

"We go on. We fight."

It was an easy answer, but it seemed enough to satisfy her. She nodded and bowed her head.

"And one day it'll be over."

"I don't like to lose, Commander."

Aston raised her head and Recker saw her strengthen at his words. For the shortest of moments, he felt like a fraud and that he didn't deserve the respect. Then, he hauled himself back from the brink.

"And by hell we're going to win this one," he said.

This time, he almost believed it.

———

Sign up to my mailing list here to be the first to find out

about new releases, or follow me on Facebook
@AnthonyJamesAuthor

OTHER SCIENCE FICTION BOOKS BY ANTHONY JAMES

Survival Wars (Seven Books) – Available in Ebook, Paperback and Audio.

1. Crimson Tempest
2. Bane of Worlds
3. Chains of Duty
4. Fires of Oblivion
5. Terminus Gate
6. Guns of the Valpian
7. Mission: Nemesis

Obsidiar Fleet (Six Books – set after the events in Survival Wars) – Available in Ebook and Paperback.

1. Negation Force
2. Inferno Sphere
3. God Ship
4. Earth's Fury

5. Suns of the Aranol
6. Mission: Eradicate

The Transcended (Seven Books – set after the events in Obsidiar Fleet) – Available in Ebook, Paperback and Audio

1. Augmented
2. Fleet Vanguard
3. Far Strike
4. Galaxy Bomb
5. Void Blade
6. Monolith
7. Mission: Destructor

Fire and Rust (Seven Books) – Available in Ebook, Paperback and Audio.

1. Iron Dogs
2. Alien Firestorm
3. Havoc Squad
4. Death Skies
5. Refuge 9
6. Nullifier
7. Scum of the Universe

Anomalies (Two Books) – Available in Ebook and Paperback.

1. Planet Wreckers
2. Assault Amplified

Printed in Great Britain
by Amazon

19803240R00174